The Funeral of Tanner Moody

JOHN JAKES
ELMER KELTON
ROBERT J. RANDISI
And Others

The Funeral of Tanner Moody

LEISURE BOOKS NEW YORK CITY

To all of the legends of the West.

LEISURE BOOKS ®

July 2004

Published by

Dorchester Publishing Co., Inc.
200 Madison Avenue
New York, NY 10016

ISBN 0-8439-5224-5

ACKNOWLEDGMENT

My heartfelt thanks must go out to Marthayn Pelegrimas, who created Tanner Moody. She used the name in her story "The Taylor of Yuma," which appeared in my anthology *Tin Star* (Berkley, 2000). Her Tanner Moody was a deceased prison guard who only appears in the story when he is dug up from his grave. I fell in love with the name, though, and with her permission stole it. Hers is the first story to appear in the book.

—Robert J. Randisi

TABLE OF CONTENTS

I would rather be ashes than dust!
I would rather that my spark should burn out in a brilliant blaze
than it should be stifled by dry-rot.
I would rather be a superb meteor,
every atom of me in magnificent glow,
than a sleepy and permanent planet.
The proper function of man is to live, not to exist.
I shall not waste my days in trying to prolong them.
I shall use my time.

—Jack London

Prologue

The White Elephant Saloon
Fort Worth, Texas
December 1902

Legends are made up mostly of lies, and Tanner Moody's was no different. In fact, the legend of Tanner Moody could probably be held up as the prime example of that. Moody himself had been heard to say he knew what part was deserved and "what part comes out the hind end of a bull." Yet enough of it was true to make Tanner's legend legitimate.

I'd left Denver under a cloud and was heading for New York, where there was a new job possibility. But I'd wanted to stop first in Fort Worth, Texas, for a meal at the White Elephant Saloon, for old time's sake. I wasn't sure, once I went east and settled there, if I'd ever get out west again.

I took a cab to the White Elephant Saloon and was surprised to walk in on a crowd of people milling about, holding drinks and conversations. I nabbed a passing waiter who was carrying a tray of drinks and asked, "What's going on here?"

"Are you kiddin'? You don't know?"

"No idea," I said, "or I wouldn't ask."

"It's a funeral."

I looked around. "A lot of people here for a funeral. Who died?"

He told me. That was the first I'd heard that Tanner Moody had died.

I knew Tanner Moody, but I cannot say that we were friends. Still, it was a shock to hear that he had died, and of natural causes, to boot. It is usually expected that a man like Tanner will meet his end at the wrong end of a gun. After all, it is how men of legend usually die. Immodestly, I expect to go that way, myself.

I decided to have the meal I had come for and use the time to figure out how I felt about Tanner's demise. Since he was in his seventies it couldn't be called untimely. Considering the kind of life he'd led, it was amazing he had lived that long. The same might even be said for the rest of us who had somehow made it into the new century—Wyatt Earp, Bill Tilghman and me. Tilghman was still marshalling, and probably would be wearing a badge until the day he died. The last I heard of Wyatt he had refereed a fight in San Francisco that had turned controversial and, as a result, had headed for the gold fields of the Klondike.

2

Me, I'd spent the last few years in Denver, either promoting or writing about sports, and was on my way to New York.

Tanner was more than twenty years my senior, yet I considered him a contemporary. On that level it was difficult to deal with his death. It meant that another one of us was gone, and we had that much less of a hold on the past. The "hey-day" of the legend was fading fast, and those of us who were still here were just hanging on.

By the time my steak was gone I'd decided I had no choice but to go pay my respects and say good-bye to Tanner Moody.

The main room of the saloon looked much the way my friend Luke Short had decorated it thirty years ago, when he owned it.

When Luke went into partnership with Jake Johnson his plan had been to make the White Elephant Saloon one of the largest and most elegant gambling establishments in the entire Southwest. He started by hanging crystal chandeliers from the high ceilings, then arranged large canvases painted with classical scenes on the walls. The imported poker and faro tables were inlaid in rosewood frames. Green velvet drapes hung in front of every window and thick carpet covered the floor. Waiters in formal attire served drinks from the bar.

On this day, however, the activities going on were varied and—in some cases—rather odd. There were people coming and going, and even more who were milling about. Those who had already paid their respects to the deceased were now trying to kill time, determined for their own reasons to remain until the end of the day. On the other hand, those who had not yet visited the casket that was set up in one corner of the room were trying to find someone to talk to, or some way to put it off until the last moment. It was at this time that an idea began to dawn on me.

In point of fact I was on my way to New York to meet with a man named William Eugene Lewis. He was the younger brother of my good friend, the writer Alfred Henry Lewis. William had interviewed me more than twenty years ago, when he was a cub reporter, and since that time had followed my career. He was now, he believed, on the verge of becoming the managing editor of the *New York Morning Telegraph* and—when that position was indeed attained—intended to offer me a job on the newspaper as a reporter. My foray into journalism had begun in Denver and it had become my way of fitting into the new century. My wife, Emma, was already in New York, securing lodgings for us.

Now I was thinking, what better way to enter the new century than to write about the old, and what better representative of the old century was there than Tanner Moody? Rather than give in to the ultimate conceit and write about myself, or about my friends, Tanner was the person I should write about if, indeed, I intended to do this.

But to help me decide whether or not to do it, I had to first find out more about Tanner than I already knew. At this point, I had only memories from our few meetings, or what I had heard about him through stories. What I had to do now was identify some of these people who had come to his wake, who might even be staying for the burial, and listen to their stories. What were their experiences like with Tanner Moody? Did they love him, hate him, wish he was alive so they could kill him, or mourn his death?

But no one knows better than I the lies that legends are built upon. So this is what I decided to do. If I ever managed to get it all into print I would say: Dear readers, devour these stories of the legend of Tanner Moody, absorb them, enjoy them, but remember to believe perhaps half of them, and take the other half with a grain of salt.

And so with that in mind I moved in among the mourners and the revelers, intent on drinking, and listening, and retaining what I heard, putting off my own visit to Tanner's casket so that would be the finale of my tale . . . Bat Masterson paying his respects to Tanner Moody.

One

The New York Morning Telegraph, Feb. 4, 1903
The Legend of Tanner Moody
First of a series by Bat Masterson
Exclusive

When I entered the saloon and became an official attendee of Tanner Moody's wake I recognized a few of the people there. Not friends, but acquaintances who exchanged head nods with me as I approached the bar. Not any great friends of Tanner's, either, if I remembered correctly.

I obtained a beer from a bartender with gray hair and a heavily lined face, who informed me it was on the house because of the wake. I wondered who was footing the bill for this, since it had to be costing a fortune.

"This been goin' on all day?" I asked the barman.

"Since nine A.M. Folks was waitin' outside the door to get in. I seen people who hated Tanner Moody, some who were friends with him, and others who just wanted to get a look. We even caught some folks trying to take souvenirs off'a him."

"Souvenirs?"

"Locks of hair, pieces of his coat, stuff like that."

Tanner's casket was off in a corner of the room by itself, and from time to time mourners would wander over to pay their respects. I wondered why they didn't have a guard on the casket if folks were stealing from it.

"How long is he going to be laid out here?"

"Three days. Today was the first."

"Who's payin' for this wake?" I asked.

"Beats me," the man said. "All I know is my boss told me drinks is on the house. Some folks has already staggered outta here drunker'n a skunk. I'm surprised we ain't seen some gunplay."

I looked around. There weren't very many men wearing guns. It was the twentieth century and guns weren't as necessary—or as plentiful—as they once were. I had one in a rig under my arm, but that was only because there were still men around who—even in a new century—would have liked to catch me without one.

"Where's the law?"

"In and out," the bartender said. "These young fellas wearin' uniforms."

"Isn't there a sheriff?"

"Not like in the old days, there isn't. Now that we

have a police department the sheriff just sort of struts around behind his badge and stays out of trouble."

"Why don't they leave somebody with a . . . uniform here to watch over things?"

"You got me again, friend," the man said. "I'm jes' servin' up the drinks."

And he wasn't the only one. The White Elephant's bar was too long for one man to handle. The bartender at the other end was half this one's age, and was serving drinks to the mourners with a smile. I remembered when Luke Short first had the bar installed— that and the crystal chandeliers. I knew that Luke had sold the saloon to Jake Johnson back in '84, but I had no way of knowing how many times it had changed hands since then. Hence, I had no idea who the present owner was.

"Bat Masterson?"

I turned at the sound of my name, moving my hand within snatching distance of my gun. The man who had spoken my name looked at me from beneath a white Panama hat, and from behind a big nose and sagging jowls.

"You are Bat Masterson, aren't you?"

"Who's asking?"

"My name's Bob O'Dell," the man said. "I'm with the *Fort Worth Telegram*."

He was probably the grubbiest journalist I'd ever seen, which made me wonder a bit about my new profession.

"I'm Masterson."

"I knew it was you," he said excitedly. "Mind if I

ask you a few questions? Were you a friend of Tanner Moody's? Or an old enemy? Here to mourn or—"

"Actually," I said, cutting him off, "I'm covering the wake and funeral for a newspaper myself. I don't think talking to the competition would be good journalism, do you?"

O'Dell frowned and stared at me, taken aback.

"You're a . . . newspaperman now?"

"That's right.'

"I, uh, hadn't heard. What paper?"

"I was the sports editor for *George's Weekly* in Denver for a while, but I'll be writing this up for the *New York Morning Telegraph*."

I admit I was stretching the truth just a bit, but it was worth it to see the crestfallen look on the face of the man when he heard the name of the paper.

"That's a, uh, big newspaper."

"Yes, it is," I said. "If you'll excuse me, I want to circulate a bit and talk to people."

"Uh . . . oh sure, go ahead," he grumbled. "Don't want to, uh, hold up a colleague."

I grabbed my beer and left O'Dell standing at the bar.

There were other journalists present, but none of them had the nerve to approach me as Bob O'Dell had—which was just as well. They were likely of higher stature than he, and I wouldn't have wanted to take the same position I had with him.

I was, however, approached by others, some of whom I didn't mind talking to and catching up with. Some were even men with reputations of their own, although they had not—nor, truthfully, would they ever—attain the stature of a Tanner Moody, or a Wyatt Earp. One such man was Harry Morse. Morse was a longtime lawman and private detective who, in 1883, captured the notorious Black Bart, who, for six years, was the most successful highwayman in history.

Morse was in his late fifties, and looked well fed and surprised when we came face to face.

"Masterson."

"Hello, Harry."

"Didn't expect to see you here."

"I didn't know about it," I said. "It's just a coincidence that I stopped in."

"Some coincidence," Harry Morse said, "but in looking around I notice a lot of the fraternity in attendance."

"What fraternity would that be, Harry?"

Morse smiled at me and said, "Legends, Bat, legends—like Tanner, like you . . . and like me."

I ignored that remark.

"I didn't know you knew Tanner Moody."

"We had some dealings a time or two," he said. "In fact, back in sixty-eight—"

It was well known that Harry Morse loved to talk about his exploits. I was not about to stand there and be regaled with them, however, so I headed him off.

"I don't really have time for that now, Harry," I said. It may seem odd that I cut him off at that point, but I wanted to move around the room and eavesdrop on conversations. I did not want to be trapped for an hour or more by one person who was impressed with himself. True, Morse had many fine accomplishments to his name, but he managed not only to relate them every chance he got, but exaggerate them, as well. I shook his hand and moved on . . .

As I walked around I realized I could hear snatches of virtually every conversation going on around me. Rather than approach people the way O'Dell had done—or get collared by someone like Harry Morse—I decided I would get the real story from folks by eavesdropping. At least, it was worth a try.

I decided to start with the unlikeliest of mourners, and an elderly woman caught my eye as she approached Tanner's casket. I watched as she stared down at him, and I got lucky when a man moved up to stand beside her. They started to talk and I maneuvered myself so that I was within earshot . . .

Poor Ole Moody

by Marthayn Pelegrimas

"My mother has never set foot in an establishment that serves alcohol. She, sir, is a lady," the man said in a too-loud voice to a waiter offering a glass of champagne. "We have come only to pay our respects to the deceased, not to imbibe."

"Oh, hush up, son."

She looked to be no more than four feet tall, bent in that way folks get when they start shrinking back closer to the earth they're getting ready to inhabit for eternity. Her gray hair, streaked with a few wisps of black, had been pinned up tightly beneath her small gray felt hat. The same fabric carried through in her simple straight skirt and matching cape. The only adornment was decorative black braiding that trimmed the curve of her hem. As she walked across the carpeting, the pointed toes of her button boots showed she had remarkably tiny feet.

Her son, a large man with puffed red cheeks, was

only a head taller than his mother. After offering her his arm and having it pushed back at him, he walked purposefully, staring straight ahead, apparently not wanting to be included in the scene.

The bar was long, the full expanse of one wall, but in spite of the kind of business that was conducted within the four walls, the atmosphere was somber. There were no gamblers at any of the tables, no flashy women trying to proposition, no boisterous patrons. The focus of everyone's attention was the hand-carved casket that rested on a mahogany platform especially fashioned for viewing the body of Tanner Moody.

It being early, Elvira Clifford was the only female in the saloon. She managed to nudge her son away from her as she got closer to the casket. This moment was too sad and heartfelt to share.

"Poor Moody." She reached out her hands, then realizing she was still wearing gloves, slowly pulled the gray leather from each bony finger. Tucking the gloves inside the small bag hanging from her elbow, she stroked the cold cheek of her old friend, then bent down to kiss him tenderly. "Poor, poor Moody."

"Are you all right, Mother?"

She didn't turn to look at him. "Edward, please, don't smother me. Go sit down."

Edward Clifford resented his mother's callousness when he was a boy, but now, at fifty-five years of age, he had gotten quite used to her abrupt manner. Shrugging, he walked to a table in a dark corner.

She leaned closer to Tanner's ear and whispered. "I should have listened when you warned me against marrying Charlie Clifford. You remember Charlie, don't you, Moody? He was that kid who worked for your father, helping with the chores after your mother . . . You know, the one with the mess of wild blond hair. I used to go on and on about that hair of his. Drove you crazy. You finally told me that Charlie was all the time getting himself in trouble and I should stay away from him.

"I used to think it was because you were jealous. Or maybe I just hoped that you were. But after you left, Charlie was real attentive. But when Edward came along, Charlie started getting back into that trouble you warned me about until it got so bad I told him to change his ways or his address. We'd been married about three years by then. Guess you can figure out which way he went. But I don't have any regrets. I got Edward and Sarah out of the deal."

She gripped the edge of the casket, studying the ivory silk lining for a moment.

"Hey, Moody, guess you found out if that heaven Preacher Tabor shouted about is real. And if it is, I truly pray for you, dear one, that they opened those gates wide when they saw you coming."

A handsome man entered the saloon. Dressed in a black frock coat, his head was covered with a black Stetson and in the middle of his face grew a wooly mustache. He walked with confidence. Coming in from the cold morning air, sunshine still bright in his eyes, he almost knocked the old lady down as he stopped in front of the casket.

14

"Oh, madam, please forgive me, I didn't see you there."

His eyes slowly grew accustomed to the darkness and as they did, he took in his surroundings. All the windows had been covered with black crepe, and the same fabric had been draped across the front of the building as well. Pine boughs were arranged in large brass vases on either side of the coffin, with several sprigs of wild flowers tucked amongst the needles.

When the old lady failed to respond he asked, "Are you all right, madam?"

"Fine, fine. My lord, can't a person be alone with her thoughts?"

"Yes, certainly. I apologize."

The stranger moved aside, standing nearer to the foot of the casket.

After a few long moments passed in silence, the woman, apparently having reflected upon her bad manners, asked: "Friend or relative?"

He wasn't quite sure how to respond. While he thought, she became impatient. "I said, are you a friend or a relative?"

"I guess you'd call me an admirer."

The old woman seemed amused. "Well, I guess you could call me an admirer, also."

"Then you didn't actually know Mr. Moody?"

"Oh, I knew him, that's for sure. Back when we were just children, down in Aguilares; his father had some land there."

"Aguilares? That's near Laredo, isn't it?"

She nodded. "I've been reading so much about Moody for so many years now. And every time his father's spread was referred to as a 'ranch' I'd have a good laugh."

"And why is that?"

"Oh, things weren't as organized as they are now. Back then you fought for what you had and just tried hanging on to it for as long as you could. His father was from Georgia, you know, a real Southern gentleman. Had no idea what he was doing half the time, which put him at the mercy of a lot of heartless folks. There was never a lack of work or trouble—if not from the land itself then from the people on both sides of the Rio Grande."

"And how well do you remember his mother?" he asked.

She swayed a little and he reached out for her elbow.

"May I escort you to a chair, madam? You seem a bit fatigued."

"Yes, I think I do need to sit down. My son and I have come a long way."

As they walked toward one of the tables that had been lined up along the wall, Edward hurried to his mother's side.

"Mother, can I help—"

"This kind gentleman and I are having a conversation. Why don't you go get something to eat? I'll be fine."

Edward was used to taking orders from his mother and just nodded. "I'll only be an hour."

16

"She'll be safe here, among friends," the stranger told him.

She watched Edward walk away, then slowly lowered herself into the chair the man held for her.

The man sat facing her, and they remained still for a while, watching a crowd of gentlemen enter the saloon. At first the men talked loudly but soon, remembering the gravity of the event, removed their hats and walked solemnly toward the casket. Just when they calmed down, the bartender clanged a spoon against a large brandy snifter, catching the attention of everyone in the room.

"Gentlemen . . . and lady," he said, bowing politely in Elvira's direction, "I have just received a telegram from Young's Pier Theater in Atlantic City. I'd like to share it with you." Taking a sip of the champagne in front of him, the man read: " 'The world and my heart mourn the loss of a great man such as Tanner Moody. I am forever indebted to him for his continued support and friendship. Signed with love and admiration, Annie Oakley.' "

A polite round of applause went up in the room.

"Poor ole Moody," the old woman sighed. Withdrawing a monogrammed handkerchief from her bag, she dabbed at her eyes. "Did you notice the scar on his face?" she asked her companion. "On the right side, under his eye?"

"Yes, I did. But I just assumed, considering the eventful life he led, that a few injuries would have been inevitable."

"Oh, that didn't come from sheriffing or any outlaws he might have offended. That one came from his own mother. She decorated his back with some interesting marks, too."

He didn't know how to react to what she told him. Trying to conceal his surprise, he chose instead to introduce himself. Maybe after she reciprocated, he'd think of some way to respond.

"I must have left my manners at the door. Please allow me to introduce myself. My name is Joseph Spiller."

She nodded. "Glad to meet you Joseph, I'm Elvira Clifford. Moody always called me Ellie, though. Did I tell you I knew him from the day I was born? Our families homesteaded next to each other. It was Aunt Ruby, Moody's daddy's sister, who was the midwife. She helped my mama, even though we were Mexican. She was a gracious lady, like her brother—they had that Southern charm. Good manners travel much further than bad ones, I always say."

A young woman entered the darkened room and upon seeing the casket ran toward it. Throwing herself on top of the box, she wailed.

"Now, who do you suppose that is?" the woman asked. "It isn't as if Moody's dying could have come as a shock to anyone. He was seventy-five years old, after all."

Mr. Spiller shifted in his chair. The old woman was obviously mentally alert. He had no reason, thus far, to doubt her accusations concerning Moody's upbringing.

"My, my," she said, and fanned herself. "It is getting a bit close in here. Too many people."

"Would you care for some air, Mrs. Clifford? We could take a walk . . ."

"Oh, no, but thank you for the offer. I came to sit with Moody and that's what I intend to do. However, if you've other business, Mr. Spiller, please don't let me keep you."

He glanced toward the door. "No, I'm fine."

"Did I tell you Moody's father was from Georgia? Bibb County."

"Yes, you did."

The old woman leaned back in her chair. "But his mother wasn't."

He noticed a sudden change in her tone as she spoke.

"No, that woman came from up North. A Yankee through and through, yes, that's what she was. Did you know Mrs. Moody, sir? The stepmother?"

"No, I never had the pleasure."

"Well, if you had, I'm sure you'd have thought her to be quite gracious—that is, until you got to know the woman. Until you actually walked over the threshold of their home. Ate at their table. Which I did on many occasions." Her words triggered memories she'd been fighting back most of her life. And a frown creased her wrinkled face as she remembered.

"Don't be afraid, Ellie, I won't let nuthin' or nobody hurt you."

As they crouched under the back porch, hiding, Ellie pretended to be more frightened than she really was. Oh, she'd seen that old stepmother rant and rave for years; everyone in the whole county talked about how bad-tempered she was. Moody tried comforting the ten-year-old. Lying there on their stomachs, his arm hung protectively across her back. She snuggled closer, smelling clover and sunshine in his hair.

It took all her courage, but she finally told him. "I love you, Moody."

He laughed. "And I love you too, Ellie. I love you as if you were my own sister."

She hadn't meant that kind of love. She'd meant the kind that made a person's heart swell up so big you'd swear your chest would burst. Like when the milkweed pod popped and all the feathery seeds flew out, caught up in the breeze, filling the air, covering the trees and grass. She meant the kind of love that would tie them together forever. The kind that would make him want to marry her.

And just as she was working up the courage to explain the depth of her love, that horrible woman came and spoiled everything.

"Tanner! Tanner Moody! You come out from there."

Her face was in front of them, red with anger. She appeared more frightening than usual. "I see you— both of you."

"No." Tanner whined. "I'm not goin' nowhere. An' neither is Ellie."

In spite of her fear, the little girl shouted, "I'm tellin'! I'm tellin' my ma an' she'll tell Mr. Moody. So, you'd better just leave us alone!"

That only made the stepmother laugh. "Tanner knows what happens if he says one word of our private business to his father. Don't you, son? Tell Ellie what will happen if she runs around telling tales like that."

Ellie looked at him but he only stared ahead. For the first time she could feel the fear shivering through him.

"Go on home, Ellie. I'll be okay."

The stepmother roared at her to go away and terror, rushing through her clear down to her legs, fueled the run home.

Later Ellie tried telling herself she had gone for help, but then wondered at the fact that she never told one single person about the incident. She kept thinking that maybe if she kept quiet, Moody would get it a little easier. Maybe if . . .

She was so ashamed of herself she avoided poor Moody for days. But when she saw him next, he had a long gash on his cheek. He told her how Mrs. Moody had grabbed his arm. He'd fought back but she had more leverage with him down on his belly like that. She'd practically pulled his arm right out of the socket. An old broken jar lay buried just beneath the dirt until Moody was dragged across it. Then its jagged edges cut through the skin of his tender face.

"Mrs. Clifford, would you care for something to drink?"

It took her a second to realize where she was. "Whiskey would be nice. But don't tell my son."

Mr. Spiller waved for one of the waiters to come to their table. After he'd ordered two drinks he asked when she'd first met Tanner Moody.

21

"Like I said before, Moody and I knew each other from the moment I took my first breath. He said he was the one who slapped my bottom to force a cry out of me. He became my brother, my protector. He was five years older than me.

"Oh, he was so handsome. Stood straight. His father had taught him to be proud. And his mother, I don't remember her at all. She died when I wasn't more than four years old. But I do remember the sadness in that house. It was the fever that took her and for a while it looked as though Moody's father would die from it, too. But, praise God, he recovered. Moody was his only child, you know. Of course there was Aunt Ruby to help out but she had six kids of her own. So for a while it was just the two of them. But folks all said there was never such a diligent, loving father as Mr. Moody was.

"Then one day, like the plague, Leila Johnston came to town. Her husband had been killed, working in a mine up North, and she came to live with some relatives. They were the only people she had. Them and her four children. What a pack of brats."

The woman by the casket let out another long wail and for a moment all attention was on her. A waiter went to offer a cup of water, but she pushed him away.

"Stupid woman," Mrs. Clifford snapped.

"Just very distraught."

"You're a kind man, Mr. Spiller. I was very kind also when I was your age. But life and all the horrible situations and characters it thrusts on a person makes it mighty difficult to remain civil."

"I'm sure you're right," he said. He thought a moment about a few questions he had for the old lady but before he could voice any of them, a shot was fired. His hands went to his ears, which rang from the unexpected blast.

The bartender ducked for cover and most of the men in the room dove under tables. Several raced out the front door. The old woman sat stiffly.

"Don't no one come near me!" the female by the casket shouted. She held a pearl-handled revolver high over her head. The single bullet had ruined a large painting of Tanner Moody that had been hung against the back wall.

Edward Clifford came charging through the door. He stood there a moment, waiting for his eyes to adjust to the dimness. "Mother!" he shouted into the large room.

"You! Git in here!" the young woman screamed, pointing with the barrel of her gun.

When the man failed to move fast enough, she shouted again.

"Edward," Mrs. Clifford said as loudly as her voice would allow.

Mr. Spiller stood. "Here, we're over here."

The older man slowly became aware of the danger but was still confused as to the nature of the situation. Surprised at his own courage or stupidity, he wasn't quite sure which it was, he started toward the woman holding the gun and demanded to know what was going on.

"Stop right there! I'm taking this son-of-a-bitch Moody for a little ride."

Edward had no idea how to respond to such a statement. "I think I'll go sit with my mother now."

"I think that's the best place for you, don't you, mister?"

Meekly, Edward sat down. "Are you all right?" he whispered to Elvira.

"Hush, I'm fine."

The next person to enter the White Elephant Saloon was the sheriff. "Now, miss," he shouted, standing at the door with his hands up in front of him. "I'm sure you don't want to . . ."

"No, Sheriff," she said, pointing the gun at his head, "I'll tell you what I want. I want justice and revenge. Both have been too long in comin'. My family has suffered for too many years. Every one of us has suffered."

"Come down to my office," the sheriff said. "Let's not have any more trouble here. What you're doing is sacrilegious."

She threw her head back and roared a deep, hearty laugh. "This here's a saloon, Sheriff. An' this here dead hero of yours, the respectable Mister Tanner Moody, is a murderer. I'm just here to make sure this bastard don't git no Christian burial. He don't deserve no more nice words or tears. This lowlife killed my grandmother an' he's gonna pay. At long last!"

The sheriff edged his way past the bar. "If what you say is true, miss, we'll look into that matter later, but now I don't think this is the time or place for . . ."

She raised her arm and took aim. This time she hit two glasses off the bar. "See, Sheriff? I know how to use this. I didn't come to hurt no one. So just let us get this casket outta here and we'll let all of you get back to your mournin'. Come on, Joe, give me a hand."

Joseph Spiller stood up and walked over to the woman in the dirty velvet dress with the ragged lace trim. The Cliffords sat dumbfounded.

"Now, Mattie, honey."

"Grab that end," she ordered, pointing to the foot of the casket. She had a mannish figure and it looked for a moment as if she were going to lift the other end of the mahogany box herself. But then she pointed her gun toward a young waiter cowering in the corner. "You! Git over here an' grab the other end. I got a wagon out back we can load it into."

"Hold on one minute there, miss." Turning to the waiter, the sheriff said, "Don't you move."

"I've been waiting my whole life to give Mr. Moody here what he deserves. I think eternal damnation is a pretty nice reward for all the pain he brought my family."

The sheriff had managed to get to within ten feet of the woman. "Now, Mattie . . ."

"Don't you dare call me by my Christian name. Not you."

"I apologize, Miss . . . ?"

"Johnston."

He could see her hand shaking and knew he had the advantage; all he had to do was talk to her rationally, point out how unreasonable she was being. "Miss Johnston. I don't quite understand why you think Tanner here had anything to do with harming your grandmother."

"My mother told me, my aunts and uncles all knew it too. When my grandmother came down to live with them dirty Moodys all she wanted was to be a good mother to that murderin' no-good piece of trash. You see, Sheriff, my mother was the oldest. Old enough to know what she seen was real. An' she seen all of 'em watchin' her beloved mother die. No one lifted a finger. Can you imagine how that affected my mama's life? What kind of a parent she was to us kids? She weren't right in the head after seein' that kinda thing."

Mrs. Clifford let out a moan and, grabbing her shoulder, fell onto the table.

"My mother needs a doctor!"

Mattie grinned. "Guess there is a God after all. Now we can all have the pleasure of watchin' someone else's mama die. An' when I leave here, y'all will know just what it's like to git no help from no one at the time you need it most."

"Sheriff, call for the doctor," Edward ordered, ignoring Mattie. I demand you—"

"You're in no position to demand nothin'!" the crazed woman screamed.

"Listen to me, Mattie." Spiller reached out to grab her arm but she moved away. "I don't think we should do this."

Amazement spread over her face. "We planned this, Joe. That night we spent in Kansas City, I spent half of it tellin' you how my family got ruined. You said you understood. You promised to help me." Then, moving closer to him, she whispered, "Didn't we even talk about how we could ransom the bastard?"

Spiller nodded. "I know, honey, but I've had some time to talk to that old woman over there and I think maybe your mother didn't tell you things the way they really were. This just doesn't feel right. Maybe—"

"Grab that end, Joe, or so help me, I'll shoot you. I'm the only one left who can do this an' I'm gonna do it or die tryin'."

Elvira Clifford moaned and the sheriff held up his hands. "Miss Johnston, there's only one of me and two of you. It seems my responsibility right now is to help that woman. Tanner's already dead an' there ain't much I can do to help him. So if you're determined to make off with him, I reckon there ain't too much I can do about it." Having made his decision, the sheriff marched over to the old woman, scooped her into his arms and headed for the door.

"Suit yerself," Mattie said, to the surprise of everyone in the room.

Edward trailed behind, clutching his mother's purse, "It'll be all right, dear, don't you worry. Eddie won't let anyone hurt you."

"Where are you staying?" the sheriff asked.

"Down at the Lindell Hotel," he shouted to the man's back as they hurried down the street.

"We'll call Doc Bell from the hotel, then," the sheriff told him.

Elvira opened her eyes. "Where are we going? What are you doing?"

"I'm here, Mother!" Edward shouted to her. "Just stay calm."

"I am calm! I'm calm, just put me down!" Her feet

kicked at the air as the sheriff looked straight ahead and kept walking, ignoring her words.

The bartender stood in the doorway watching the three. "Who'd have thought it?" he asked himself. "Always figured that damn lawman was a coward."

A man scribbling on a piece of paper looked up. "Why's that?"

"Never been no cause for him to show any backbone until now, I guess."

"You two! Shut up over there!" Mattie Johnston's orders could be heard clear across Main Street. "Git your butts over here and clear away all this trash."

"No." The bartender shook his head. "I won't touch any part of that tribute. People been bringing pictures and items dear to them in honor of Mr. Moody for days. I'll take no part in desecrating any of them."

"I'm only gonna ask you once," she said.

"You have my answer."

"And here's mine." She raised her pistol and fired, hitting the man in his left shoulder.

"There now, rest until the doctor gets here," Edward told his mother.

"I don't want to rest," she snapped, sitting up on the edge of the bed.

"Sheriff, I want to thank you for helping my mother. I'm Edward Clifford." He extended his hand.

The sheriff shook hands with him. "It's a pleasure, Mr. Clifford. Name's Clark."

"So what do you both propose I do now?" Elvira asked. "I've come all this way to see Moody and now you're keeping me here, against my will, waiting for a doctor who will scold all of us for wasting his . . ."

Before she could finish, she fell to the floor.

"Mother!" Edward and the sheriff dashed to lift the frail woman onto the bed. She lay unconscious.

"What should we do?"

The sheriff pulled a blanket over her small frame. "Nothin' to do till the doc gets here."

"What's taking him so long?"

"Relax, Mr. Clifford, we just called a few minutes ago. You stay here. I'll go fetch one of the women downstairs to come help your mother get more comfortable."

Before Edward could protest, the sheriff left the room.

He tried patting his mother's cheeks to revive her, then searched the room for her smelling salts. As he tore through the drawers of the bureau, he whimpered. In all his fifty-five years he had never been without his mother. What would he do? What would become of him? She had always been there for him—she was the strong one. She'd outlived two husbands and three children.

The sheriff returned with the doctor. "Look who I found on the stairway. Doc Bell, this here's Edward Clifford."

The doctor removed his hat. "Mr. Clifford, I presume this is your mother?"

"Yes."

"And has she been ill?"

"No. Never. Not a day in her life."

"Well, you two wait downstairs while I examine my patient. I'll let you know when I'm done."

Reluctantly, Edward left the room with Sheriff Clark.

"Poor ole Moody," Elvira Clifford moaned. As she opened her eyes she saw the distinguished man in the black suit standing at her side. "Are you the undertaker?"

"No, Mrs. Clifford, I'm the doctor. Seems you fainted. Your son is very worried about you."

"Is he here?" She looked around the room but without her glasses couldn't make out too much.

"It's just the two of us."

The frail woman pressed her head into the pillow. "Could you bring me my pills?" she sheepishly asked. "They're in the bottom of that hatbox."

The doctor returned with a small vial. "So, you're having heart problems?" he asked. "How long have you been taking these?"

"Almost a year. I know Doctor Adams, back home, thought I wouldn't make it past spring, but when I heard Moody was dead, I had to keep myself alive long enough to come see him."

Pouring a glass of water from the pitcher on the bureau, the doctor helped the woman swallow two small pills.

"And you've managed to keep your condition a secret from your son?"

She smiled. "That's been the easiest part of all this. But I have to admit, the dying part is getting more difficult."

Doc Bell removed a tarnished stethoscope from his bag. "Let's just have a look here," he said, adjusting the right earpiece. "Now take a few deep breaths for me."

For the next few moments doctor and patient listened—he to her weak heart and she to the ominous silence.

It was obvious he didn't like what he was hearing but still she asked, "So? What do you think?'

He had to turn his back to her. Carefully returning the instrument to its proper place, he took his time clasping the bag shut. When he finally moved to face her, he'd managed to get the nervous tic at the corner of his mouth under control. His wife always said it was the only thing that gave him away. Fool thing, he thought, what kind of a way is that for a man of medicine to act? But every time bad news had to be delivered, the infernal twitching started up again.

"Are you comfortable, Mrs. Clifford? Is there anything I can do for you? Would you like me to telephone your doctor?"

"Sit." She pointed to the rocker in the corner. "Pull that chair closer and sit by me. I came here to get a few things off my chest and that's just what I'm going to do. 'Cause I don't think I'm leaving this room alive."

The doctor dragged the chair across the worn floorboards, then positioned it near the bed. Reaching up, he patted the woman's hand. "Now, Mrs. Clifford . . ."

"No need to feel badly about any of this, Doctor, I've had a very . . . ahh, I guess you'd call it an eventful life. I've done practically everything I ever wanted to do—and quite a few I didn't. But there's only one regret and it's been nagging at my heart, eating away at it almost my whole life."

Footsteps roared up the stairs outside the room,

then voices, followed by a loud knocking on the door.

"Doc, I hate to bother you but there's some trouble down at the White Elephant."

"Anyone close to dying?" the doctor asked.

"Ahhh, no, I don't think so."

"Come back when you know for sure, then."

Elvira Clifford would normally have told the doctor to go tend to those other folks, but this day was about as far from normal as they came.

After the commotion died down, Doc Bell turned his attention on the old woman. "Now, Mrs. Clifford, what did you want to tell me?"

"It's about me and Moody. When we were kids back in Aguilares. Lord, how I loved that boy."

His smile! Every day when he stood there grinning at her like he did, she loved him a little more. Maybe her cheeks flushed because of that one tooth on the left side that was missing. Poor Moody. The buckle from his father's belt was meant for his shoulder and back but had caught his mouth. The stepmother said when he got older, another tooth would grow in to fill up the space. But it had been Moody's fault, she said, for moving when she was trying to teach him a lesson.

He was so skinny back then. Tall and thin. Hand-me-downs hung on him like scarecrow clothes, all faded and worn. But Ellie knew he'd grow up to be a big strong man and then he'd ask her to be his wife.

Of course she'd say yes. She rehearsed how she'd

sweetly smile and nod coyly. Like it had come as a surprise. And they'd leave Texas and the stepmother would never bother them again.

But then came the one day that everything went wrong.

It was in the fall. Leaves were turning and, thankfully, things were cooling off. She was supposed to meet Moody back where the fence had come apart and they would go fishing. She waited and waited. When she was sure he'd forgotten, she went looking for him.

The cast iron cauldron was always filled with something—it didn't matter the time of year or day. That woman was forever out there, back of the house, cooking up something. When Ellie came through the long grass, she could see the stepmother poking and stirring whatever it was with a long pointed stick.

"Mrs. Moody?"

"What do *you* want?" She never even bothered turning around. All her politeness was saved up for her husband. She had none to spare for anyone else.

"Is Tanner around? We were supposed to—"

"Ain't seen that brat all day. But when I do he's gonna be real busy. Too busy to trot off with you. He's gonna . . ."

The little girl stopped listening when she spotted him, crouching by the side of the house. He motioned for her to go home. She could see his eye had been bruised.

"Thanks Mrs. Moody, I gotta go home now."

The woman stopped what she was doing and

abruptly turned. Her eyes caught what the girl was looking at and that's when she spotted Tanner Moody. "Git over here, boy!"

"I'm not comin' anywhere near you! You just wait till my father comes back. I'm tellin' what you done to me."

"Your pa's not comin' back till after supper. An' by the time I get finished cryin' to him 'bout what a horrible brat you are, I'll have all the sympathy around here. Not you. Now, git over here or you can make it harder on yerself an' make me come after you."

The poor boy stood there a moment, confused. Even though he was fifteen and almost as big as the stepmother, she outweighed him. And to hit a woman was unthinkable. His choices were narrowed down to two: stay or run.

"Run to my house!" Ellie shouted. "You can stay there until your father comes home!"

The woman grabbed the little girl roughly by the arm. "Stay outta this, missy, this don't concern you."

"Let her go!" he shouted.

But the woman didn't listen and wrenched the girl's arm, causing her to scream. "Tanner, you get your good for nothin' butt over here now."

He lunged at her. Leila Johnston stabbed at his leg with the sharp end of the stick she still clenched in her hand. Ellie could see a small pool of blood wetting the hem of his trousers.

Tossing the girl a few feet, Leila laughed. He tried grabbing for the stick but the woman was faster. Then she started stabbing upward, toward his chest and Ellie was more afraid than she'd ever been in all her ten years on earth.

All she had was her self and that's what she used. Charging toward the woman's back, she ran, butting her like a crazed billy goat.

Leila Johnston fell forward across the top of the large iron pot. Steam rising from the liquid inside, scaled her arms as she tried holding herself up. The children stood watching in horror, not sure what to do. Gravity won out and the stepmother's weight brought the pot over, sending a tidal wave of indigo over the woman and the dried grass. Blue spatters freckled everything within a few feet of the disaster. The bombazine curtains she had been dyeing slopped onto the ground.

Tanner picked the stick up that had flown out of her hand and landed close to his feet. Standing over the woman, he held the pointed end toward her. But before he could say anything, she grabbed and tried pulling him down to her level or herself upright—Ellie was never sure, even though she had played the scene out in her memory for decades.

The fire that had burned beneath the pot still roared and as Leila struggled, her hair caught in the flames. Grabbing her head she screamed from the shock and pain.

"Help me up!" she shouted over and over. "Help me up! God damn you, help me!"

But they didn't move in her direction.

They ran away instead.

They ran until nothing looked familiar and they were sure no one could ever find them.

When they finally stopped, Ellie turned to him, tears rolling down her dirty cheeks, blue dye splashed on the front of her pale pink smock. "What are we gonna do, Moody? They'll throw us in jail. They'll . . ."

He stood over her, almost two heads taller. "I won't let nothin' bad happen to you, Ellie. Promise."

"But I . . . I . . ."

He hugged her. Probably to quiet her down but she pretended he was her sweetheart and held on for dear life. Her fear emptied out in loud sobs and she could feel the front of his warm shirt getting damp.

"Now listen to me. We don't know how bad she is. We have to act like nothin' happened. We'll go fishin', then to your house. I'll sneak back, when I'm sure Pa's home. I'll tell him what happened. He listens to me. He loves me more than her . . . I know he does. It'll be my word against hers."

She knew, even at that young age, that her life would be changed if talk of her hateful act got around town. She knew no boy would want to deal with a horrible girl like her. She'd have no life: no husband, no children. What if the sheriff came and took her away? She forced her breathing down to a calmer rate. Then she looked down at herself.

"Moody. What about this?" She pointed to the stains on her blouse.

"When we get back to your house, you'll change.

I'll take it with me an' walk back by the river an' throw it in."

"But, Moody, what about . . ."

"Don't worry, Ellie. I'll take all the blame."

He was her champion, her hero. And when he said he'd make everything all right, she believed.

The doctor rocked slowly in the chair. "What happened to Mrs. Moody?"

"Such horrible burns. The top of her head looked like she'd been scalped. Her neck got the worst of it, though. She died after three days of suffering. Out of her mind from the pain. Back in '41, we were pretty much on our own. The women did what they could but it wasn't near good enough. There wasn't a doctor for miles. That poor woman never remembered what happened.

"But Moody told his father the truth . . . well, all of it except the part about it being me who pushed her. Never told a soul that I had killed her."

"And what about the stories I've heard how Tanner Moody had a blowup with his old man and left the state?"

"Mr. Moody thought he was protecting his son. Thought the law would come for him and lock him up for sure if they thought the boy had hurt his stepmother. So together, they made up a story. Waited awhile of course, until gossip died down. Then made it look like they had such a row that things could never be the same between them again. Mr. Moody gave his son some money and after a quick good-bye, I never saw him again."

"And you had to go on living in Aguilares as if nothing happened?"

She nodded. "I always figured when I grew up a bit, I'd go ask Mr. Moody where his son was. Then I'd go to him. I owed him so much. I'd thank him for everything he'd done for me." She frowned. "But Mr. Moody wouldn't tell me. He wouldn't tell anyone. That man loved his son so much.

"One night when I went to visit him and beg one more time for Moody's whereabouts, the poor man broke down crying and told me how sorry he was for putting the boy through all that misery. He swore he'd never tell anyone where Moody was. Never. It was the only way he could keep him safe—the only thing he could do for his son. Mr. Moody lived alone on that land for years before he died of influenza in the winter of '56."

"And what became of Leila's children?"

"At first they all claimed they saw Moody push their mother. The stories grew with each year. First they claimed to be out in the yard playing when it happened. Then they were fighting the vicious boy off their beloved mother. They were finally all sent back up north to live with cousins. Mr. Moody just couldn't handle that wild pack himself. Their lies grew with each generation and so did their hatred for poor ole Moody."

The doctor sat back, trying to take in everything he had just heard.

"Doc, no matter what anyone says and no matter

how he might have turned out, Tanner Moody was the bravest, most courageous man I've ever known."

"And you still love him? Even after more than sixty years of not seeing him?"

"Oh yes. That first love never fades from your heart, does it?"

A gentle knock came at the door. "Doctor? It's Edward Clifford. May I see my mother now?"

"What do you want me to tell him?" the doctor whispered. When she didn't reply, he stood to check the old woman's breathing.

"Come in, Mr. Clifford," he said just loud enough to be heard.

Edward was wracked with great sobs of grief as Doctor Bell explained that Elvira's heart had simply given out. And that was all he had time to say before the sheriff returned.

"That Spiller fella jumped on her," the sheriff said over his shoulder as Doc Bell hurried to catch up. "It was just about the only way to get the gun away from her. Jesus Almighty, this has been one peculiar day and it ain't even noon yet."

It looked more like a riot than a wake. People crowded the street outside the saloon. The sheriff had to push ahead, threatening anyone who would not move with a night in jail.

"Let the doc through. Move aside. Bill!" he shouted to one of the waiters, "open the door!"

Joseph Spiller sat propped against the wall beside Tanner Moody's casket. His coat was draped over a chair and he appeared shaken, clutching his shoulder. Blood seeped through the white of his shirt.

Doc Bell knelt beside the man. "Let's have a look . . ."

Spiller pushed his hands away. "My shoulder only got nicked. It's my leg that caught the worst of it."

He would have missed the wound entirely. The black wool of the man's trousers was soaking up the blood, making it almost impossible to see.

Removing a pair of small scissors from his bag, the doctor started cutting, making a large hole in the trousers, preparing the area for a more thorough examination.

"Where's the lady?" the doctor asked as he worked.

"They took her upstairs. Someone said there are rooms up there."

"Used to be Luke's place. How bad is she?"

"Got a good sized bump on her head. She was unconscious when they carried her away. How's Mrs. Clifford? I really . . ."

"She died about ten minutes ago."

Spiller looked stunned.

"So, you two were in this together? That's what the sheriff says, anyway."

"Started out that way."

The doctor stopped for a moment to study the man. "Doesn't look like either one of you thought this thing through very far."

He shook his head. "Guess not."

When Doc Bell was finished cleaning the man's wounds, he instructed Sheriff Clark to take Spiller down to his office where he could stitch the leg up.

Then he headed for the stairs to have a look at Mattie Johnston.

She was sitting on the bed wrapped in a quilt embroidered with violets.

"Well, miss," he said, "let's have a look at you."

She glared as he approached, never moving while he removed his jacket and then washed his hands in the basin on the side table. She wouldn't give any of them the satisfaction of seeing her in pain.

"Look up here," he said as he lifted her chin. "Follow my finger." He watched her eyes, checked the pupils. Then turned her head so he could have a better look at the lump in the middle of her forehead.

"Does this hurt?" he asked as he carefully moved her head from side to side.

"No."

"How about this?" He massaged her scalp, checking for other bruises.

"No."

"Well, you're going to have a severe headache for—"

"I'm fine! Stop fussin'. Ain't never needed a doctor before, don't need one now."

It wasn't the words but her tone that got to him. "Maybe you don't need a doctor, but because of your actions here today, several people have been badly hurt."

She sniffed in his direction. Then under her breath she muttered, "Serves 'em right."

The doctor stood back. "Now that's enough."

"What the hell do you know about anything?"

"I know you've been misinformed. That what you think happened—did not. At least not in the way you've been told."

Mattie tried getting up but fell back. "I know what I know. All you people think that Moody bastard was a damn hero. A saint!"

"No," he interrupted, "Tanner Moody was never a saint. He did many unlawful things but the majority of his deeds were honorable."

"And just how do you know that?" she asked. "What makes you so sure that what *you* know is real? Or what I heard ain't? What makes you so sure that the people who tell you their stories are honest?"

"Well . . ."

"Each one of us gotta decide what's the truth. An' my truth tells me Tanner Moody started the hatred in my family when he killed my grandma Leila. An' that hatred has been born over an' over with each of us. Look at me, Doc. See that shinin' deep in there? It sure ain't love. Naw, love is somethin' my ma never had much of. Cause she never got much after her ma was killed. Hate an' revenge. It's what our family is about, thanks to good ole Tanner Moody."

"Why didn't you track him down? Why didn't any of your family have the courage to confront him when he was alive if you all felt like this?"

"The man never sat still. He was always runnin' from us. Hidin' out."

"You honestly believe Moody did all the things he did in his life just to avoid you?"

"That I do."

42

The doctor had run out of words. Reflecting for a moment while he put on his coat, he picked up his bag, and walked toward the door.

"Cain't take the truth, huh?"

"The sheriff will be up. Stay in bed."

"Keep on walkin', Doc!" she screamed as he closed the door. "Give Moody a great big ole kiss for me!"

A group of men walked into the saloon as Doc Bell walked out. "Yep," one of them said, "Tanner Moody was my brother's best friend, they fought Indians together up in Montana."

"Did I ever tell you how Moody and I rode with Quantrill's Raiders, during the war?" the other one asked.

The doctor knew that last part was totally untrue. And in spite of himself, he had to stop and have a good look at the man capable of telling such a lie.

He had an air of respectability about him. Could have been a judge. But the admiration he commanded from his friends by telling his story, was something he probably never got any other time during his life. And because of his encounters today with Mattie Johnston and Elvira Clifford, Doctor Bell was wise enough to have learned that the legend of Tanner Moody had rubbed off on everyone.

Two

The New York Morning Telegraph, Feb. 5, 1903
The Legend of Tanner Moody
Second in a series by Bat Masterson
Exclusive

Rarely do we get to see the legend as a child, but in my first article I told the tale of Elvira Clifford, a woman who had known Tanner Moody when they were children together, and who loved him all her life, and never told him. It is important, reader, for you to remember that certain parts of these stories I tell have been embellished, for I was not there for each and every word and action that took place. So it is my job to fill in the blanks for you.

After eavesdropping on Elvira Clifford, and finding out what happened later from her son, and from the doctor—both of whom were kind enough to speak with me—I went to the room I had taken at a nearby hotel. By this time I had come to realize that I would indeed be writing this series of articles, and I had to make sure that I had enough paper and pencils to take down all the details. After a good night's rest I'd do some shopping and then return to the White Elephant to see who the second day of Tanner Moody's wake would bring in.

I returned to the wake the next morning after breakfast and a short trip to a nearby mercantile store for the proper supplies a newsman should have. I was greeted by the same bartender, who supplied me with a cup of coffee when I turned down his offer of a beer that early in the morning. As I turned away from the bar I found myself face to face with another ghost from Tanner's past. The man was tall and well dressed, and white had taken over his hair and mustache, but I was still able to recognize Mr. James B. Hume, perhaps the greatest Wells Fargo detective of all time. In fact, for years he was their chief of detectives and had, indeed, hired Harry Morse to work for Wells Fargo. It was while working for Hume that Morse captured Black Bart.

Hume turned and as we came face to face betrayed surprise only by a raised eyebrow.

"Bat Masterson."

"Mr. Hume," I replied. "I confess I'm surprised to see you here—but then, why should I be? Harry Morse was here, as well, a short time ago."

"Really? It's been some time since I last saw Harry. How did he seem to you?'

"Well," I said. "And you?"

"In fine fettle, Bat," Hume said. "A little worse for the wear of years, but then who isn't?"

"Too true."

"And what about you? You look well."

"I'm doing fine, in fact," I said. "I'm here quite by accident." I went on to explain how I had come to be in attendance, and then we repaired to the bar to catch up a bit. I received a refill on my coffee and Hume accepted a mug of beer from the bartender.

"A newspaperman," he said, after we had talked a while. "There's not many of your stature who have made it into the twentieth century, Bat, and fewer still who have, eh, changed professions."

I couldn't very well argue with that, and there was no umbrage to be taken. Especially not after he added, "I admire that."

"We'll see how admirable it is after I have written my first article for the *Telegraph*," I said.

"And do you have something planned?" Hume asked.

"This," I said. "I'll write about the funeral of Tanner Moody. How well did you know him, James?"

"Not well, I'm afraid," he said. "Our paths crossed several times when he was wearing a badge . . . Just well enough to want to pay my respects. I'm afraid I have no escapades for you to write about."

I thought both Tanner and Hume lucky that their

paths had not crossed while Tanner was still on the wrong side of the law. I had no doubt they would have bedeviled each other to no end.

"No," Hume said, placing his empty beer mug on the bar, "I'm afraid you'll have to get your tale from another quarter. If you'll excuse me, I'll pay my respects and be off. I have business to attend to."

"Still Wells Fargo business?"

"What else?" Hume asked. "I'm seventy-five, and while my erstwhile aide Jonathan Thacker bears the bulk of the work, I still maintain the title of Chief Special Officer. I'll die before I'll retire."

As I watched him walk toward the casket to pay his respects, I could see that pain and age had caused him to lose the erect posture he had maintained for most of his adult life. I'd heard stories of various ailments assailing him, but it was good to see him still up and operating, even at a diminished capacity.

I finished my coffee, put the empty mug back on the bar and surveyed the room. It was already filling up with people—mourners, curious onlookers, more souvenir hunters, no doubt—and I started a slow circuit, continuing my search for the next chapter in my Tanner Moody tales . . .

It was midafternoon when a man arrived who attracted quite a bit of attention. He was an elderly gent in his seventies, wearing an expensive Spanish suit. He was silver-haired and tall, but as he moved across the room, working his way through the crowd, he appeared to favor his left shoulder. Watching him just a little longer, it became clear that his left arm was almost useless.

He walked to the bar and ordered a shot of whiskey, which he tossed off quickly. He cast a glance or two toward Moody's coffin, but made no move to walk over to it. I decided to approach him and see what had brought him to Tanner Moody's wake.

His name was Don Felipe Talamantes and he had met Tanner Moody many years ago. I introduced myself, stating that I was attending in the capacity of a journalist.

"I am familiar with your celebrity, senor," he said. "It would be my pleasure to share a drink with you."

He had a second whiskey in front of him but I said, "Just a beer will do."

He said, *"Cerveza, por favor,"* to the bartender.

"You were a friend of Senor Moody's?" he asked, when I had my beer in hand.

"An acquaintance, I would say," I replied. "But I'm planning to do some articles about him, based on his life and on the people who have come to attend his wake and funeral. If I may ask, Don Felipe, what brings you here? Were you and Moody friends?"

"Perhaps not even acquaintances, Senor Masterson." He pointed to his left shoulder. "My one encounter with him left me with this."

"He shot you?"

"Sí."

"And yet you're here to pay your respects?"

He heaved a great sigh and said, "It is a long story,

and part of it I learned from a man who did know Senor Tanner. He worked with him on a ranch that was owned by a man who competed with my father."

"And that man was . . . ?"

"Alas, I never knew his name. We came together quite by accident some years later. He is dead now, but he told me a story, and perhaps if I relate it to you in his words you will better understand. Do you have the time?"

"Don Felipe," I said, "at the moment, time is all I have."

"*Muy bien,*" Don Felipe said. "This man he was the—how do you say—the straw boss . . ."

Straw Boss

by Elmer Kelton

Yes, I knew Tanner Moody way back when nobody else did, hardly. I always expected to attend his funeral someday, but I thought it might come a lot sooner than this. Even early, he seemed like he was born for trouble. It wasn't that he went looking for it so much as it always seemed to come looking for him. There was something about him, an air I guess you'd call it, that was like a challenge to those people who *were* looking for trouble.

This was not long after the Mexican War and way before the War of Northern Aggression. Tanner was just old enough that his whiskers were beginning to turn dark. He had grown up in the South Texas brush country, so close to the Mexican border that when the wind was right you could smell the chili cooking. Sun and wind had made his skin so brown that he could pass for a Mexican if he wanted to, and he spoke the language like a native. That came in handy sometimes.

He was a cowboy when I first came to know him, or maybe I ought to say *vaquero*. People didn't use the word *cowboy* much at that time. It didn't get respectable until later. His daddy had come from Georgia into Mexican Texas and brought the Southern farmer's stock-handling methods with him. But Tanner learned the Mexican way of working cattle and breaking horses. Those were not always to his daddy's liking. For one thing, he loved to rope cattle with a rawhide *reata* just for the pure hell of it. It tickled him to set a wild one back on its rump. Naturally the old man didn't approve of roughing up his stock. That led to some hot arguments and finally a knock-down, drag-out fight that sent Tanner looking for new territory away from the old man's bailiwick.

This was at a time when border jumpers were working both sides of the Rio Grande. Mexico had lost two wars, one to Texas and one to the whole United States. General Santa Anna had signed away the whole of Texas to save his own skin after the Texians captured him at the battle of San Jacinto. But a lot of his countrymen didn't agree that he had the right to make such a lop-sided trade. They didn't place near as high a value on Santa Anna's life as he did. So in the Mexicans' eyes it was pure patriotism if a man went raiding over into Texas and brought back a lot of gringos' cattle and horses. And of course the two wars had left most of the old Texians with a gnawing grudge against Mexicans in general, so they saw no crime in swimming across the Rio Grande and bringing back cattle and horses that understood nothing but Spanish.

Ofttimes the same animals kept changing hands like a counterfeit dollar, swimming south one night and back north a night or two later. Some people swore that they saw cattle develop web feet from crossing the river so many times.

There had been peace treaties after both of the wars, but there was mighty little peace. When people start hating one another because of the race they were born into, it's hard to tell them much about right and wrong. The part of Texas between the Nueces River and the Rio Grande was fought over time and time again. Mexico claimed it, but Texians said the agreement with Santa Anna made it theirs. It came to be a mean place to live in.

Tanner did his share of border jumping before he was old enough to shave. It's easy at this late date to say he did wrong, but he didn't see it that way. He just followed the mood of the violent times he growed up in. Attitudes have changed a right smart since then, but it's not fair to judge people of that day by today's rules of etiquette. I don't reckon Tanner ever thought about explaining or apologizing for any of it. Everybody was doing it, Texan and Mexican. He was just better at it than most of the others, and he survived. Many a man, white and brown both, disappeared in the brush or in the river with no tombstone to show that they had ever lived.

When I first knew Tanner he came to work for a gringo outfit that branded its stock with a T Cross. You might think that would be a hard brand to alter, but most of the ranches across the river had big and intricate brands. It wasn't hard to wrap one of those around the T Cross and cover it plumb up. Not that they all bothered. Texas brands didn't mean any more over there than Mexican brands meant in Texas.

Directly across the river from the T Cross was the ranch of old Don Carlos Talamantes. Don Carlos had been a colonel under Santa Anna, though he never liked *el presidente* much and plotted against him a right smart. He was real bitter over losing Texas because he had claimed land north of the river. Naturally he lost it when Texas took its independence. He blamed Santa Anna about as much as he blamed Sam Houston and the Texians. His way of getting even was by raiding the Texas ranches within a night's ride of the river. He gathered anything that couldn't outrun him. The T Cross wasn't his only victim, but it took the biggest losses because it was the handiest to him.

You can imagine that this didn't set well with old man Jesse Threadgill, who owned the T Cross. He was not a stranger to war himself. He had fought alongside Houston at San Jacinto and later rode with the Texas Rangers in the Mexican War. I heard it from a sporting woman who saw him out of his underwear that he had more scars than she could count in the little time that he held still.

Tanner was brought up to believe that when you

worked for a man and took his pay, you *worked* for him. You stayed loyal to him whether you believed in what he was doing or not. You didn't make bad talk against him behind his back. If a day came when you couldn't abide him anymore, you just up and left. Then you were free to say what you wanted to.

Old Jesse's answer to Don Carlos was to try to steal back as much of his own stock as he could find and take the don's for good measure. The two old reprobates treated it almost like a game except that now and then somebody got hurt real bad. It looked for a while like they might have to expand the cemeteries on both sides.

That was the situation Tanner rode into when he signed on with the T Cross. Old Jesse had known Tanner's daddy back in Georgia before they both came to Stephen F. Austin's Texas. I was straw boss at the time. Jesse told me to take Tanner under my wing and see that he made a hand. There wasn't much tolerance for a man who *didn't* make a hand.

A big part of the job involved moonlight work south of the river. If a man had any scruples about it, he didn't have much business being in that part of Texas in those days. Tanner had already had some experience in that line because his daddy played the game too.

Most of the time Don Carlos and Old Jesse went along with their men on the raids. You couldn't say that either one of them called on his men to do something he didn't do himself. You had to give them credit for guts, even if their notion of honesty fell short of the mark.

So far as I know, Tanner got his first bullet wound at the hands of Don Carlos himself. We had been roused out of our bedrolls when one of the river sentries came riding in to report a raid in progress. We spurred out hell-for-leather in the hopes we could head them off and save Old Jesse's cattle. Half of them had probably come from Don Carlos's herd, but possession was what counted. We intended to keep it.

The raiders had gathered up a hundred head or so and were pushing hard to get to the river and cross before daylight. We were maybe a mile from the *rio* when we overtook them. They were a mix of cows and calves, bawling their heads off trying to find each other. Steers were generally a lot quieter, but when you're getting them dirt cheap and in the moonlight you don't waste time being choosy.

The raiders started shooting before we reached them. We didn't know whether they were firing at us or trying to stampede the cattle and get them to the river before we could stop them. Gunfire causes some people to stop and turn back. For others it's like a shot of whisky that makes them wild and reckless. That was the effect on Tanner. He let out a screech that years later would be called a rebel yell, and he set those big-roweled Mexico spurs to jingling against his horse's ribs.

I yelled at him to slow down and take some care, but I had just as well have been whistling into my hat.

He rode straight toward the lead cattle, yelling at the top of his lungs and trying to turn them back against the raiders. Some of the cattle broke out around him. Others slowed down or milled in confusion. Shots were being fired all around them, front and rear. They didn't know which way to go.

Up to that point Tanner had not fired. The best we had in those days were some old-fashioned cap-and-ball pistols. You had to reload after every shot. If your enemy got to you while the barrel was empty, your milk might turn to clabber real quick. Tanner was holding his shot till he had a can't-miss target.

Don Carlos had a son named Felipe, who always regretted that he had been born too late to fight the Texians at the Alamo. He was sure that if he had been there he could have saved Santa Anna from the disgrace of San Jacinto. I guess he envied his old papa for having been such a strong military man, and he tried to measure up to him any way he could. He had built himself a reputation as a fearless raider and fearsome enemy of the *tejanos*. Wherever he saw danger he flung himself into it, trying to prove he was Papa's equal.

All of a sudden him and Tanner had their horses nose-to-nose and the muzzles of their pistols not much farther apart. Felipe took time to swear a few words about the moral character of Tanner's mother. Tanner didn't waste any conversation. He just squeezed the trigger.

It was Felipe's good luck that both horses were

faunching around and threw Tanner's aim off by a few inches. The lead ball smashed Felipe's shoulder and knocked him off of his horse. He was in some danger of being trampled by the cattle, but they broke around Tanner and his horse. You could say Tanner probably saved his life, though that was not his intention after coming so close to killing him.

Tanner was fumbling to reload when Don Carlos came charging up. He saw his son on the ground and knew that Tanner had put him there. The old man was a good shot, but it is hard to hold your aim from the back of a running horse. He was probably distracted too by what had happened to his son. His bullet burned across Tanner's ribs and killed a cow that was running by. The jolt made Tanner drop his pistol. He didn't get down to look for it. He put spurs to his horse and put himself out of range in case the don got reloaded.

Don Carlos, though, dismounted and waved the running cattle around his son. One of his vaqueros helped him lift Felipe onto the don's horse. The old man mounted behind him and started making heavy tracks straight toward the river. His vaqueros gave up the cattle and followed him. There would be other nights and other cattle.

So far as we knew, nobody on either side got killed in that little sashay. That was the way with lots of those nighttime gunfights, more noise than blood. It was hard to hit what you couldn't see, especially when your horse kept scotching away from the shooting.

Tanner never did find his pistol. The cattle had tromped it into the dirt. Years later a cowboy found it, rusted too bad to ever use again. He hung it over a mantle as a keepsake because by then Tanner Moody's name carried a lot of weight.

The spy system being the way it was along the river, it didn't take Don Carlos long to find out the name of the man who had crippled his son. A week or so after the raid somebody took a shot at Tanner from out of the thick brush. The shooter missed by a few inches. At first we figured it was a random thing and anybody who worked for the T Cross was a target. Tanner was the only one who believed he had been picked out of the bunch. A few days later it happened again. Tanner happened to be wearing one of those wide-brimmed Mexican sombreros. The bullet tore a hole through the top of it and lifted it right off of Tanner's head.

This time the shooter got only halfway across the river before we caught up to him. He hollered back that Tanner Moody was a *cobarde,* a coward. His horse came out on the other side, but the shooter didn't. He washed up later on the Texas bank with half a dozen bullets in him. We were all shooting at him, so it would be hard to say which of us killed him. Tanner made no claim.

Jesse Threadgill didn't take it lightly. I remember him saying, "Tanner, I promised your old daddy I'd watch out for you. I'd hate to have to tell him you got killed takin' care of what's mine. It's best you get away from here for a while."

Tanner took it wrong at first. "You firin' me?"

"No," says Jesse, "I'm sendin' you on a trip. Time you get back, maybe the wind will change."

Most people assume the cattle drives didn't start till after the big war, but the truth is that they commenced a lot earlier. Cattle weren't worth much money. Looking back, it's hard to imagine people being willing to fight and die over them. Down on the Texas coast they were being butchered for nothing more than their hides and tallow to be shipped to the East on boats.

Not everybody was willing to settle so cheap. An owner could get more by driving them afoot to markets like New Orleans or Chicago. A few herds were walked as far as New York. Those were long and expensive trips. Going east, drovers had to circle around a lot of towns and contend with farmers who didn't want Texas cattle tromping their fields. Worse than that, they had to make a lot of river crossings, the most dangerous thing of all. If he lost many cattle the owner might not come out much better at the end than if he had settled for selling hides and tallow.

Old Jesse said, "I'm fixin' up for a drive to New Orleans. I want you on it, Tanner."

Tanner frowned like he'd bit into an apple and found half a worm. "It'll look like I'm runnin' away. I ain't no coward. I've got a mind to ride down there and meet Don Carlos face to face. Then we'll see who's a coward and who's not."

"Don't fool yourself into thinkin' he's one. You've got to give the old scoundrel credit. He's got more nerve than a mouthful of bad teeth. I wouldn't be surprised if he showed up here one day and slapped his glove in your face, darin' you to duel him."

"I'd do it. I'd shoot him so full of holes that he wouldn't float."

"I ain't at all certain you would win. More'n likely he'd want to fight with knives. You fancy cold steel between your ribs?"

I could tell the thought shook Tanner a little. He asked, "When we leavin'?"

It took us a while to sort out five hundred steers old enough and fleshy enough to travel plumb to New Orleans. Trail herds later on would be a lot bigger, but five hundred was considered a bunch at the time. They would be driven slow enough to graze along the way and not lose a lot of weight. Butchers in New Orleans wanted them to arrive ready for the skinning knife. As we cut out the steers we kept pushing them to the north end of the ranch, as far from Don Carlos's reach as we could. Jesse set Tanner to watching the steers, figuring he was safer there than down along the river.

It was Tanner's first cattle drive, though I had been on a couple and had some notion of what to expect. People nowadays have got romantic notions about the trail, about the grand adventure and all that. Mostly it was long days and more long days of dust and boredom and saddle-sore butts with occasional short spells of pure panic when we crossed a river. The fact is that most cowboys or vaqueros couldn't swim. They hadn't been around enough water to learn. We lost one of our

60

Mexican hands in the Sabine, thrashing around and hollering for help. None of us was close enough to reach him in time. He went under and didn't come up. We never did find him.

It chills you plumb to the bone to see a man die like that, fighting for life and losing. It left a mark on us all, and Tanner the most. He didn't eat much for the next couple of days and had a strange faraway look in his eyes. Something was building up inside him.

It was too bad for the Louisiana farmer who picked the wrong time to try and stop us from crossing his land. He came riding up cussing and shaking his fist. I promised him we would go way around his field, and I offered to pay him for what grass our cattle ate or tromped down. But he was in a bad humor from the start. Maybe his wife had kicked him out of bed or something. Anyway he fired his pistol into the air to try and stampede the cattle.

They were too tired to run. The only thing that stampeded was Tanner. He spurred his horse and slammed into the farmer's. He jumped out of the saddle and took the farmer down with him. Then he commenced to pound on that gentleman until we felt obliged to drag him away before he got charged with murder. Tanner wasn't ready to quit. He wanted to finish his little set-to, but we threatened to tie him in his saddle. We figured the local constabulary might have a prejudice against Texas drovers. Old Jesse would not have appreciated the way we ran his cattle that day till we had crossed the parish line.

By night Tanner had cooled down and admitted he might have hit that farmer a little harder than he had to, but he didn't offer to go back and apologize. Fact is, I don't remember Tanner ever apologizing for anything.

Old Jesse met us in New Orleans. He figured out about how long it ought to take us to get there, and he only missed it by a couple of days. He had already made a tentative deal to sell the cattle. The buyer looked them over and paid Jesse in cash. Then Jesse paid off all of us hands and said it was all right for us to stay and enjoy a vacation as long as we started home the next day or two.

Tanner had never seen a city like New Orleans. San Antonio was the biggest place he had been, and it wasn't much of a town back in those days. After you had seen one old rundown cathedral you had seen them all. The local Mexicans had their fandangos, but lots of times they made a gringo feel awful unwelcome.

New Orleans, though, was wide open, the friend-liest place you could imagine, especially if you had money in your pocket. There was music and wine and whisky and some of the liveliest women us Texas boys had ever seen, dressed like Christmas packages and painted up like a child's toys.

Tanner had had very little experience with women, and these New Orleans beauties dazzled him. You couldn't hardly blame him. He had grown up in the brush and had never seen anything like the city had to offer. He pretty soon got himself paired off with a little French gal who called herself Babette. She was prettier than a spotted pup. I think she got the idea at first that Tanner owned part of the herd and had money. I don't know who told her that. But after she had been with him a while the money didn't matter to her. She took a shine to Tanner for what he was, and not for what she thought he owned. And Tanner, well, he went around with a glazed look in his eyes and a smile you couldn't break off with a chisel and a hammer.

Tanner had never gotten much book learning, but in a couple of days—and nights—that girl taught him things he never would have learned in school. She couldn't have found a more eager pupil, and she seemed to be enjoying the lessons as much as he did.

I tried to warn him that he would be going home broke, but he considered the money well invested. The more I saw of Babette, the more I tended to agree with him. I felt like going to school myself. Later on Tanner got a reputation as being something of a ladies' man. I know where it started.

But good times all too often come to a bad end. A big planter from upriver came in to town. It seemed he felt like he had staked a prior claim on Babette. It didn't help that he found Tanner and Babette in the middle of a lesson. Having no patience with claim jumpers, he drew a little palm-sized gun from his swallow-tail coat and took a shot at Tanner. He wasn't much good at hitting a moving target, though. The bullet smashed a pitcher full of water and soaked everything around it.

Tanner took a notion to make the planter eat that

little pistol. He was at some disadvantage, for he was in his bare feet and kept slipping around on the wet floor. I wasn't there, so I have to rely on what Tanner chose to tell me later. Some things you don't invite even your best friends to watch.

Tanner said it was even worse than the fight he had had with his old daddy. The planter had a knife in one of his boots and tried real hard to whittle on Tanner's liver. He did manage to cut Tanner in several places, none of them vital. They wrestled around on the slick floor and managed to overturn and bust just about every piece of furniture in the room. Tanner finally got the best of it, for he had been working hard and was in good physical shape. The planter had slaves who did all his heavy lifting, so he was a little flabby.

They were both worn to a frazzle, but Tanner managed to get the planter facedown on the floor and take the knife away from him. Then he proceeded to cut a swallowfork in the man's right ear, the same mark he had been putting on T Cross cattle. He said if he had had a hot iron he would have branded the T Cross on the planter's left hind cheek, but he had to settle for the earmark.

By that time Babette had lost interest in romance. She wrapped herself in a robe and ran out of the room screaming. Tanner figured the gendarmes would be showing up shortly, and he didn't want to have to explain the difference between a swallowfork and an underbit. He kept the knife and the little pistol for remembrance and left town ahead of the rest of us.

He always had a soft spot for New Orleans after that, though he was a long time in returning to visit.

We took our time in going home, for Louisiana was far different from the dry country we were used to, and we wanted to see it. We rode a little different route than the one we had followed with the cattle because we figured some of those people weren't real anxious to see us again. Most especially we didn't want to see the farmer Tanner had had his little dust-up with. Some people take a long time in turning loose of a grudge.

We found out that Don Carlos hadn't turned loose of his, either. The spy system didn't waste much time letting him know that Tanner was back in the country. The old ranchero's son Felipe was going to have a crippled shoulder the rest of his life, thanks to Tanner's marksmanship. Tanner was not proud of having shot him in the shoulder; he had tried for his heart. Rumor had it that Don Carlos was offering a thousand dollars in Mexican silver for anyone who would deliver Tanner to him alive. Failing that, he would settle for Tanner's head in a sack.

Tanner took all this as a compliment. He had never been worth so much in his life. "My old daddy ought to be proud of me," he said. "Nobody ever offered anything like that for him."

I have to admit that all this made Tanner a little cocky. Instead of keeping his head down and staying as far out of sight as possible he went to town when the work allowed, and sometimes when it didn't. It was a mixed town, part gringo and part Mexican. You never knew who might be your enemy. And not all the enemies were Mexican, as it turned out. Money can play hell with a man's loyalties.

We were on a cow hunt a good twenty miles from the river and feeling pretty safe against raiders from across the river. We had made camp beside a creek so small it should have been ashamed of itself. We didn't give it much thought when somebody hailed us from out in the brush and asked if they could come in to the campfire. The evening had turned chilly after the wind switched around to the north. The voice was gringo, not a trace of Mexican accent in it.

I hollered back, "Come on in." There was just me and Tanner, a boy named Johnny Rascoe and a couple of good loyal Mexican hands.

The visitors were three gringos with sort of a coyote look about them. We took them to be Texas outlaws who made their living raiding down into Mexico. While that didn't make them friends of ours, exactly, it sort of made us feel like they were allies in a long fight.

They were strangers. We never did know how they came to recognize Tanner so easy. Photographs were scarce in those days, and I doubt Tanner had ever had one made. He didn't have any scars or marks that showed. But right off, even without waiting to sample our coffee, one of the three nodded at Tanner and said, "I believe you'd be Tanner Moody."

That set off an alarm in my head, and I suppose in Tanner's too. He waited and sized them up a minute before he said, "So my mother always claimed."

Quick as a lizard getting off of a hot rock, the lead

outlaw reached for his gun. He was fast, but Tanner was faster. All I saw was a blur, then Tanner's pistol belched fire. The outlaw sort of bowed, like he was being introduced to the king. He never did get to fire his pistol. Tanner grabbed it out of his shaking hand and swung it around to point at the other two outlaws. One had his own pistol halfway out of the holster but froze there. The other didn't try at all.

Tanner said, "You boys have wore out your welcome. Get on your horses and ride, and take this one with you." The one he had shot was staggering around holding his belly. I wouldn't have given a lead peso for his chance of seeing the sun rise. We never did know whether he made it or not.

The only thing Tanner said was, "Don Carlos ought to be grateful. I just saved him a thousand dollars."

The experience took the edge off of Tanner's cockiness, however. He realized the three men could have shot him from out in the darkness. He might never have known what hit him. Their mistake was in coming in close for a cinch shot, a little cocky itsownself. The next ones might not do it that way.

Jesse threatened to fire Tanner for his own good, but Tanner wouldn't hear of it. He said he would keep on working whether he got paid or not, knowing the old man wouldn't settle for that.

Jesse was exasperated. He said, "Young men don't think they'll ever die. Old men have seen enough death to know they will, and they do everything they can to keep it from happenin'. Do you have any idea what it costs to have a decent gravestone carved these days?"

Tanner said, "Take it out of my wages. I wouldn't have much need for the money anyway. Take the rest and buy the boys a drink."

Jesse said, "I'd give a thousand dollars to have your nerve, but I wouldn't give two bits for your judgment."

I don't believe Tanner had ever thought seriously about the possibility that his situation could bring tragedy to somebody besides himself. He had gotten to be friends with a kid of about eighteen named Johnny Rascoe. Johnny was an orphan, or at least that's what he told us. You never could be sure because a lot of young drifters in those days were trying to get away from a bad deal at home, a strict daddy or maybe a stepfather or stepmother they couldn't get along with. Tanner's break with his own daddy probably gave him more than usual in common with Johnny. At any rate the two got along a lot like brothers. Tanner taught him to play poker, and he told him more than I would have about Babette. Guess he thought the kid ought to know something about women before he got exposed to them himself.

Several of us went out on a cow hunt one day. We thought a time or two that we saw somebody way off in the brush, but we never were sure of it. Even with a lot of the leaves shed in the wintertime, you couldn't always tell a cow from a horse or a deer at a couple of hundred yards. We were uneasy enough that we stopped and fixed supper before dark, then smothered the fire with dirt so it wouldn't put out any light. We then moved off a little ways and made dry camp.

Sometime in the dark hours after midnight Johnny got up. Tanner was half awake and asked him where he was going. Johnny said he had to relieve his kidneys. He walked out into the mesquite. In a little bit we heard a scuffle and Johnny calling for help. We jumped out of our blankets and ran toward the sounds, but it was so dark we couldn't see anything. We heard horses moving southward in a lope and went to catch our own. By the time we got mounted we knew we couldn't do much until daylight. We searched around, lost in the dark, and didn't accomplish a thing.

Awhile after sunup we cut across the tracks and followed them toward the river. We found Johnny lying on the bank, shot and left for dead. He was still breathing, but barely. He managed to tell us that a couple of gringo outlaws had mistaken him for Tanner. They were talking about how they were going to spend that thousand dollars from Don Carlos. When daylight came and they could see they had made a mistake, they shot Johnny out of frustration.

Tanner had tears in his eyes. "Why didn't you tell them who you was?" he asked Johnny.

Johnny said, "They didn't believe me. I decided to let them keep on believin' I was you 'til we'd left you a long ways behind." He coughed up blood and asked, "Am I goin' to die?"

Tanner couldn't answer him. None of us could.

Johnny took hold of Tanner's arm. "I've got a mother . . ." He never did finish. To this day, I don't know who or where his mother was. We carried him back to the ranch headquarters and buried him with none of his kin there to see or to know where his bones were laid.

A real change came over Tanner. He had always held back a lot, but now he really drew up into himself. "By rights it ought to be me in that grave," he told me. "Johnny died in my place."

"It wasn't your doin'," I told him. "There wasn't nothin' you could've done to prevent it."

About the only thing he could've done was to have gone and turned himself in to Don Carlos and let the chips fall where they would. But that would've been suicide, one sin Tanner never subscribed to.

The longer he brooded over it, though, the nearer he came to doing that very thing. Watching him, we could see him gradually coming around to a decision. We wondered among ourselves what it would be, though we wouldn't have asked Tanner himself for all the cows in South Texas.

What he did was go to town by himself one afternoon. He wouldn't let any of us go with him, but three of us waited until he was out of sight and then trailed him. We knew some of Don Carlos's spies lived in town, though we had no idea which ones they were. We wouldn't have been surprised if Tanner had taken it in his head to shoot every Mexican male he came across, he was that wrought up.

What he did was go into a cantina that was a favorite with the local Mexicans as well as some of those who visited back and forth across the border.

He pounded on the bar to get their attention—he already had it anyway—and said in Spanish, "I know some of you are friends of Don Carlos. I want you to deliver a message to him. Tell him I am going to camp on the Texas side of the river. If he wants me he is welcome to come and meet me halfway. We can shoot it out in the middle of the river. Tell him not to send any of his hired assassins. I'll shoot them on sight. Tell him this is between him and me. Tell him we are going to end this once and for all."

People who were there said the cantina was as quiet as a graveyard. Tanner turned and walked out, showing them his back if they wanted to take a shot at it. Nobody did. I guess they were all stunned by his audacity, and maybe afraid he had eyes in the back of his head. There are stories in Mexican folklore about the devil taking human form. Some of those folks were probably thinking they had just seen him.

By the time we got to town Tanner had come and gone. He had stopped at a mercantile and bought a little food to camp with, then had headed down to the river, to a spot where so many cattle had been crossed in one direction or the other. When we reached him he had made a camp of sorts and was waiting. But not for us.

He told us, "This is between me and Don Carlos. Ain't no part of it yours. I want you-all to go back to the ranch."

We tried to argue with him, but he acted like he didn't hear us. It was like he had shut himself in a little room where he couldn't hear nothing or see nothing. So we headed back toward the ranch, as he had told us to do. But we didn't go far. We stopped about three hundred yards from the river where he couldn't see us, and we set about to waiting just the way he did.

We spent a cold, miserable night there. He had the advantage of us. He had his blankets, and he had bacon and coffee and I don't know what else. We didn't have anything. We didn't even dare to build a fire because we figured he would see it.

Come morning we looked down toward the river. We could see over onto the other side. There must have been a dozen riders there on Mexican soil. The chilly morning breeze bought us little fragments of the voices as Tanner and Don Carlos hollered back and forth to one another. We couldn't tell what they were saying.

In a little while Tanner mounted his horse and walked it out into the edge of the river. Don Carlos did the same on the other side. He stopped and motioned to the men who had come with him. The message was plain. They were to stay back. It was not their fight.

We got on our horses and loped down to the river in case we had to back Tanner against that bunch on the other side. There was nothing to stop them from coming over except the old man's orders.

The horses had their feet on solid riverbottom the first several yards out into the river. But then the water got deep, and they started swimming. Lots of the time in that situation a rider will slip out of the saddle to let the horse have more freedom. They'll hold onto the saddle strings or the horse's tail. But Tanner and Don Carlos didn't do that. They stayed mounted.

Don Carlos fired first and missed. We wondered how he could have expected to hit a target with his horse plunging up and down, trying to stay afloat. Tanner fired second, and missed too. Then both men came up with a second pistol. They were trying not to waste this shot, for then they would have to try to reload from the backs of struggling horses.

The horses were almost touching heads when Don Carlos fired his second shot. Tanner took it in the arm. He almost lost that second gun. But he managed to bring it up. We saw fear in the old man's face. Tanner was too close to him to miss.

Don Carlos's horse made a strong plunge and turned over onto its side, throwing the old man out into the water. It was clear that the don, like most of us, could not swim. He began thrashing around in desperation, the way we had seen one of our Mexican vaqueros do in the Sabine River crossing.

His voice came clear and filled with panic. "*Ayudame!* Help me!"

Tanner still had the loaded pistol in his hand, aimed at the drowning man. We thought he would fire and put the old warrior out of his misery. But he held back, letting the river do the job.

Though we had had our troubles with Don Carlos, it was hard not to feel sorry for him in his helplessness. His raids had cost Jesse a lot of cattle, though

Jesse had always managed to get some of them back along with a goodly number of the don's. Still, it was hard to watch him die that way, gasping for air and swallowing that muddy river water.

Tanner must have had the same feeling, or maybe he remembered the boy in the Sabine. He reached down with his good hand and grabbed the old man's flailing arm. He pulled him up beside his own horse and turned the animal toward the south bank. By this time the don's horse was swimming downriver, out of reach.

Tanner got a fresh hold around Don Carlos's shoulder and managed to hang onto him until his horse found solid footing. He carried the don up onto the dry riverbank and let him slide to the ground in front of the Mexican riders.

At the distance we couldn't tell whether Tanner said anything or not. I doubt that he did. We held our breaths, for he was at the mercy of Don Carlos's men. But they made no move against him. The only ones who moved rushed to the old man's aid. Tanner turned and put his horse into the river again, headed north. He showed the crowd his back just as he had done in the cantina, giving them a chance to shoot him. None of them did.

His arm was still bleeding when he got to us. He frowned. "Thought I told you-all to go back to the ranch."

I said, "Guess we didn't hear you."

He accepted that, and some help with his arm. We got it wrapped so it wasn't bleeding anymore. I told him, "This won't change Don Carlos's habits. He'll keep on jumpin' the border and runnin' cattle. It's in his nature, just like with Old Jesse."

Tanner didn't argue about that. He said, "And one day somebody'll put a bullet in him. He'll die like an old warrior ought to. There's no dignity in drownin' like a rat."

Tanner wouldn't admit it, but I suppose he admired Don Carlos for coming out to face him man to man.

He said, "I don't guess my daddy would be very proud of me now."

I said, "I don't see why not. We are."

"Yesterday I was worth a thousand dollars. Now I think the reward is off."

Tanner Moody rode away a while after that, into adventures most of us can only read about. He could be tender as a baby or fierce as an eagle, whatever the situation called for. He lived a fuller life than just about anybody I ever knew. But I doubt that he ever stood taller than he did that day on the Rio Grande.

Three

The New York Morning Telegraph, Feb. 6, 1903
The Legend of Tanner Moody
Third in a series by Bat Masterson
Exclusive

In my last article I related the story of Don Felipe Talamantes and how his brief encounter with Tanner Moody had left him cripple, and yet in debt. Don Carlos died many years later, after Tanner Moody's legend had begun to grow. He made his son, Don Felipe, promise to attend the funeral of Tanner Moody—if, indeed, Felipe outlived the legend—and pay respects to the man who had saved his father's life.

And so while Don Felipe may have hated Moody for leaving him with a useless arm, he loved his father—and the memory of his father—enough to keep his promise.

After telling me the story Don Felipe excused himself, made his way over to Moody's casket, and paid respects on behalf of Don Carlos. He then spit on Moody's corpse, turned and left.

I never did see who cleaned off that bit of spittle . . .

There was another room in the White Elephant that was sort of a private club where gentlemen could go to drink, eat, read a newspaper, or simply converse without all the gambling going on around them. Also, it was a place where women were not allowed to go.

The room had been added by my friend Luke Short, and apparently the present owner chose to continue to offer his patrons the alternative to gambling.

As I entered that room I saw that most of the tables—a least a dozen—were each occupied by two or three men, smoking cigars, holding drinks, and discussing—for the most part—Tanner Moody.

I didn't know any of them on sight, so I decided to take one of the remaining tables for myself, order a drink and just sit back and listen.

I asked a passing waiter for a brandy, which would be easier for me to nurse than a beer (I hate warm beer). Once I had the drink in my hand I began my eavesdropping.

The two men seated at the table to my right talked a bit about Tanner Moody, but it was clear they had never known him. They were just talking about aspects of his legend that everyone knew—all of the exaggerations, the gossip, the dime novel legends rather than the true story.

I turned my attention to the table on my left, and found three men there talking about cattle prices. After all, we were in Texas, and the stockyards were not very far from where we were sitting. If they had ever been talking about Moody, they were done.

I leaned back in my chair, the better to hear the three men at the table behind me. The conversation immediately caught my attention . . .

They were all in their seventies—Moody's age—which interested me right away. As contemporaries of his there was a chance that one of them may have actually known him. In point of fact, they all sounded as if they had known him, talking about "ol' Moody" and calling him "Tanner" from time to time. I finally decided to try and find out for sure what their connection was.

I stood up and turned to face them.

"Gentlemen," I said, "forgive me, but I couldn't help but overhear your conversation. It sounds to me like one, two or all of you actually knew Tanner Moody?"

"We all did," one of them said, but he eyed me suspiciously. "What's it to you?"

"I'm a journalist," I said. "I'm writing about Tanner Moody for the *New York Morning Telegraph*."

"Never heard of it," the first man said, but the other two were more impressed.

"A New York newspaper?" the second man asked.

"That's right."

"Have a seat, sir," the third man said.

"Thank you."

The third man made the introductions. His name was Jake Higgins, the first man was Vern Wells and the second man was Dick Chambers. I had never heard of any one of them, on either side of the law.

I had to give them a name, so I told them I was my friend, Alfred Henry Lewis. None of them seemed to recognize the writer's name, but they probably would have recognized my own. I chose to keep that to myself, for the time being.

"So, how did you all know Tanner Moody?" I asked.

Vern Wells was still not ready to talk to me, and continued to eye me dubiously. I don't know what he thought I might be after, but the other two men were much more talkative.

All were wearing dark suits, but it was easy to see that none of them had a private tailor. I just couldn't tell if it was by choice, or they couldn't afford one.

"You gonna write about us if we tell?" Higgins asked.

"I sure am," I promised. "I'm after human interest stories, and I'm eager to talk to men who actually knew Moody."

Chambers sat forward, as if he was about to impart some great secret.

"We didn't only know him," he said, "we rode with him."

"As deputies, you mean?"

"Hell, no!" Higgins said. "We rode the owlhoot trail with him, didn't we, Vern?"

Wells looked at him and said, "You talk too much, Jake."

"Come on, man," Higgins said, "this here's a reporter. This is our chance to tell our stories, to get ourselves known."

To ride Tanner Moody's coattails, he meant. I was starting to think I had made a mistake.

Wells shook his head.

"We're three old men, Jake," Wells said. "You think we still got time to become legends?"

"Maybe not legends," Jake said, "but we can still tell our stories, can't we?"

"Mister, these two are full of hot air," Wells said, ignoring the others, now.

"And you're not?"

"Sure I am," he said, "I just ain't lettin' it fly your way."

"And why is that?"

" 'Cause it would be a waste of time." Wells said. "I think you're blowin' some hot air, yourself. If you're here at Moody's wake, then you want Moody stories. Ain't I right?"

"Well . . ."

"I tell you what," Wells said. "I'll tell you a Moody story you might not hear someplace else."

"What story is that?"

"Back in the fifties is when Moody first started thinkin' about ridin' the outlaw trail," Well said. "He was in his twenties then and hadn't decided which way his life was gonna go yet. You interested in hearin' that?"

"I'd be very interested in hearing that, Mr. Wells," I said.

"And after that you'll wanna hear about us?" Higgins asked hopefully.

"Well . . . sure, Mr. Higgins," I said. "Sure, why not?" I looked at Wells. "The fifties, you said?"

"Mid-fifties, prob'ly . . ."

Love and Bullets

By Peter Brandvold

Tanner Moody swung down from the saddle and mounted the stoop of a remote Southwestern cantina. Boots chinging, he parted the batwings and ordered beer and tequila, spending the last of the money he'd made panning for gold in Timbuctoo Gulch, California.

He took the beer and shot glass to a table in a dim corner, near a square joist trimmed with *ristras*. Sitting, he lifted the beer to his lips and saw the girl.

He froze, staring over the lip of the mug into the room's far corner. She sat with a big Mexican wearing a bullhide serape, drooping black mustaches, and a long-barreled pistol on his right hip. Tanner Moody had been riding the trail from California for the past two weeks. He was broke, hungry and thirsty, and any woman would have looked good to him.

But this woman's beauty tied a firm half-hitch knot in his lower intestine. It wasn't just the rich, black hair and aristocratic face, the low-cut blouse revealing the globes of her full, round breasts. It was her beauty swathed in her sexy, dusty trail garb—the slitted riding skirt revealing an alluring portion of one tan thigh. The gold-and-silver trimmed sombrero hanging down her back by a leather thong. The two pistols holstered on her slender hips. The scuffed, silver-tipped boots.

And it was her haughty, earthy manner. She and her big companion were arguing. He grunted and pounded his fists on the table, and she did the same, keeping her voice low but obviously not cowed by her companion's size or his rage.

Finally, she bolted to a half-crouch, yelled, *"Bastardo!"* and slapped the man across the face. It was a hard slap, resounding around the room, for a moment silencing the chickens in the yard and the flies buzzing around the windows and the beer puddles on the floor.

The bartender and the only other man in the room—a short, balding vaquero nursing a beer and tequila at the bar—ceased their conversation and turned to the man and woman in tense silence.

The woman stood glaring down at the big Mexican, who sat his chair, glaring back at her. Moody saw the flush building in the man's dark, hatchet face, and fearing for the girl's safety, he covertly unfastened the leather thong holding his big Colt's dragoon in its holster.

But the woman's companion only stared up at her

until, finally, the woman eased back down in her chair. The two said nothing after that, just sat in tense silence, staring at their beers and empty shot glasses.

Tanner Moody sipped his beer and studied the woman covertly, half-hidden by the support post from which the spicy *ristras* hung. She sipped her beer and expertly rolled a cigarette with her long, thin fingers. As she shook her hair back, placed the quirley between her lips and struck a lucifer on a table leg, Tanner's throat thickened.

The woman inhaled deeply on the cigarette, tossed her head back, and blew smoke at the ceiling. Doing so, she jostled the big, silver crucifix nestled in her ample cleavage. Her bosom shifted behind the sweat-damp cloth of her blouse, revealing the fact she was not wearing a stitch of underclothing.

Tanner Moody's chest grew tight as catgut. Throwing back the tequila shot, he set the glass on the table and noticed his right hand shaking.

The woman turned her head toward the bar and said something to the barman in Spanish. Tanner knew a modicum of Mexican Spanish, but the woman had spoken too quickly for him to follow. He assumed she'd ordered another round of drinks. Her big companion growled a short string of words at her, but she ignored him.

Tanner was surprised when the bartender appeared off Tanner's left shoulder and set a shot glass on the table beside Tanner's beer. "Tequila," the man said. *"Por la senorita."*

Tanner's heart drummed. His ears warmed. He

glanced around the support post at the girl's stony profile framed by swirls of ebony hair. She did not look at him. She brought the cigarette to her lips, shaking her hair back again, and blew smoke at the window in the adobe wall.

The big Mexican glanced at Tanner, then turned to snarl at the girl through square, yellow teeth. She ignored him.

Tanner looked at the shot glass on the table before him. Glancing up, he saw the man staring at him sternly, black eyes wide as saucers.

The girl stared cooly out the window.

The crucifix flashed in the sunlight, attracting Moody's savoring eye to the delectable breasts, clearly outlined within the damp, clinging blouse, and from there to her brown left thigh, nearly the flawless whole of which was revealed by her slitted, doeskin riding skirt embroidered with red and blue zigzags along the hem.

Except for the buzz of flies and the chickens clucking in the yard, the room was silent. Tanner didn't turn his head to the bar, but he sensed the lone customer and the bartender glancing tensely between him and the girl's companion.

Tanner swallowed, calmed himself, and reached for the shot glass. No sooner had he plucked the tequila from the table than the girl's companion bolted to his feet suddenly, his chair pistoning back against the wall with a crash.

Turning toward Tanner, he raked the flintlock saddlering carbine from the sheath on his right thigh, slapped the barrel into his left hand, and pulled the trigger.

The cannon exploded, flames sparking across the room like a burning Apache arrow.

At the same time, Tanner lowered his left shoulder under his table, and stood, flinging the table forward and left as he pivoted right. A half second after the .67-caliber ball slammed into the table with a deafening *thwack*, Tanner jerked his Arkansas toothpick from the leather sheath hanging down his back, sighting instinctively, and let fly.

The big, hatchet-faced Mexican was still extending the flintlock when the knife flashed in the sunlight angling through an unshuttered window. Somersaulting, it plunged hilt deep with a fleshy, bone-grinding thud.

The dark man just stood there, the flintlock still in his hands, head thrown back as if for a better look at the knife cleaving the bridge of his nose and covering his face with blood.

When he finally dropped like a felled pine, dead, the girl stood and peered down at him. Finally, she sauntered over to Tanner. He now stood with his big dragoon out, covering the rest of the room.

A foot shorter than he, she looked up at him obliquely from under the brim of her gold and silver trimmed Mexican sombrero, her hair dancing about her bare shoulders. He was vaguely surprised to see that her eyes were blue.

After several seconds she glanced at the puddle of spilled tequila beneath his boots.

Her chest rose and fell as she breathed. The crucifix moved slightly. A faint mole on her chest darkened.

"You spilled your drink, amigo," she said huskily. "Would you like another?"

Tanner Moody had no idea what in hell he was doing. A girl had bought him a drink in a remote roadhouse, he'd killed her companion, and now he was following her along a horse trail winding through the foothills of the San Juan Mountains, galloping hell-bent-for-leather, eating the dust kicked up by her fine bay mare with a roached mane and silver-mounted Mexican saddle.

He was still broke and hungry, but for the first time in over a year, he didn't feel world-weary . . . or alone. Every vein and artery fairly bubbled with electricity, and the two shots of tequila had nothing to do with it. He felt like a kid chasing an inviting, alluring girl through the woods back home.

Sophia was her name. That's all she'd told him before she'd said, after knocking back her own tequila, "Get your horse and try to keep up."

He'd didn't cotton to pushy women, but this one had him thoroughly under her spell.

Now they crossed one ridge after another and rose into cedars and pines. The trail grew rocky, more serpentine. The air freshened and carried the tang of juniper and forest rot.

They followed a stream bubbling and crashing over boulders. The girl, he reluctantly had to admit, rode the superior mount, and the claybank had trouble keeping up. She disappeared around a sandstone scarp. Rounding the scarp, Tanner reined to a halt, finding only the bay, its saddle empty, reins dangling.

Hearing a throaty laugh, Tanner turned his head left to see the girl running up the slope, disappearing into the firs and lodgepoles.

"What the hell?" he muttered, his pulse racing, the frog in his throat having grown to javelina-size. He wasted no time swinging his right boot over the saddle horn, hitting the ground, and heading up slope at a run.

Pushing through low-hanging pine branches, he saw a wide, dark pool churning at the base of a high falls.

The girl stood deep within the falls, in a cleft in the black rocks behind it. He couldn't see her clearly, but he saw enough to see that she was naked, tipping her head back on her shoulders and running her hands through her hair.

"Come," she called, beckoning. *"Vamonos!"*

Lowering his gaze, he saw her skirt, blouse, and boots strewn about the rocks before him. It wasn't long before his own clothes mingled with hers. Naked, he waded into the stream, wincing at the chill and at the sharp stones cutting into his feet. He waded around behind the falls and, half-crawling, half-climbing up the ledge of slippery black boulders, joined the girl behind the falls.

Water thundered into the obsidian pool on his right. The mist from the falls enveloped him. The air was rife with the smell of fresh water, minerals, and ferns. He'd never felt so cleansed and fresh, so alive.

The girl stood naked and wet, wearing only the silver crucifix in the deep hollow between her breasts, laughing with excitement. Running her hungry eyes up and down his long, lean, well-muscled body, her features sobered, and she extended her arms. He walked to her, wrapped his thick arms around her, kissed her open mouth as she ran her hands down his back and buttocks, digging in with her nails. Her lips tasted like peach halves fresh from the ice box, with a tincture of tequila.

He gently pushed her back against the ledge, and took her.

He took her again in the pool on the other side of the falls, their feet wedged in the sandy bottom, the girl bent forward over a flat rock and swinging her head back and forth as she cried with pleasure, like a mare being taken by a stud.

He took her again on the sandy bank, in the traditional way, her legs wrapped around his back, her hands tugging gently at his long, brown hair, clawing at his beard.

When they finished, they lay side by side, facing each other. She snuggled against his chest, kissing him softly, chuckling giddily after the hour's passion. His chest heaved as he sucked the thin air and nibbled her ears. He felt light-headed, giddy with adrenaline, somehow disembodied.

He no longer cared that he was flat broke and jobless, homeless. All he had at the moment was this bewitching girl who couldn't possibly be real but she was, and that was more than enough.

"Who are you, anyway?" he asked her, smoothing the hair back from her ear and gazing lovingly but incredulously into her dark-blue eyes. He was propped on his left elbow, lying on his side in the sand.

"I am Sophia Alvina Cabeza de Vaca," she said ironically, fingering his bulging left bicep. The crucifix dangled from her cleavage alluringly.

"Wait a minute," he said with a frown. "Your old man's that big Mexican rancher, ain't he—the one with that land grant that extends all the way to Las Vegas?"

"*Sí,*" she said, her eyes fluttering.

Tanner blew air through his lips, staring at her as if seeing her for the first time. He'd known she was no peon—no girl who looked and dressed like she did came from field workers. But he'd had no idea she hailed from the richest family in northern New Mexico and western Kansas.

She must have sensed the apprehension in his eyes, for she entwined her hands behind his neck, snuggled close, and said, "But I no longer live with them or have anything to do with them. In fact . . ." She stopped, reconsidering her words, and lowered her eyes.

"In fact what?" Tanner asked.

She shook her head.

For a moment, she remained silent, staring at his chest. "Maybe I will tell you sometime . . . if you stay." She kissed him, then scrambled to her feet and began gathering her clothes. "Come. It will be dark soon."

"What about the man I killed? Who was he?"

"He was unimportant."

Staying where he was, Tanner grunted caustically. "Where we going?"

She was stepping into her skirt, pulling the garment up her long, coltish legs. "I will show you," she ordered, like a girl used to giving orders and being obeyed. "*Vamos!*"

Tanner still didn't move. As mesmerized as he was by this girl, he was growing weary of her orders.

Topless, wearing only her skirt, she squatted before him, took his big, bearded face gently in her hands, and kissed him, probing his mouth with her tongue. She licked his lips as she pulled away.

"Please," she said with a smile.

On the way to wherever they were going, they held their mounts to walks, riding side by side except where the twisting, climbing trail narrowed. She probed him about his past, and, in spite of her own secrecy he found himself opening up to her, telling her about his adventures and travels throughout the West, his successes, his failures. He told her he was drifting at the moment, jobless, considering heading back to Texas to look for work on a cattle ranch.

He hadn't seen another soul in weeks, and it felt good talking to someone besides his horse.

As they crossed a cedar-stipled ridge high up in the mountains, where black-tailed deer and elk scat grew more and more plentiful along the game trail they followed, he turned to her and beetled his brows ironically. "Now, I spilled my guts. What about you, senorita?"

She only laughed and spurred her mount into a run

down the ridge, leaving Tanner once again in her dust. Cursing, he spurred the claybank after her and didn't slow the horse until they came to a notch in a high, mountain wall carpeted in pines and strewn with boulders. They seemed to be heading directly toward the wall, but there couldn't be a way through it, and they certainly couldn't climb a grade that steep.

When he'd spurred his horse up trail, the shadow of the ridge engulfing him, gloving him in a penetrating, high-country chill, the girl lifted her head and called in Spanish what Tanner recognized as, *"It is Sophia! I am coming in . . . with a visitor!"*

Tanner scanned the ridge, where a man's silhouette suddenly appeared as if growing out of the trees and boulders. The man wore a high-peaked hat and carried a long-barreled rifle with a lanyard. He lifted the rifle in one hand, and waved it slowly from side to side.

Sophia turned to Tanner sitting on his claybank directly behind her. "Come."

Tanner and Sophia crossed a low knoll and twisted around behind a scarp, negotiating a crevice little wider than a wagon, ducking under the pine bows lining the trail. The trail straightened as it turned again toward the ridge, revealing an arched passage resembling a giant, black mouse hole in the gray-green granite. Only when he entered the tunnel, riding abreast of Sophia now, did he see daylight at the other end, about a hundred yards on.

Riding out the other side, he found himself in a grassy bowl-shaped canyon filled with aspens and pines. Down the canyon's center, a narrow, mossy-banked stream trickled, glistening in the late-afternoon light.

"Well, I'll be goddamned," Tanner said, halting the claybank and rising in the saddle to look around. "Why, no one would ever know this was here, unless you rode right up on it!"

"*Si,*" Sophia said. "That is how I found it. Quite by mistake. When I was a little girl out riding my first horse." She glanced around at the high, rocky walls completely enclosing the canyon. "It was my secret place."

"This hangin' canyon's on your father's spread?"

"Of course."

Tanner felt a prickling along his spine. He'd had no idea he was on the spread of Don Luis Maria Cabeza de Vaca. But most of this country belonged to the old Spanish aristocrat, so not being on it would have been a feat.

As they rode ahead, Tanner saw the wooded base of the canyon's northwest wall. About fifty feet up the wall, the dark maw of a cave opened.

Beneath the wall, spread across the aspen- and birch-studded meadow and on both sides of the stream, were a dozen or so army tents flanked with camping gear—cook fires, spits, canvas awnings, hammocks. Several wagons were parked side by side at the meadow's west edge. Rope was strung from scattered trees in a wide circle, enclosing a good section of the stream. Inside, horses cropped grass or stood shading each other.

Tanner Moody's primary interest was the men scattered about the meadow—the men who, spying the newcomers, were now drifting toward them, hands on their prominently displayed pistols and revolvers. Several men who'd been tending a large cook fire in the center of the camp, grabbed long guns and headed their way.

They were a rugged, ornery-looking lot, both Mexican and American. Some were dressed like vaqueros, others like Texas and Arizona drovers. Still others wore the buckskins, mocassins, and beaded tunics of mountain men. Several, though dressed like white men, appeared to have some Indian blood.

All were armed and eyeing Tanner Moody with dangerous caution, squinting and snarling, grumbling among themselves like pack dogs confronting a new cur on the street.

"Leave your gun in its holster," Sophia said firmly but quietly.

Only then did Tanner realize his hand had reached for the big dragoon on his right hip. He released the bone grips, slid his hand to his thigh as he watched the men approach, encircling him and Sophia, close enough now that he could hear their voices. Some spoke Spanish, some English, some an odd, guttural hybrid of the two, with a little Yaqui thrown in.

"Who's this?" one of the men asked in Southern-accented English—a short man dressed like a gambler, though his expensive silk shirt and wool vest had acquired a rough patina of trail dust and camp smoke.

He had long blond hair, a bib-like, dark-blond beard, and an aquiline nose. On his hip he wore a

Walker Colt. In the waistband of his broadcloth trousers was wedged an old flintlock pistol, its brass furniture badly tarnished. Looking back up the trail, he said, "Where's Pepe?"

"Dead," Sophia said nonchalantly. She lifted her left hand to indicate Tanner. "This man killed him."

A collective rumble rose from the group. The blond man cocked his head and squinted an eye at Tanner but said nothing.

"With a knife," Sophia said proudly. She pointed to the bridge of her nose. "Right between the eyes. You would have been impressed, Pinto."

Apparently, most of the men spoke English, though Tanner saw a couple of the Mexicans muttering to the others, translating.

One of the Mexicans stepped up. He was stocky and hatless, with a gray and black calico shirt under a black vest. His black hair was thick down both sides of his head and face, but his pate was nearly bald. Two Pattersons jutted up from the hand-tooled holsters tied low on both hips.

"This man killed Pepe?"

"*Si*," Sophia said without emotion. "Pepe needed killing. In Del Norte last night he would have shot a deputy town marshal if he hadn't been too drunk to shoot straight. If the deputy himself had not been too drunk to recognize us, I would have cancelled tomorrow's job."

"Pepe was your man, senorita," said the stocky Mexican, as if reminding her of a fact.

Flushing a little, Sophia glanced at Tanner. Shuttling her glance back to the stocky gent staring evilly up at Tanner, she said, "Pepe made the first move on Senor Moody. He had no choice."

The Mexican's low voice rose, half-sneering, half-accusing. "Senor Moody is now your man, senorita?"

Tanner returned the stocky man's malicious stare, then raked his gaze across the others. Their own expressions had turned more threatening. Their jealousy and acrimony was almost palpable.

This would be a good time for Tanner to turn and ride back the way he'd come. These men were outlaws. Crooks and killers, all.

The Mexican blinked slowly at Tanner, then turned his swarthy, smoke-smudged face to Sophia. She sat her saddle stiffly, her bee-stung lips set, eyes confident and calm—every ounce the alluring Spanish outlaw queen.

"You know you will always have my loyalty, senorita," the stocky man assured. "But Pepe—he was my *cousin*!"

As he shouted the last word, he pivoted toward Tanner and reached across himself for his pistols. The Mexican fired his right pistol as Tanner clawed the big dragoon from his holster. Tanner pitched back in his saddle, letting the .44 ball cut a shallow swath across his chest while raising his dragoon in his right hand.

As the Mexican leveled his left Patterson, Tanner shot him through the heart, the bullet punching him back against two others. The men eased him to the ground, staring up at Tanner Moody with increased hostility but also with newfound appreciation.

Tanner held the smoking pistol out before him, the

hammer cocked. The hair along his back pricked. At any moment he could be shot by the men behind him. The notches on his pistol belt were proof he'd been to see the elephant a time or two. But here he was outnumbered at least twenty to one, and if these men wanted him dead, he had only seconds to settle up with his maker.

The thought had no sooner passed through his brain than the blond-haired gent called Pinto threw up both arms and yelled, "Hold up!" He lifted his gaze to the men behind Tanner, then turned to those on both sides of him.

Glancing over his shoulder, Tanner saw that several men had drawn their revolvers. They stood frozen now, like statues.

Pinto squinted up at Tanner shrewdly, then turned to Sophia, who sat her mount as she had when Tanner had last regarded her. Only now she smiled proudly at Tanner, as though at a prized thoroughbred.

Turning to the others, Pinto yelled, "It seems we have a new *segundo*."

Sophia smiled. Throwing up an arm triumphantly, she yelled, "Let's feast!"

When the others had begun heading for the cook fires, Sophia turned to Tanner. Apparently sensing his anger and confusion, she said with customary impudence, "You are free to ride away now."

She smiled smugly. Turning her horse and galloping toward the cook fires, she glanced behind her. "But you will miss all the fun we would have, you and me . . ."

* * *

He would leave in the morning. Early. Before anyone else was up.

That's what he told himself through the lengthy feast and celebration, through several stone mugs of beer and tequila, through several Spanish trail-driving ballads performed by two guitar- and fiddle-wielding ex-vaqueros.

He repeated it to himself as he and Sophia made drunken love on the mossy river bank, under a shrunken moon. The dying cook fires sparked orange in the distance, the voices of the revelers calling out drunken platitudes about brotherhood and loyalty.

When their passion had released them, Tanner lay naked atop her, holding her gently down with his body, smoothing her silky hair back from her temples. The night was cool and starry, but their bodies were warm and damp from coupling.

"Tell me why," he said. "Why are you with them? You're a rich girl." He shook his head, trying to reason through the food, alcohol, and passion fogging his brain. "Why are you ridin' the owlhoot trail?"

Her bare chest rose and fell beneath him. She stared up at him, her eyes slowly losing the luster they'd attained as they'd made love. The blue orbs acquired a far-away look, as though she were gazing at the velvet sky beyond his shoulder.

"Because," she said, pausing to breathe deeply, "my father is a pig."

"How?"

Sophia returned her eyes to his. Hers were flinty, the stars barely reflected in them. "Ask Pinto to show you his back sometime. My father had him whipped nearly to death for cheating at cards in Durango. He'd have died if I hadn't intervened."

Tanner stared down at her, as befuddled as before.

"Did you meet Paul, the drover from Texas who can't speak? My father accused him of fouling a well with lye, so he made him eat lye. Only Paul wasn't the one who'd fouled the well. My brother had done it after Papa had him horsewhipped for stealing a gun from his office."

Sophia paused to let the information sink in.

"One-Eye Loomis," she continued, "had his eye plucked out by Papa's men for making eyes at the *segundo*'s daughter." She stared at him. "Should I go on?"

"All these men have been hornswoggled by your old man?"

"My father is a powerful man, Tanner. He and my uncles and brothers control nearly a hundred thousand acres and four towns. They own two banks and seven mercantiles, several liveries and taverns. Everyone not related to my father by blood he considers his slave."

His brows ridged with thought, Tanner lifted himself slowly off the girl and propped his head in his left hand, facing her on his side. After a time, he said, "So you've gathered them all together to get even with your old man?"

"Something like that."

"What'd he do to you?"

She rolled atop him, running her hands through his hair, brushing one cheek against his beard. "I confess, I intended only to use you to kill Pepe. But after I saw you, felt who you were, I fell in love with you."

He took her face in his hands, kissed her gently. His heart swelled with emotion so raw it unsettled him.

She tightened her grip on his neck, kneading the muscles. "You will stay?"

He shook his head resolutely. "I'm not a murderer."

"We do not kill," she said, "unless we have to. The stage we are striking tomorrow," she continued, "will be carrying money for beeves my father sold in Alamosa. I learned this from a friend who works at the stage depot in Del Norte and who has no more love for my father than I."

"How much have you stolen from him?"

She shrugged. "A few thousand dollars. We strike his mercantiles and gambling dens, but mostly, we steal from the stagecoaches carrying the money he makes from business transactions. So far, it has not been much—enough to celebrate in Santa Fe or Las Vegas now and then. But that is not the point. The point is to confound the *puta madre*." Her blue eyes brightened, like those of a little girl who'd just been given a much-anticipated doll.

She continued, "Maybe after I have had my fill of hiding out and sleeping on the ground, I will go east to live off my father's money. Would you like to go east with me, Tanner Moody?"

"I ain't exactly the eastern ty—"

She squeezed his arm. "I am just talking. It is nice to have someone to talk with. Pepe didn't talk . . . or listen. But I have talked enough." She closed her lips over his, brought his right hand to her heaving breast. "Make love to me once more. Then we will sleep. . . ."

100

* * *

Late that night, Tanner and Sophia retired to her cave and slept, entangled in each other's arms. Tanner wasn't sure how much time had passed before he felt her slide away from him, heard the sibilant sounds of her dressing.

The cool, black pit of sleep engulfed him once again. He was thrown out of it by three loud revolver shots.

"Wake up, you worthless bastards!" Sophia yelled somewhere to Tanner's right, her voice echoing around the canyon. "We have work to do!" She repeated the order in Spanish, punctuating it with, *"Vamonos!"*

Instinctively, Tanner had reached for his gun when he'd heard the shots. Hearing Sophia's voice, he released the big dragoon holstered beside his soogan and collapsed against his saddle. His head ached and his mouth tasted like a dry tequila bottle.

"Hey, gringo." Her voice was nearer now.

A boot toe nudged his side. He looked up to see her lovely, hatted visage smiling down at him, her dark hair curling about the shoulders of a brown wool poncho. She held her revolver low in her right hand, as if threatening another shot. "You ready to—" She pooched out her lips sexily. "How do you *Americanos* say it? Ride the long coulees?"

Pushing onto his elbows, he regarded her groggily. She holstered her pistol and smiled down at him, blue eyes flashing in the weak morning light penetrating the cave.

How could a man—even Christ himself—ride away from such a girl?

Grumbling, he tossed the blankets away, reached for his pants. For now, it seemed, he was an outlaw.

An hour later, the gang had breakfasted on coffee, frijoles, and bighorn sheep leftover from last night. They saddled their mounts, forked leather, and rode for two and a half hours through the northern slopes of the San Juans. In a wide valley bisected by a stage road, they waited behind a knoll.

Watering his horse from his hat, Tanner looked up suddenly. In the distance, thunder rumbled. Only it wasn't thunder, but the thuds of the team and the clatter of the stage rising on the breeze.

Sophia said, "Let's ride."

Tanner and the rest of the gang followed her out from behind the knoll, lining themselves stirrup to stirrup across the road and into the meadows on both sides. Sitting his claybank beside Sophia's mare, Tanner frowned against the late morning sun.

The dusty auburn stage approached behind the racing team. In spite of his reluctance to cross this line he'd never before considered crossing, Tanner's heart thudded with excitement. He was ambivalent about his place here, but he had to admit he'd rarely felt so aware, so alive.

Not yet seeing the gang, the driver popped the blacksnake over the backs of the six-hitch team, encouraging them. Suddenly, the shotgun messenger snapped his arm out, pointing down the road. Poised to crack the whip again, the driver froze suddenly, staring at the gang blocking his trail.

As if to prove the gang wasn't a mirage, Sophia drew

her revolver and fired two quick shots in the air. Instantly, the driver rose in his seat, planted both boots on the footrest, and sawed back on the reins, cursing and yelling, "Whooooooahhhhhhh! *Whoahhh, now!*"

As the carriage squawked to a halt behind the lathered team, Sophia lifted a purple bandanna to her face and gigged her horse along the trail. Guns drawn, Tanner and the others masked their own faces with bandannas and kerchiefs, and quickly surrounded the stage.

While Tanner and several others held their guns on the driver, Sophia halted her mare near the shotgun messenger, extending her cocked revolver. The man held his barn blaster in both hands but without conviction, fearfully looking from Sophia's gun to the other nineteen gang members surrounding him, and back again.

"If you know what is good for you, amigo," Sophia said coolly, "you will drop that iron pronto!"

The messenger was several years younger than the driver, to whom he turned for counsel.

The older man regarded the milling outlaws who'd surrounded the stage. He nodded grimly beneath his broad-brimmed, sun-bleached hat. "Reckon they have us greased for the pan, Ty."

Ty dropped the shotgun, which cracked off a wheel and clattered in the road dust and rocks.

"Wise decision," Sophia said. "And what are you carrying for us today?"

The driver said something Tanner didn't hear. Moody had neck-reined his horse right, swinging wide around the stage and canting his head to peer around the sides of the canvas curtains drawn over the windows. They fit too snugly to allow more than mere glimpses of the toneau's dark interior. Several of the other outlaws were trying to look inside, as well.

A rope of uneasiness knotting deep in his stomach, Tanner brushed past the other men and rode around behind the boot to the other side.

Sophia laughed caustically. "I have it from a good source you are carrying more than two old ladies and a spinster schoolteacher. Produce the strong box or my *companeros* and I will fill you both so full of holes you won't hold a teaspoon full of snakewater!"

Tanner reined his horse to the right rear window. Leaning out from his saddle, he started to shove away the curtain for a look inside. He froze when he saw something move in the window right of the door. A big, silver-plated Navy pistol moved through the window, its barrel turned toward Sophia.

"No!" Tanner shouted.

Clawing the dragoon from his holster, he fired without aiming. The bullet slammed the gun against the window frame, a smoking, black hole appearing in the wrist, just above the white shirt sleeve. A scream rose from inside the toneau as the hand opened, releasing the gun before darting back inside the carriage.

Before Tanner knew what was happening, the shade nearest him snapped up, and the maw of a Hawken rifle was rammed toward him. The shade's violent *thwack*, coupled with Tanner's shot, fiddlefooted his horse. The horse's sudden jerk to the right and forward was all that saved him from the Hawken's ball.

At the same instant that he felt the bullet lift hair at the back of his head, the stage door opened. A black-haired man in a Spanish-cut suit and wielding revolvers in both hands leapt to the ground, extended one revolver, and fired. As one of Tanner's brethren screamed behind him, the man fired his second gun, evoking a pained shout to Tanner's right. The man was thumbing back the right revolver's hammer when the outlaw named Roth shot him twice in the chest and once in the chin. The gunman was stumbling back against the stage when another man bolted through the stage door, both fists filled with iron.

As he triggered his revolvers, Tanner extended his own dragoon. As he pulled the trigger, several other gang members did, as well, drilling the man through the chest and belly, dropping him.

Tanner didn't lower his gun. While two other gunmen bolted out the other side of the stage, another man bolted out Tanner's side. The man dropped to a knee, cursing in Spanish, his long, reddish-black hair brushing across his brown forehead as he raised his carbine to his left shoulder. He didn't get the shot off before Tanner and Sophia, forking her mare to Tanner's right, both pinked him, spinning him around and draping him across one of the other fallen.

Holding the claybank's reins taut in his left hand and extending the dragoon with his right, Tanner tossed a look into the stage. The other door was open. Through it he saw two other men lying dead in the road. One gang member lay dead, as well. The others held the reins of their skittish, fiddlefooting mounts taut, their smoking guns held skyward. Surprised, be-fuddled looks beetled their brows.

Dust and smoke plumed about the sun-blasted stage. The jehu and shotgun messenger had been cowering on the floor of the driver's box. They both looked down and around the stage now, sheepish, worried.

Sophia's mare pranced a circle in the road's powdery dust. The girl's hair bounced on her shoulders, and the sun reflected off her tan thighs revealed by the slitted riding skirt.

"He sent guards this time," she said angrily, halting her horse at the rear of the stage, studying both sides. She gigged the mare to the coach's left side, and crouched to peer within. A padlocked box sat between the coach seats, like a blocky footrest.

"Well, the joke is on him! Bernardo, grab the strongbox!"

"Forget it," Tanner said as the portly Bernardo began to dismount his short-legged mustang.

Tanner gigged his horse quickly around the stage. Sophia frowned at him, flushing with annoyance. "What do you mean?"

Another man yelled as he pointed west along the trail, then hipped around in his saddle to peer east. From both directions, two large groups of riders galloped, sun flashing off rifles and revolvers and silver-mounted saddles.

The oncoming horses shook the ground like a moderate quake. Tanner and the others looked up and down the valley, trying to believe what their eyes were telling their brains—that a good fifty armed riders were bearing down on them from both ends of the valley. As they rode within a hundred yards, he saw several men shuck long rifles from their scabbards. Others held revolvers barrel up, waiting.

Tanner snapped a look at Sophia, staring east, a shocked look in her eyes. "*Su puta madre . . .*" she said, so softly that Tanner could barely hear her over the shouted exclamations of the other outlaws and the growing rumble of the oncoming riders.

He followed her gaze east. The point rider—apparently her father—was close enough that Tanner could make out the long, angular face with ostentatious mustaches, spade beard, and deep-set eyes. He wore a peaked sombrero with rainbow stitching, and a ruffled orange shirt under a cream vest trimmed with silver. From a shoulder holster, revealed when his vest flapped wide, jutted one revolver. In two holsters riding high on his hips, he wore two more.

His horse was so black it appeared purple in the glaring sun, with one right rear stocking. It was decked out with a silver-trimmed Navajo bridle, the decorative 'dobe dollars flashing with every long, fluid stride.

When Tanner looked at Sophia again, a savage, challenging smile curled her lip.

His heart pounded. The gang was badly outnumbered and didn't have a chance in a fight here on the valley floor. They needed high ground.

Looking around, he shouted, "To the ridge!" and reined his horse toward the north wall of the canyon. The other men hesitated for only a moment, glancing uncertainly from him to Sophia, then to the red sandstone ridge. Tanner spurred his horse toward the slope. The others followed suit, yelling and palming their revolvers.

Galloping, Tanner looked back toward the stage around which the dead men lay strewn. Sophia still sat her mare in the road, staring east.

Both groups were within fifty yards, and several of the men had begun triggering their revolvers.

"Sophia!" he shouted. "Goddamnit, *hurry!*"

She turned to him as if from a trance, and he beckoned. After hesitating for several seconds, jerking her gaze from him to the group approaching from the east, she lifted her revolver and snapped one shot down valley and one up.

Then she spurred the horse toward the ridge, the graceful mare instantly leaping into a ground-eating lope.

Both groups of pursuers were only thirty yards from the stage and closing, angling off the trail and across the meadow toward the rise. Their bullets whistled in the air around Tanner's head. He scowled and winced as several blew up dust around Sophia's mare's pounding hooves.

He emptied the dragoon at three approaching horsebackers, hitting none but slowing their pursuit.

As Sophia passed, slapping the mare's rump with a braided quirt, she yelled, "We will return their fire from the ridge!"

Tanner jammed his empty dragoon into its holster and spurred the claybank into the dust kicked up by Sophia's mare, ducking under two more musket balls, which tore into the hill with vicious thuds. "First we have to get there!"

As he galloped behind Sophia's long-striding mare, Tanner glanced behind him. The group of pursuers which had galloped in from the west were slightly ahead of those from the east, and were closing on a cluster of five gang members heading for the ridge. One of the outlaws was blown from his saddle. The others triggered half-hearted shots behind them but quickly ran out of bullets.

One-by-one, the remaining four were blown from their mounts to tumble back down the hill, bloody and dead.

Two other outlaws to Tanner and Sophia's right dismounted and laid down a field of fire, dislodging three pursuers from their horses and blowing the horse out from under another. Tanner and Sophia made the ridge top, where they slipped out of their saddles, grabbed their rifles, and hunkered down behind rocks.

His back to a boulder, Tanner reloaded his .44-40, holstered it, and picked up his Colt's revolving rifle. He rested the barrel in a cleft in the rock, ignored a ball snapping a branch of the dwarf cedar to his left, and lined up a shot. His target—a big, whooping and hollering man in snuff-colored sombrero and green cotton neckerchief—turned his Appaloosa around a low scarp, and stormed up the mountain, triggering his Walker Colt. Tanner pulled his own Colt's trigger and watched the .44 ball blow a hole through the man's chest, slamming him back on his horse's rump. He bounced off the horse's right hip, hit the ground, and, as the horse veered off, rolled into a boulder with a crunch of breaking bone.

Tanner was about to shoot another approaching gunman, when the revolving rifle misfired and jammed. As Tanner ducked behind the rock, the rider galloped up the slope, triggering two pistols. Tanner had cleared the jam and was positioning the next cylinder beneath the firing pin, when Sophia rose from behind the rock to his right and fired three quick shots down the mountain.

"Mierda!" rose the rider's cry below a frightened horse's whinny. It was followed by the thump and snap of another body hitting the turf.

Tanner peered around the rock. Hearing a cacophony of gunfire but seeing no other immediate threats, he took the time to reload his dragoon, calmly filling the six cylinders with powder, caps and balls.

Holstering the gun, he ran crouching down the mountain where the claybank stood ground-tied with the mare. He fished in his saddlebags for his spare Navy Colt, which he wedged behind his cartridge belt, then wheeled and ran back up toward the ridge crest.

He was nearly there when he spied movement in the corner of his left eye. He turned to see one of Sophia's father's men aiming a big, gold-mounted, French blunderbuss around a cracked boulder. The cannon exploded, belching fire and heavy black smoke, tearing a fist-sized widget from the pine behind Tanner, where his head would have been if he hadn't ducked.

Tanner clawed the spare Navy from his belt and fired. The man with a carefully trimmed beard and waxed mustache disappeared behind the tree, then reappeared, staggering and dropping the musket, falling on his face with a groan.

Tanner ran to the rocks, to the notch from where Sophia fired her five-shot pocket pistol. On a rock beside her, she had three more pistols, which she'd apparently taken off the bodies of her two dead brethren nearby. Her beaded leather ammo pouch lay at the rock's base.

Holding up for a moment, she shouted down the mountain in Spanish. Tanner could make out only two words, *Papa* and *puta*, or whore. *"Come get your whore"*—is that what she'd said?

As Tanner fired at her father's men, most of whom had now dismounted and holed up behind the trees, rocks and fallen logs along the mountainside, he glanced right and left along the ridge crest. The other outlaws, unable to withstand the onslaught, were dropping like sparrows in a lightning storm. They had the high ground, but Sophia's father's men were slipping across the ridge and flanking them.

Tanner picked a man out of the brush and fired, the bullet thumping into the log the man had ducked behind. As he thumbed back his Colt's hammer, he saw Sophia's father. Short, broad and leonine under the peaked sombrero strapped taut beneath his gray-bearded chin, he jogged out from behind a tree and crouched behind a boulder. He'd barely gotten down before Sophia cursed angrily in Spanish and fired two shots at him, chipping rock shards from his cover.

From behind the boulder, he shouted up the mountain—something that sounded to Tanner like, *"My*

111

cheap whore of a daughter will die like an incorrigible dog!"

Sophia responded with another epithet-laced harangue. She'd just fired another shot when Tanner, firing at a man moving through a trough down the grade on his left, heard her yelp.

He turned to her. She stumbled sideways and pressed her back to the rock, dropping her pistol and clutching her chest with her right hand. Her face bleached, expressionless. Tanner thought she might have only been nicked. Scrutinizing her, he saw blood well up around her glove and his stomach turned a flip.

"Sophia!"

Her knees bent and her chin dipped toward her chest. He caught her as she fell, eased her gently down.

She sat stiffly, shocked, as he peeled her hand away from the wound, and grimaced. It was bleeding bad, soaking her blouse around her breast and shoulder.

Breathlessly, she said, "He has been hunting me for a long time. He finally—"

"No, he hasn't," Tanner cut in quickly, frantic. "You're going to be fine, Sophia."

His pulse drumming in his temples, he ripped off his neckerchief, folded it, and pressed it over the wound.

She cried out in pain, and his own heart clenched with anguish. "Hold that tight."

"Bastardo," she shrieked, sobbing, drawing her lips back from her teeth and shaking her head. *"Bastardo, bastardo, bastardo!"* She leaned back against the rocks, cursing and crying, "He has won!"

Someone was crawling on his hands and feet along

the ridge, staying low behind the barricade. Tanner swung around and extended his rifle.

"What happened?" Pinto Kramer asked. His eye found the blood on Sophia's blouse, and his bearded face tensed, his jaw dropping with alarm. "Senorita!"

Bullets spanged around them. Men from both sides shouted angrily. Pinto looked at Tanner. "You have to get her out of here. When we've cleaned the reprobates off this mountain, we'll catch up to you."

Tanner opened his mouth to reply but stopped when a bullet ricocheted off the nearby rocks. He crouched protectively over Sophia. "Come on, girl," he said, urgently snaking an arm under her legs. "I'm gettin' you outta this war zone."

Crouching to keep their heads below the rock barricade, he lifted her gently. He was swinging her down the opposite slope from the shooters, when her eyes fluttered closed and her breath grew faint.

"No," he muttered, shaking her. "Sophia, no."

She raked a breath and groaned, tipped her head against his shoulder. Clutching her tightly, he hurried down the grade, straightening when they got beneath the firing line.

Their horses had fled the shooting, and he had to carry her a good seventy yards before he found them cropping grass behind a rocky finger jutting out of the hillside. He cooed to the claybank, calming the mount, then eased Sophia gently atop the saddle. Holding her there, he swung up behind her and again pressed the neckerchief to the wound, trying to slow the persistent blood flow.

"Please, I can't die," she rasped, "before I've killed my father . . ."

"You ain't gonna die," he said, his quaking voice betraying his own doubts. "At least, not if I got anything to say about it."

He gigged the claybank down the slope, toward a brushy, rocky canyon in which he hoped he could lose her father. He kissed the back of her head. "Hold on. We got the wind to split."

As he rode with the girl in his arms, Tanner Moody cursed his luck, wondering at all that had happened to him since drifting over that last pass from California. After nearly dying from pneumonia in Timbuctoo Gulch, he'd headed east hoping his luck would change.

It had changed, all right. Seduced by the charming Spanish beauty with a penchant for thievery and firearms, he'd not only wavered from the straight and narrow, he'd kinked it up like a hangman's noose. His name had never exactly tallied with the Bible, but he'd never joined an outlaw gang to rob stagecoaches, either. And now, here he was, fogging the long coulees, trying to save himself and the woman he loved.

When they'd ridden for two hours, Tanner reined the claybank to a halt atop a pass between two conical peaks strewn with sliderock. Maybe he could find a safe shelter here in the trees where the horse and Sophia could rest for a time.

Staring along his backtrail, his spine stiffened.

Three shadows angled around a scarp and down toward the canyon floor. The flashing, silver tack identified them as Don Luis's men.

As he sat there, Sophia slumped in his arms, groaning and sighing, Tanner watched two more riders descend the scarp and disappear into the boulders and thumbing rock of the canyon's floor. He waited, watching, but no other riders appeared.

Heeling the horse eastward, he descended a park then climbed to an area of spectacular, toothy cliffs stippled with cedars and pines and great, red, jutting scarps. The air freshened. Unseen eagles screeched.

He uncorked his canteen and held it to Sophia's lips. "Drink," he said, shaking her gently.

Her eyes fluttered. She shook her head then snuggled back against his chest, her body racked by occasional pain spasms.

The image of her standing naked in the waterfall flashed behind his eyes, and his heart twisted. He'd known her for such a short time, but he loved her with everything in him . . . and he was losing her. His jaw hard, his eyes grim, he corked the canteen, draped it over the saddle horn, and gigged the claybank down the other side of the pass.

A half hour later, he found himself in a gulch, the deer trail he'd been following rising along steep, evergreen-shaded, talus-carpeted slopes. A spring bubbled around the rocks on his right. He followed it to a bowl-shaped pool at the base of a sheer, basaltic wall.

He looked up. The walls on three sides stabbed a thousand feet skyward.

Box canyon.

He cursed. This time, Sophia barely stirred, mumbling in Spanish, raking her head along his chest, throwing her arms out fitfully. She was as warm as a Navajo rug heated before a fur trapper's blazing fire.

He needed to get the blood stopped and her wound cleaned. She needed rest; this jolting was going to kill her if she didn't bleed to death first. But there was no damn time.

Cursing under his breath, he held her gently while easing himself off the horse. He took her in his arms, carried her over to the shaded slope on the right side of the spring runout, and laid her gently beneath a pine.

She stirred. Her eyes fluttered open.

His voice came gently. "How you doin'?"

"Better now that we've stopped," she said thinly. She swallowed and licked her lips. "Have you seen my father? Is he behind us?"

Tanner nodded.

"Then the others are dead," she said, glancing off, her eyes glazing with tears. Suddenly, she clutched his arm and said with surprising vigor, "Kill him! Leave me here and go kill the son of a bitch!"

Tanner stared at her. The question had been haunting him. "Sophia, why are you so damned determined to kill your father?"

She lay back against the pine needles. Her eyes acquired a thoughtful cast, then began to fill with tears. She shook her head, rubbed her eyes with the heels of her hands. "Don't ask me. I can't relive what he did to me." Her voice rose. *"Please, kill him!"*

Tanner sat back on his heels, feeling as though he'd been punched in the gut. So that's what had started all this—old Don Luis being unable to resist his own daughter. Tanner couldn't help imagining it now, and rage burned within him. He leaned forward and kissed her. When he pulled away, he said with a resolute nod, "I will."

He glanced back along the rubble-strewn canyon. Finally, he turned to her. "I'll leave the canteen. You keep that rag pressed to your chest, understand?"

She offered a thin smile. "When he is dead, we will go to *Pueblo de Los Angeles*. I have heard the weather is lovely there. We will swim in the ocean . . ."

He leaned down and kissed her forehead, lingering, reluctant to leave her. Finally, he stood and retrieved his canteen and bedroll. He arranged the bedroll into a comfortable pillow. Gentling her head onto the pillow and setting the canteen near her right hand, he kissed her.

"Hold on, girl," he said. "You keep thinkin' about that ocean we're gonna swim in."

He winked at her, then shucked his rifle from his saddle boot and began walking back along the spring.

He'd moved maybe seventy yards when he stopped suddenly, hunkering down behind a natural levee. A shod hoof had clipped a stone. Spanish voices rose, gaining volume as riders approached along a game path.

Tanner looked around. Hearing but not yet seeing the riders, he climbed over the levee and hunkered down behind a boulder near the stream. He waited until the riders sounded only a few yards away, then strode calmly onto the trail.

The four men snapped alive, startled, exclaiming as they sawed back on their reins. Their peaked sombreros shaded their flushed, unshaven faces. They were strung out along the trail in a shaggy line. The man closest to Tanner stared hard, nostrils flaring, both hands frozen on the butts of his two, long-barreled Navies.

Tanner held his rifle down low, his upper lip curled, challenging them to draw. He wondered vaguely where the old man was.

The sun beat down on the rocks. The stream gurgled over pebbles. Blackflies buzzed around a fox carcass on the other side of the stream.

The long-legged Arabians facing Tanner swished their tails and blew. The nearest one lowered and extended its head, sniffing Tanner cautiously.

Finally, the man slightly behind and left of the point rider bunched his lips and swept his revolver from its holster. Tanner snapped up the Colt's barrel and punched the trigger, over and over.

These men may have ridden roughshod for old Don Luis, but they hadn't had their fast-draws tested recently. In less than four seconds, all four men lay dead in the trail. Tanner had flung himself back behind the boulder to keep from getting trampled by the bolting horses, two of which had bucked ahead as the others scattered right, left, and behind.

When he'd set down his empty rifle, unsheathed the dragoon, and was standing in the trail again, he raised his gaze from the bleeding bodies to the gray-bearded man trotting his black horse along the stream. Don Luis had one of his ivory-gripped .38's out as he halted his thoroughbred twenty yards up-canyon, raking his eyes across the sprawled bodies disbelievingly.

He scowled at Tanner, eyes wide with outrage, but did not extend the weapon. The craggy face under his gaudy sombrero was weathered and brown as an Indian's.

He glanced at the bodies again. Tanner stared at the broad-shouldered, taut-bodied oldster, willing the man to fire on him. But when Don Luis returned his eyes to Tanner, he lowered the pistol to his thigh. His hand opened, and the gun clattered to the rocks.

The old man held up his right hand. "Two fingers, gringo, uh?"

The man removed his left Colt with the two fingers and dropped it like an andiron still hot from a smithy's forge. It clattered amongst the rocks. He reached behind his right thigh, delicately unsheathed his carbine, and tossed it down, as well.

Turning to Tanner, he raised his hands and lifted his chin with maddening arrogance. "I am unarmed."

Tanner bunched his lips with rage and lifted the big dragoon, thumbing back the hammer. Alarm widened Don Luis's mud-brown eyes. Tanner began squeezing the trigger, but his finger stopped of its own accord. It would pull no farther.

Tanner cursed, squinted down the barrel of the extended gun. Finally, he grunted disgustedly and removed his finger from the trigger, lowered the barrel a few inches. As much as he wanted to, he couldn't shoot an unarmed man. Even one as evil as Don Luis. Even for Sophia.

The lines in Don Luis's face softened as Tanner lowered the dragoon to his side.

Tanner cursed, choked back sobs of seething rage. "Go home, you old dung beetle." He took two steps forward and raised his arms, shouting, "Get the hell outta here!"

The black horse spooked, nearly throwing its rider from the saddle. When Don Luis got it under control, he turned it around and cantered back the way he'd come. He glanced cautiously over his shoulder until he'd rounded a bend in the trail and disappeared behind a thumb in the canyon wall.

Cursing aloud, asking himself if he was a man or a goddamn mouse, Tanner quickly smashed the hacendado's guns on the rocks and ran back to where he'd left the girl.

He slowed as he approached her. The back of his neck chilled.

Her chest lay still. Through the frame of her tangled, black hair, her blue eyes stared glassily up at the pine bows shading her resting place.

"Sophia," he said, his voice catching. "Sophia." He stumbled heavy-footed toward her and dropped to his knees. His shoulders shook as, slumped over her lifeless body, tears streaked his cheeks and dampened his beard. He swept his hat from his head and cursed.

He'd crossed over the line for her, he'd killed for her, and now she was gone, leaving him here . . . alone.

Shadows were gathering when he heard a pebble rolling down the bank behind him. He snapped his head up instantly and threw himself left, spinning his body around as a pistol popped atop the rocky bank before him, the slugs chewing up pine needles to his right. Hitting the ground on his back, his right arm went up, and his hand disappeared behind his neck.

The blade flashed as his hand snapped outward, releasing the toothpick. The long, slim knife caromed through the shadows and buried itself in Don Luis's chest with a bone-crunching thud.

Staring through the powder smoke webbing around the old man's gray-bearded head, Tanner watched him stumble back against a tree, groaning and clutching his chest. He dropped the pistol he'd apparently been carrying in a hideout holster or on his horse.

Don Luis stiffened. His knees bent. He dropped and rolled down the bank until he lay near his daughter, the hide-wrapped handle of Tanner's toothpick protruding from his heart.

Tanner stared down at the two bodies for a long time. Finally, he removed the toothpick from the hacendado's chest, swept the blade across the old man's tiger-skin chaps, and returned it to its sheath.

He squatted before Sophia, gently lifted her. He sobbed again as her head lolled lifelessly, arms hanging limp, her bloody crucifix dangling from its chain around her neck.

Leaving her father to the scavengers, Tanner buried her under rocks along the canyon's wall. He muttered a few words over her grave as more tears streaked his face. Then he took a long drink from his canteen, mounted his horse, and headed back for the straight and narrow.

Four

The New York Morning Telegraph, Feb. 7, 1903
The Legend of Tanner Moody
Fourth in a series by Bat Masterson
Exclusive

I had the impression, listening to Vern Wells tell me the story of a young Tanner Moody being seduced onto the Owlhoot Trail by a dark-haired Mexican beauty, that he was telling the truth. The fact that he did not want to tell me his own story—as his two friends did—supported that belief.

Wells sat and rolled his eyes while his companions—Higgins and Chambers—regaled me with stories of their own exploits. I considered the time I spent listening to them payment for coming away with the other story. I left them sitting there, probably believing they were about to become legends of the old West.

As I reentered the main room of the saloon the place seemed to be bursting at the seams, despite the lateness of the hour. I went back to the bar and asked the bartender to bring me a cup of coffee.

I had decided that I was going to write a long series of articles about Tanner Moody and so far I had only three stories.

I turned and surveyed the room, looking for my fourth . . .

Standing at the bar offered an excellent vantage point from which to watch the whole room. It had been from there that I'd spotted Don Felipe Talamantes, and now I was able to clearly see the two men who had entered. They stopped just inside the door to study the room, themselves. This, if nothing else, pointed out that they were the kind of men who were on the watch for danger. As it happened, I was acquainted with one of the men. His name was William Pinkerton and, together with his brother Robert, he ran the famed Pinkerton Detective Agency, which had been founded by their father, Allan. In 1884 Allan, already suffering from a variety of ailments, stumbled, bit his tongue, and died. Oh, he didn't just die because he'd bitten his tongue, but gangrene set in, and he finally succumbed to septicemia—although, I must admit, I'm not even sure what that is.

William was in his fifties now, as was the man standing beside him. He headed up the Chicago office and from there covered most of the West. His younger brother, Robert, manned the New York office. I knew both brothers, so I knew the other man wasn't Robert.

I didn't know what Pinkerton's connection with Tanner Moody was—friend or foe—and I decided there was only one way to find out. Pinkerton and the other man were just beginning to move away from the doorway when I intercepted them.

Pinkerton, who had continued to eye the room, adjusted his gaze to take me in, and looked surprised.

"Mr. Masterson," he said.

"Mr. Pinkerton."

"I didn't know you knew Moody—although I don't know why I should be surprised."

"Same here," I said. "Was it you or your daddy he worked with? Or your brother?"

"Moody had some dealings with my father," Pinkerton said, "but we're actually here so Mr. Conway can pay his respects. Peter Conway, meet Bat Masterson."

"It's a pleasure," Conway said, extending his hand—a nicety William Pinkerton had skipped. Conway was smaller than Pinkerton and not as well dressed. Although they were the same age, he seemed to carry the years with more vitality.

"You knew Moody?" I asked.

"Yes," Conway said. "It was years ago, during the war. I was attached to the War Department then."

"Working for Allan Pinkerton?" I asked.

"That's right."

"I'm covering this funeral as a journalist for the *New York Morning Telegraph*—"

"Journalist?" Pinkerton interrupted. "When did that happen?"

"Very recently," I said to him, and turned my attention back to his companion. "I wonder if we could talk a bit about that time?"

"I don't see why no—"

"I'll be at the bar while you two reminisce," Pinkerton said, and walked away.

"You work for William now?" I asked.

"Yes."

"Not like working for Allan, is it?"

Conway hesitated, then said, "It's a different time."

It was a very tactful answer.

"Why don't we get a drink," I asked, "and you can tell me your story . . ."

Tanner Moody
And the Prophet Mountains

By James Reasoner

A plume of smoke rose over the Prophet Mountains, west of the town of Flat Rock. I stood on the porch of the Halliday House, the only decent hotel in town, and watched it climb into the sky, wondering what had caused it. A forest fire, perhaps. Being newly arrived from the East, I knew little of such things.

Shouts from across the street drew my attention. I looked over there and saw a man pounding on the door of a squat, squarish stone building. "Sheriff!" the man yelled. "Sheriff, there's smoke in the Prophets!"

The door opened in response to the commotion, and I had my first look at Tanner Moody.

He was a large man, though well-proportioned enough so that he didn't seem overly massive at first glance. He wore what I had already come to think of as typical garb for this cattle and mining country: boots, denim trousers, a bib-front shirt, and a leather vest. The only thing unusual was the star pinned to the vest. A gunbelt was slung around his waist, with the walnut grips of a revolver jutting up from the holster. His features were rugged and possessed a good deal of power. He spoke quietly, but his rumbling voice carried easily across the street.

"What are you yammerin' about, Laird?"

The man who had summoned him pointed toward the peaks rising west of town. "There's smoke up there, Sheriff. Looks like something's wrong."

Sheriff Tanner Moody stepped out into the street to get a better look. "Haven't heard anything about any Apaches raidin' from across the border. Reckon I'd better ride up and have a look." He turned to look at the townsman. "You seen Wade?"

"No, sir, not all day."

Tanner Moody grunted. "If you see him, tell him where I've gone."

"You're not takin' a posse with you?"

"Don't know that I need one."

I took that as my cue. As the townsman hurried away, I stepped down from the hotel porch and strode quickly across the street. As I approached the sheriff, I extended my hand and said, "Sheriff Moody? I'm Peter Conway."

Out of habit and Western politeness, perhaps, Tanner Moody shook my hand. "New in town, ain't you?" he said. "Sorry I don't have time to talk—"

"I know, you have to ride up into the mountains. I was thinking that perhaps I might accompany you."

His eyes ranged over me, and I knew what he was thinking: *You? Why would I want to take a dude like you with me?*

"I'm from the War Department," I added.

That answered his question. He grunted and nodded. "Got a horse?"

"I made arrangements at the livery stable to rent one as soon as I arrived."

"Go have it saddled up, then," he said as he started to turn back to the sheriff's office. He added over his shoulder, rather scornfully, "Unless you know how to saddle a horse yourself."

"As a matter of fact, I do."

I didn't waste any time, because I was sure that Tanner Moody wouldn't. I stopped at the hotel only long enough to retrieve my Henry rifle from my room, and then I headed for the livery stable as quickly as I could.

The sheriff kept his horse at the same stable, a fine-looking buckskin, tall enough and sturdy enough to support his weight. He was already mounted when I got there. "Hurry up," he told me. "I ain't got time to waste."

A few minutes later I led my rented horse out of the barn and stepped up into the saddle. The animal was a bay gelding, a good horse, if not quite the equal of Tanner Moody's mount. The sheriff left Flat Rock at a gallop. I was close behind him, thankful that I had done considerable riding in my youth and had kept up the habit in Washington, D.C.

We headed straight for the mountains, which were, as mountains usually are, farther away than they appeared. The ride gave me time to think about the assignment that had brought me out here.

With a war going on, it was more vital than ever that a steady supply of gold and silver flow into the government's coffers so as to maintain a strong economy. In recent months, however, shipments from the ore-rich Prophet Mountains had been severely disrupted by the activities of bandits and outlaws. The local authorities had been unable to quell this tide of lawlessness.

Of course, to some this came as no surprise, considering that many were of the opinion that Tanner Moody was no better than an outlaw himself.

Before coming out here, I had done some investigating of the man's background and found that apparently there was some justification for that belief. From a young age, Tanner Moody had associated himself with ruffians and desperadoes and gunmen. I could find no evidence that he had ever committed a serious crime himself, but the prevailing sentiment was that he had just never gotten caught. There was no doubt he was skilled in the handling of firearms. He had killed men in pistol duels—several of them, in fact. But all of these killings were, in the parlance of the West, "fair fights." The other men had drawn their guns first, and Tanner Moody had fired in self-defense. But his association with criminals and the blood on his hands led people to draw the inescapable conclusion that he was a bad man.

Oddly enough, over the past few years he seemed to have put all that behind him and had worked in a succession of jobs as a lawman, serving as a town marshal, a deputy sheriff, and now the full-fledged sheriff of the county that encompassed the Prophet Mountains and the town of Flat Rock. From all accounts he had served honorably and efficiently in these positions, but people remembered his checkered past and still harbored some mistrust of him. The sheriff of Harker County, to the east, had told me, "Tanner Moody? Why, he's just about the slickest owlhoot you'll ever see! He may have those people in Flat Rock fooled, but mark my words, he's up to something. Wouldn't surprise me a bit if he's got somethin' to do with all them gold shipments bein' held up. I reckon he's as crooked as a dog's hind leg."

Well, I thought as I followed him toward the mountains, we would certainly find out. That was my job, to find the men responsible for the robberies and to put a stop to them.

Even if it meant dealing with the famous—or infamous—Tanner Moody.

He didn't slacken the pace until we were in the foothills of the mountains. The smoke had stopped rising while we were riding, and that seemed ominous to me. We rounded a bend in the trail. Tanner Moody hauled back on the reins and brought his mount to a stop. I followed suit. He leaned forward in the saddle and uttered a heartfelt "Damn."

About two hundred yards ahead of us was what was left of a wagon. It had been burned so that the iron frame was all that remained. The mules that had pulled it lay on the ground, dead, shot down in their traces. Several huddled shapes were on the ground not far from the burned-out wagon. I knew them for what they were. I had seen dead bodies before.

Tanner Moody hitched his horse forward in a walk. There was no hurry now. As I rode alongside him, he said, "I was afraid of this. Carling, the superintendent up at the Jeremiah Mine, said he wasn't goin' to tell me the next time he sent a shipment out. Reckon the damn fool didn't trust me."

I didn't say anything.

Tanner Moody spat. "Looks like bein' close-mouthed didn't do him much good. That bunch must've got wind of the wagon leavin' the mine."

"You mean the band of outlaws responsible for these robberies?"

He looked over at me. "Sure. That's why you're here, ain't it? The War Department doesn't think I can catch them." He snorted. "Hell, your bosses probably think I'm one of the bunch myself."

"You do have a certain reputation, Sheriff," I ventured.

He reined in and turned his head to glare at me. "I know more about my rep than you do, Conway. I know what part of it's deserved and what part comes out the hind end of a bull."

"Of course," I murmured.

He was still angry as he rode on, but I sensed that not all of it was directed at me. He was upset because the wagon carrying the gold shipment had been attacked and burned. No doubt the deaths of the guards bothered him as well. Perhaps he *wasn't* involved with the outlaws, I thought. His reaction seemed genuine, and I pride myself on being a good judge of such things.

Tanner Moody carried a Henry like my own in a saddle scabbard. When we rode up to the scene of the atrocity, he swung down from the saddle and pulled the rifle from its sheath. His eyes swept the surrounding terrain, the rugged, brush-dotted foothills that were all around us.

I felt something inside me tighten as I looked at the bodies of the guards. Probably they had been shot, but it was difficult to tell because they, like the wagon, had been set afire. The charred remains were so grisly I had to look away. "Who would do such a thing?" I heard myself asking.

"Snake-blooded skunks," Tanner Moody said. "Men who like killin'."

The distaste in his voice was evident. I found myself with a certain admiration, even a liking, for the man.

That changed in the next instant as he turned quickly and raised his rifle, pointing it at me. I barely had time to exclaim, "What—" before Tanner Moody shot me in the head.

I returned to the land of the living full of pain and disorientation. The pounding in my head was accompanied by a sharp sense of nausea. I turned my head and retched. The movement made my head hurt worse, but when the spasms finally stopped I felt a bit better.

"That's usually what happens when a fella wakes up from bein' knocked out."

The rough voice belonged to Tanner Moody. I had no trouble recognizing it, and I drew some comfort from the fact that my brain seemed to be functioning fairly well.

I opened my eyes and saw the sandy ground where I had emptied the contents of my belly. Turning the other way, I blinked and looked up at a dark figure looming over me. From the size of it, I knew it belonged to the sheriff. He leaned over and said, "Let me give you a hand."

He seemed awfully solicitous for someone who had shot me not long before. I sensed that only a short time had passed since his attack on me. But I was too weak to sit up by myself, so I allowed his strong hand to close over my arm and lift me into a sitting position.

I found myself looking at another corpse, but this one wasn't burned. It belonged to a bearded, roughly-dressed man I had never seen before. He wore a buckskin shirt with a large blood stain on the chest where he had been shot. His eyes were open and stared glassily at the sky.

Tanner Moody straightened and prodded the dead man in the side with a boot toe. "Know him?" he asked me.

"I never saw the man before. Who is he?"

"The fella who was about to shoot you in the back

when I spotted him from the corner of my eye."

I frowned in confusion. "I don't understand."

He spoke as if I were a particularly thick-headed child, and at that moment, I suppose I wasn't much better than one. "That hombre was about to back-shoot you, so I shot him first."

"No," I said, "You shot me. In the head." I lifted a hand to the center of the pain and found a raw furrow on my scalp, just above my right ear. I winced as my fingertips explored the injury.

Tanner Moody gave a bark of laughter. "Hell, Conway, you think I shot you? You'd be dead if I had." He thrust the barrel of his rifle toward the man on the ground. "That's where my bullet went. But the son of a bitch got off a shot as he went down, and it clipped you on the head."

I cast my mind back to that moment, trying to recall if I had heard two shots instead of one, but honestly I couldn't remember. From the way the sheriff described the action, the shots must have gone off so close together that they couldn't be distinguished from each other. Clearly he wasn't lying about the matter; the fresh corpse was sufficient proof of what he had said.

"My apologies," I muttered.

"*De nada*. I reckon I can see why you thought I'd thrown down on you. He was up there in the brush on that slope behind you. The sun just happened to glint off his rifle as he was drawin' a bead on you. Pretty dumb thing for him to do."

"To try to kill me, you mean?"

"To try to kill you *first*. He should've ventilated me, then he could have taken care of you."

I knew he was saying that I didn't represent nearly as big a threat as he did. I couldn't argue with that. After all, he was the famous Tanner Moody, and I was only a War Department bureaucrat from Washington. But I was not without experience. During the early days of the war, I had commanded a company at Bull Run before resigning my commission and accepting the position under Secretary Stanton. I had experienced enemy fire.

I climbed to my feet, forcing myself not to be too shaky as I did so. "Do you think he's one of the outlaws?" I said as I pointed to the dead man.

"That'd be my guess. The rest of the bunch left him behind to discourage anybody from comin' after them. Didn't work, though. We'll see if we can pick up their trail."

"And we'll follow them, just the two of us?"

"What's the matter?" Tanner Moody asked with a grin. "You reckon we ain't enough to handle a gang of killers?"

Actually, I didn't, but I hesitated to say as much. And while I was hesitating I was saved from the necessity of saying so by the arrival of a posse from Flat Rock. The sound of rapidly approaching hoofbeats made us look around, and we saw more than a dozen men riding up the trail toward us. A lean, dark-haired man led them. He wore a badge on his shirt. I decided he must be one of Tanner Moody's deputies.

"You're a mite late, Wade," the sheriff said as the group rode up and brought their mounts to a halt.

"Sorry, Sheriff," the deputy said. "I was down at the church with Dinah."

Tanner Moody grunted. "I forgot. You got a weddin' comin' up tomorrow."

The man called Wade didn't say anything.

"Well, spread out and look for tracks," the sheriff ordered. "Careful, though. You don't want to mess up any sign that's there."

The posse members did as they were told, dismounting and walking all around the site of the robbery, except for three men who were picked to help with the bodies of the slain guards and another who was sent back to Flat Rock to fetch the local undertaker. The bodies were wrapped in blankets and placed beside the ruined wagon. A considerable amount of cursing went on in the process. I gathered that the unfortunate guards had been known to the posse members.

"Sheriff, over here!" one of the searchers called.

Tanner Moody strode over to answer the summons. I went with him, feeling stronger and steadier on my feet now. I knew I was very lucky not to have been wounded worse by the bushwhacker.

The outlaws hadn't taken any pains to conceal their tracks. The trail led off to the north, along the east side of the mountain range. "That's mighty rugged country up there," Tanner Moody declared, "but I reckon we'll see if we can follow them."

For the rest of that day, that's what we did, leaving behind one man to wait with the bodies for the undertaker. But as the sheriff had said, the terrain was quite rugged, and as the ground became rockier, it was more difficult to follow the tracks left by the killers.

I rode along with my eyes on the ground and paid no attention to the man who moved up alongside me until he said in a raspy voice, "You're new in these parts, ain't you?"

I looked over at him. He was getting on in years, with a white beard and white hair that fell to his shoulders, but he seemed spry enough. He rode a mule instead of a horse and dressed like a cross between a cowhand and a prospector. I suspected he had followed both professions in his life.

"That's right, I just arrived in Flat Rock today," I told him, though my itinerary was really none of his business.

He reached over to shake my hand. "Ezra's my name."

"Peter Conway," I introduced myself as I clasped his callused hand. The posse had become rather spread out as it followed the trail of the bandits, so this fellow Ezra was the only one riding near me at the moment. Perhaps that was why he had approached me.

"How'd you get roped into this snipe hunt?" he asked.

"I volunteered to accompany the sheriff when he rode up here to check out that smoke." I didn't say anything about being from the War Department.

If Ezra was overly puzzled by my answer, he gave no sign of it. "You heard tell of Tanner Moody before?"

"Indeed I have. He's quite famous in some circles."

Ezra grunted. "More like notorious, some folks'd say. You prob'ly think he's an owlhoot and want to write about him."

I understood that he had mistaken me for a journalist. Well, that was a handy enough ruse, so I made no move to deny it. Instead, I said, "Sheriff Moody does have a rather colorful, not to mention dangerous, reputation."

Ezra leaned over and spat on the rocks next to the trail. "I don't know what all he might've done before he came to Flat Rock, but I can tell you this: he's the best sheriff this county's ever had. Been straight as an arrow the whole time. Ain't killed nobody but them as needed killin'. And he's had to put up with a heap, too, what with his own deputy stealin' his gal."

I recalled the sheriff saying something about Wade having a wedding coming up the next day. "You mean the woman Wade is about to marry was once romantically involved with the sheriff?"

"That's right. Him and Dinah hadn't made plans to get hitched or anything like that, but I reckon they would've got there if Wade hadn't come along and messed ever'thing up for 'em." The old man wiped the back of a hand across his mouth. I sensed that he was naturally garrulous and that if I remained silent, he would continue. After a moment, he did so. "I'll tell you the straight of it, but that don't mean I'm sayin' you need to go and write about it."

"I won't write a word about whatever you tell me," I told him honestly.

"Well, the sheriff was sweet on Dinah Macauley, and she was sweet on him, but then Wade Fletcher come to Flat Rock, and he swept Dinah right off her feet with his good looks and sweet talk."

"Then Wade hasn't been Sheriff Moody's deputy for a long time," I said.

" 'Bout a year, I reckon. He come to Flat Rock from up in Montana somewhere. Was a lawman up there, deputy town marshal, I think. The sheriff needed a deputy, so he hired him. It's worked out pretty good, except for the business about Dinah."

"That seems like a rather important matter," I pointed out.

"Yeah, but since Tanner Moody pinned on the badge, he's taken the job mighty serious-like. I reckon there's a part of him that'd like to fire Fletcher and send him on down the trail, but he can't bring himself to do that 'cause Fletcher's done a good job as a star packer. The personal part of it don't come into play, as far as the sheriff's concerned."

This was all very interesting, and it might even have a connection with the job that had brought me here, I reasoned. If Tanner Moody had attempted to leave his past behind him by becoming a lawman, then settling down with a wife might be included in that effort to be a law-abiding citizen. To have a potential mate whisked away from him could have made him bitter, could have even made him decide that the whole thing wasn't worth it. The loss of Dinah Macauley could have prompted him to turn outlaw, though he continued to hide that behind his pose of an honest lawman.

That was pure speculation on my part, of course. But if the theory was true, it would go a considerable distance toward explaining why Tanner Moody had been unable to catch the outlaws or put a stop to the robberies of the ore shipments. Until I could prove it, though, I had no choice but to continue as I had been, riding with the posse after the robbers.

Finally, after losing the trail and attempting without success to locate it again, Tanner Moody said, "That's it. They're gone."

"Yeah, I reckon so," Deputy Wade Fletcher said. "That makes what, four or five times they've given us the slip, Sheriff?"

Tanner Moody just glared at him. Even though Wade had said "given *us* the slip," I and everyone else in the posse knew what he meant. This was the sheriff's failure, not ours.

"Go on back to town," Tanner Moody growled. "I'm goin' up to the Jeremiah to see Carling."

"You want company?" Fletcher asked.

"No, you'd better get back to your bride," the sheriff said heavily. "I'll see you when I get back to town."

Fletcher shrugged and waved to the other men to turn around and head for Flat Rock. Ezra went with them. I didn't.

"Ain't you goin'?" Tanner Moody asked me.

"No, I'll go with you to the mine," I told him.

"If the War Department wants you to keep what you're doin' quiet, you ain't doin' a very good job of it."

"On the contrary, that old gentleman called Ezra is convinced that I'm a newspaper reporter. By nightfall he will have told everyone in Flat Rock as much."

Tanner Moody still glowered at me for a second, but then his expression changed and he chuckled. "You've got ol' Ez figured out, all right. He'll tell the world." He turned his horse. "Come on, if you're goin' with me."

I rode with him, glad he hadn't insisted that I leave. I wondered if that meant he didn't have anything to hide . . .

Or if he just didn't care what I discovered about him.

Timothy Carling was mostly bald, with a fringe of reddish-gray hair around a freckled scalp. He slammed a fist on the desk in his office at the Jeremiah Mine and said, "Damn it, Moody, those were good men! And they're dead!"

With a visible effort, Tanner Moody kept his temper under control. "I know that, Carling," he said. "And I want to catch their killers just as much as you do. But they gave us the slip and there's nothing I can do about it."

Carling sank into the chair behind his desk and put his head in his hands for a moment. When he looked up, he said, "There was at least eighty thousand in gold on that wagon."

I gave the man credit for first expressing his outrage over the murder of the guards and driver before taking the loss into consideration.

Tanner Moody picked up one of the straight-backed chairs in front of the desk, turned it around, and straddled it. "How come you didn't let me know you were sending out a shipment?" he asked.

Carling fidgeted with a pen on the desk and looked uncomfortable. After hesitating for a moment, he said, "I didn't think it was necessary."

"Didn't think it was necessary . . . or didn't think it was a good idea?"

"Blast it, Sheriff!" the mine superintendent exclaimed in frustration. "I have a duty to the owners of the Jeremiah to do what I think is best for their investment."

"And after the other robberies, you figured it was best not to tell me about the gold," Tanner Moody said heavily.

"You said that, Sheriff, not me."

"Did you tell anybody?"

Carling hesitated. "No, I didn't. I didn't even tell the guards and the driver until it was time to load the wagon. I figured that way there was less chance the news would get out." He looked at me. "You're from the War Department, Conway," he said needlessly. "What's the opinion in Washington?"

"That the robberies have to stop," I replied. "Secretary Stanton was adamant about that when he told me he was sending me out here."

"And what do you intend to do?" Carling demanded.

"I'm investigating the matter."

Carling's eyes cut over toward the sheriff. "Better do your looking close to home."

143

Tanner Moody stood up. "That's enough. As far as I'm concerned, Carling, you bear some of the responsibility for those men gettin' killed."

Carling came to his feet as well and glared across the desk. He might work in an office now, but he still retained some of the power in his body that he had possessed when he worked down in the shaft as a miner. I thought for a moment that he might take a swing at the sheriff. If these two big men began to brawl, I would have to step back out of the way. I thought of myself as deceptively wiry, but I had no business getting in the middle of a fight between two such bullish individuals.

No punches were thrown. Tanner Moody said, "Come on, Conway, let's get the hell out of here." He turned and stalked out of the office.

I followed him, but not before saying quickly to the mine superintendent, "I'll be in touch, Mr. Carling."

Our horses were right outside the office. As we mounted, I looked farther up the shoulder of the mountain at the shaft house and the pile of tailings from the mine. Down there below the surface of the earth, men were toiling with picks and shovels at this very moment, prying wealth from the earth. I admired them for their fortitude but did not envy their jobs. Tightly enclosed spaces have always bothered me.

The sun lowered toward the peaks behind us as the sheriff and I rode toward Flat Rock. After several minutes of silence, Tanner Moody said, "Well, I reckon you've got your mind made up that I'm an owlhoot, too, just like everybody else around here."

"On the contrary, I believe in keeping an open

mind," I told him. "I've seen no evidence to indicate that you're involved in anything illegal, Sheriff. I'd say you want to catch those gold thieves as much as anyone."

"Thanks." After a moment he went on, "How's your head?"

"It hurts like the very blazes," I told him honestly.

He laughed, but there was nothing malicious about the sound. "Yeah, gettin' grazed like that will make a man's head hurt, all right. You might ought to have Doc Yarborough take a look at you when we get back to town. He's a pretty good sawbones when he's sober."

"Not necessary. I carry a small mirror and used it to check the pupils of my eyes. They're the same size, so I'm confident there was no brain concussion. That's a sign of it, you know."

Tanner Moody grunted. Evidently, he hadn't known.

It was dark when we got back to Flat Rock. The sheriff headed for his office, and I went with him even though he again mentioned seeing the local doctor. I insisted that I was all right.

"It's your funeral," he said dourly.

When we got to the office we found Wade Fletcher sitting at the desk. He wasn't in any hurry to get up when Tanner Moody came in. In fact he eyed the sheriff rather defiantly for a moment before he climbed slowly to his feet and moved out from behind the desk. "Any luck at the Jeremiah?" he asked.

"The gang didn't double back and return the gold, if that's what you're askin'," the sheriff said. "Carling just about accused me of bein' in cahoots with them."

"That's crazy," Fletcher said, and managed to make it sound as if he didn't consider that such a far-fetched idea after all. I could tell that the deputy considered himself more suited to wear the sheriff's badge than Tanner Moody was. As if taking the sheriff's woman wasn't enough.

"Carling and everybody else around here will sing a different tune when those owlhoots are behind bars or dancin' at the end of a rope," Tanner Moody said. "Make the rounds, and then you can turn in."

"Sure thing," Fletcher said. He started toward the door.

The sheriff stopped him by saying, "Wedding still on for tomorrow?"

Fletcher smiled. "Sure. Why wouldn't it be?"

Tanner Moody shook his head. "No reason. Go on, get out of here."

Fletcher left, chuckling. I decided I didn't like the man. I made another decision as well.

"I believe I will see your local medico after all," I told the sheriff. "Where will I find his office?"

"A block and a half down the street, on the other side. His office is above the hardware store. If he's drunk, tell him I said to sober up." Tanner Moody laughed humorlessly. "Hell—even drunk, Doc Yarborough's better than some doctors I've seen."

That was encouraging, or at least it would have been if I had intended to actually pay a visit to the doctor. But that was just an excuse. With a nod, I left the sheriff's office.

Pausing on the boardwalk outside, I looked up and down Flat Rock's main street. It was late enough so that most of the businesses were closed for the night, with the exception of the saloons at the other end of town. Their windows glowed warmly, and music and laughter drifted from them.

I spotted Wade Fletcher moving along the street, checking doors to make sure they were locked. As I watched, he paused abruptly in the mouth of an alley and then moved into the area between two buildings. It was dark as pitch in there, and I could see nothing else without moving closer.

Without any firm reason for doing so, I approached the alley mouth. Why was I suspicious of him? Instinct alone, I suppose. I liked Tanner Moody, and I didn't like the deputy. As I came closer, I heard the soft murmur of voices, and after a moment I knew my hunch had been correct.

"Every dollar we keep out of those Yankee banks is one more dollar that won't pay for guns to kill good Southern boys," an unfamiliar voice said. "You're doin' just fine, Fletcher."

"You didn't give me a whole hell of a lot of choice," Wade Fletcher said, an edge of bitterness in his voice.

The other man laughed. "You're the one who killed that gent up in Montana, not me. I just figured you'd like it kept quiet, seein' as how you're packin' a badge now and about to marry such a pretty, upstandin' gal."

"Yeah, well, just make sure I get my cut before you send the loot back to Richmond."

"Don't worry. You'll be a rich man and the sheriff, to boot, once folks around here kick Moody out of office."

Well, there it was, all laid out in the open as nicely and neatly as anyone could want. I had been very fortunate to overhear the conversation that would break the whole case. In my time working for the War Department, it has been my experience that such strokes of good luck were often what allowed an investigation to be successful. But it's necessary first for the investigator to be in the right place at the right time, and *that* is a matter of sharp instincts, dogged persistence, and sheer talent, if I do say so myself. Now all I had to do was return to the sheriff's office and tell Tanner Moody what I had discovered.

I would have done so immediately if I had not stepped on a loose plank in the boardwalk and had it come up and slap me in the face.

I reeled back from the unexpected blow and let out an involuntary cry of pain. Curses followed, but not from me. Instead they came from Wade Fletcher and his confederate, no play on words intended. They lunged out of the alley and grabbed me, dragging me back into the shadows. The other man looped an arm around my neck and began to choke me as Fletcher said, "It's that damned reporter!"

I had no opportunity to tell them that I was actually a government agent, and if I had, it probably would have just made my situation worse. Of course, it couldn't get much worse, as the other man proved a second later by saying, "I'll strangle the son of a bitch!"

That was when Fletcher said, "No, take him up in the mountains to get rid of him. If he disappears, Moody'll figure he just left town when he didn't get the story he wanted. If his body is found down here, that bastard'll want to find out what happened to him."

The other outlaw grunted agreement. His arm across my throat tightened even more. The black night turned red, and then I lost consciousness for the second time that day.

I suppose I should have been happy that I passed out from lack of oxygen, rather than being knocked unconscious by another blow on the head. Such repeated injuries can be quite dangerous, even fatal. So can discovering the truth about a gang of Confederate agents and outlaws working with a turncoat deputy.

One of the lawmen in Flat Rock was as crooked as a dog's hind leg, all right, but it wasn't Tanner Moody.

I awoke draped facedown over the back of a horse, my wrists and ankles roped together under the belly of the animal. I made no sound or movement to let my captor know that I had regained consciousness. For all I knew, he believed me to be dead already, strangled to death in that alley. He would be more inclined to carelessness if he thought that he was handling a corpse instead of a live prisoner.

I was a bit proud of myself for thinking that fast under the circumstances.

Fletcher had suggested that the man dispose of me "up in the mountains." I wondered if that meant the man was taking me back to the camp used by the gang, or if I was to be dumped in the first convenient ravine. I hoped fervently it was the former. That way, if I managed to escape, I would know the location of the outlaw sanctuary.

I'm unsure about the duration of our trek into the Prophet Mountains. It was a long and uncomfortable ride. That much I can say without any doubt. But finally we stopped, and I heard the crackle of a campfire and rough voices calling out questions, the main one of which was, "What the hell you got there, Reese?"

So Reese was the name of the man who had been conducting the clandestine meeting with the deputy in Flat Rock. I filed that fact away in my head in case I needed it later.

Footsteps came over to the horse. I felt a jerk on the ropes holding my arms and legs together. That was a knife blade cutting through the bonds. Then a hand grabbed the back of my coat and hauled me off the horse. I fell hard to the ground.

"Damn nosy newspaperman who showed up in Flat Rock today," Reese said. "Fletcher wants us to get rid of him so his body'll never be found."

"Since when do we take orders from Fletcher?" another man asked. "He does what we want, if he knows what's good for him."

"He knows," Reese said. "He doesn't want Moody tryin' to figure out who killed this fella, and I agree. Better he just vanishes."

Yet another man laughed as I lay there as silent and motionless as possible. "You think those dumb townies will give Fletcher the sheriff's badge as a weddin' present tomorrow mornin'?"

"Could be. He wants the job as much or more than he wants that gal."

I opened my eyes the tiniest slit. I saw firelight and dim shapes silhouetted against it. I was lying on my right side, somewhat doubled over as I had been when I was on the horse. Moving slowly, I edged my fingers toward the top of my boot. I could tell that the pistol I carried in a sheath strapped to my ankle was still there. Perhaps Fletcher and Reese had searched me, perhaps not, but even if they had, they hadn't thought to look in my boots. They wouldn't have suspected a journalist of carrying weapons there.

More footsteps approached me. "Is he dead already?"

"I don't know," Reese said. "He might be. I choked him pretty good. Poke him with your Bowie and find out."

I couldn't allow that, of course. My ruse of unconsciousness or death had come to an end. I twisted on the ground, drawing a startled yell from the man who was approaching me. My right hand went into the boot and closed over the butt of the pistol concealed there. At the same time, my left hand reached for the pistol hidden in that boot. The left-hand gun came out just slightly behind the right hand one. I rolled over and came up with both guns pointing at the outlaws, half a dozen men who stood around the campfire gazing at me in surprise.

"Drop your guns!" I called out in a loud, clear voice. "In the name of the United States government, you are all under arrest!"

It was possible they might have surrendered. One never knows until one tries.

Instead they gave vent to sulfurous curses and "slapped leather" as the frontiersmen say.

I fired first, sending a bullet from the right-hand pistol into the chest of one of the men. He went over backward, the tails of his long coat flapping, and landed in the campfire, where he screamed as his clothes began to blaze. That scream lasted only a moment before he died. By that time I had squeezed off a shot with the left-hand gun and drilled a neat hole through the upper arm of another man. My appearance makes people regard me as something less than a physical threat, but they forget it takes quick reflexes and steady nerves to be successful in gunplay, rather than sheer brute strength, and I have both of those things in abundance.

Not enough, however, that I could face six men and emerge victorious. The four who remained would have shot me to pieces in a matter of seconds . . .

If Tanner Moody had not leaped into the circle of firelight with that Henry rifle in his hands, flame spouting from its muzzle as he fired.

I lunged forward, landing on my belly to make myself a smaller target. From that position, I continued to blast away with both pistols while Tanner Moody stood to my right, raking the outlaws with lead from

his rifle. The outlaws returned our fire, of course, and for several long seconds the air was thick with flying bullets and filled with one deafening report after another. Smoke from the burned powder stung my eyes.

But when the shooting finally died away after what seemed like an eternity, I was uninjured, and all six of the bandits were down.

Tanner Moody limped forward. I saw blood on the left leg of his trousers, but he didn't move as if he were badly injured. He reached down, grabbed the ankle of the man who was burning in the campfire, and dragged him out of the flames. I was grateful for that. The smell was beginning to be rather overpowering.

The sheriff turned his head to look at me. "You hit, Conway?" he asked.

"No, but you are," I told him.

"Not enough to worry about," he said. He toed several of the bodies and nodded in apparent satisfaction that they were dead. One of the men, however, let out a groan.

Instantly, Tanner Moody set his rifle aside, drew his revolver, and rolled the wounded outlaw onto his back. The blood that covered the man's face was garishly red in the firelight. He gasped, "H-help . . . me . . ."

"You're not hit that bad, partner," Tanner Moody told him. "We'll take you to town and let Doc Yarborough take a look at you. He'll patch you right up."

Doctor Yarborough, drunk or sober, would not be able to do the man any good. I could tell that from the wounds stitched across his chest. My estimation was that the wounded outlaw had only minutes, perhaps even seconds, left to live.

"First, though," Tanner Moody went on, "you got to tell me how Fletcher knew about that gold shipment."

"It hurts . . . so bad . . ."

"I'm sorry about that, partner. Tell me about Fletcher and I'll take you right to the sawbones."

"C-Carling . . . told him . . . He didn't . . . trust you."

I raised an eyebrow as I stood there reloading my pistols with shells from a concealed pocket inside my coat. Carling, the superintendent of the Jeremiah Mine, who had lied to us in his office. The man had played right into Fletcher's hands. I had no doubt that Fletcher had known about the other gold shipments that had been held up and had tipped off the outlaws. Fletcher was the honest lawman in the minds of the people, while Tanner Moody was the man with the shady past who was either incompetent or in cahoots with the bandits. That was the image Fletcher had fostered, and it had worked.

But wouldn't Carling be suspicious once he told Fletcher about the gold shipment and that shipment was subsequently held up? Perhaps, but Fletcher was smart enough and slick enough to divert that suspicion by saying that he must have accidentally let something slip to Tanner Moody. I could almost see the earnest, regretful expression on the deputy's face as he did so. And Carling and everyone else in Flat Rock who was so intent on thinking the worst about Tanner Moody would believe him.

Those thoughts flashed through my mind as the wounded outlaw's final breath rattled in his throat. He was gone, joining his comrades in death.

Tanner Moody stood up and swung around to face me. "Where the hell'd you learn to shoot like that?" he asked.

"I've always had a knack for firearms," I said. "Now, if I may ask you a question, how did you find me?"

"You were never lost," he said. "I stepped out of the office back in Flat Rock in time to see Fletcher and that other fella jump you. I wasn't close enough to hear what was goin' on, but I saw that owlhoot ride out of town with you thrown over a horse. Didn't know if you were dead or not, but I figured it'd be worth trailin' him to find out."

"Indeed," I murmured. "Did you overhear any of their conversation before the shooting started?"

"Enough to know that Fletcher's been workin' with the gang all along," Tanner Moody said, his voice grim.

"I believe he was forced to do so because the ringleader had knowledge of a crime Fletcher committed in Montana."

The sheriff snorted in contempt. "That don't matter. Fletcher went along with 'em and helped to get a bunch of good men killed. That makes him guilty as hell in my book."

"Oh, in mine, too," I agreed. "We'll bring him to justice." I stooped and slid the pistols back into their hidden holsters inside my boots. As I straightened, I said, "Did you ever suspect him before?"

For a moment, Tanner Moody didn't answer. Then

he said, "Yeah, I did, but I thought it was just because . . . well, because he and this girl . . . I figured I wasn't thinkin' straight because of . . ."

"That's all right, Sheriff," I told him. "I understand. Besides, if you had ever accused Fletcher, people probably wouldn't have believed you. They would think you were just trying to get even with him for the matter you just mentioned."

"What's to keep 'em from thinkin' that now?"

"The testimony of an agent of the United States War Department," I said.

It was long after midnight when we rode away from the hideout in the mountains. Before leaving, we had located the gold stolen the previous afternoon, cached in a shallow cave not far away. The bodies of the dead bandits had been left behind. We didn't have time to bury them, Tanner Moody said, and loading them onto horses and taking them back to Flat Rock would slow us down too much as well. He wanted to get to town before ten o'clock the next morning, when the marriage ceremony of Wade Fletcher and Dinah Macauley was scheduled to take place.

"I'll be damned if I'll make her a widow on her weddin' day," he said.

It seemed to me that gunning down her betrothed only moments before the ceremony would be only slightly less disturbing for Miss Macauley, but I kept that observation to myself.

When the sun began to rise over the open prairie to the east, we were only halfway back to Flat Rock, according to Tanner Moody. We pushed our horses harder. He was intent on reaching town before the wedding.

When we finally rode in, I looked along the main street toward the whitewashed church at the other end of town. Quite a few buggies, buckboards, and horses were tied up outside the building. From the looks of it, nearly everyone in Flat Rock and the surrounding area had turned out for the wedding of the popular deputy sheriff and the beautiful Dinah Macauley.

Soon there would be two more guests, Tanner Moody and myself. We were hardly dressed for the occasion, though. We were disheveled and covered with trail dust. Our faces were grimy from the powder smoke. The sheriff had tied a rag around his wounded leg, and blood had seeped through to stain it. We were about as disreputable as we could be.

That didn't stop Tanner Moody. He reined his buckskin to a halt in front of the church, swung down from the saddle, limped up to the doors, and thrust them open, letting organ music wash out from inside. The music stopped abruptly as Tanner Moody walked down the aisle.

Wade Fletcher was already there, standing in front of a black-clad minister next to a young woman in a white dress. Dinah Macauley was as lovely as I had suspected she would be, with hair as dark as a raven's wing, sparkling blue eyes, and full red lips. Those lips trembled slightly as she turned to face Tanner Moody. Her expression was a study in surprise and confusion, but then those emotions were replaced by anger.

"Tanner Moody!" she said. "How dare you try to ruin this day for me?"

"Not tryin' to ruin anything, Dinah," he said. "But I've got some business with Deputy Fletcher here. First, though . . ." He looked at the minister. "They done said the I-do's yet?"

"No," said the man of God. "We . . . we just started the ceremony."

"Good."

I never heard more menace packed into such a short word.

Wade Fletcher had been quite surprised to see the sheriff, too, but when he had glanced past Tanner Moody and seen me following him up the aisle, understanding dawned in his eyes. He knew then that the jig was up, as they say. If I was still alive, that meant his involvement with the gang of gold thieves was about to be revealed. But I give the man credit. He didn't panic. He remained cool and swung his gaze back to Tanner Moody as he waited to see what was going to happen.

Fletcher was dressed in a dark suit, a snowy white shirt, a vest, and a string tie. Despite the relatively formal attire, he had his gunbelt strapped around his waist. I suppose that as deputy sheriff, he felt that he should be armed even at a moment such as this.

"You got anything to say for yourself?" Tanner Moody demanded of him.

"When I got up this morning and you weren't anywhere around, I figured you'd ridden off so you wouldn't have to see me and Dinah leaving the church as man and wife," Fletcher said with a faint smile hovering about his lips. "I reckon I was wrong about that."

"You were wrong about a lot of things." Tanner Moody glanced at the young woman. "So were you."

I saw the flash of hurt in her eyes. He had said too much, had made her think that he was here merely as a jilted suitor. Her chin lifted defiantly as she said, "I'll thank you to leave now, Mr. Moody, before you ruin everything."

"It's already ruined. This fella you plan on marryin' is an outlaw and a murderer."

"Those are mighty strong words, Sheriff," Fletcher murmured. "How do you plan to back them up?"

That was my cue. "I'll back them up," I said as I stepped forward. "My name is Peter Conway. I'm an agent for the United States War Department, reporting directly to Secretary of War Stanton."

That brought several surprised gasps from the crowd. I saw the old-timer, Ezra, gaping at me. No doubt he had told nearly everyone here that I was a newspaperman.

"Well, hell," Fletcher said, his voice barely above a whisper. "It wasn't my fault, Moody. Those Rebs made me work with them. Otherwise I would've swung for a killing up in Montana."

At those words, Dinah turned to stare at him in horror. She was already quite close to him. Fletcher closed the distance even more with a quick step. His left arm went around her neck while his right hand jerked the gun from the holster on his hip.

Tanner Moody demonstrated the blinding speed and deadly accuracy which had won him his bloody reputation. He drew and fired in the blink of an eye. The bullet tore along the right forearm of his deputy and sailed on to smack into the pulpit as the minister leaped out of the line of fire. He was quite nimble for a man of the cloth.

Fletcher cried out in pain and dropped his gun before he ever had a chance to pull the trigger. A sobbing Dinah struck at him and pulled away. Tanner Moody holstered his gun, stepped forward, and swung a punch that crashed into Fletcher's jaw and sent the deputy flying backward. Fletcher collided with the pulpit and knocked it over. He fell, too, stunned by the blow.

In the congregation, the women screamed and fainted. The men shouted questions and curses. It was quite an uproar.

And of course, there would be no wedding today.

It came as a shock to me when I heard later that Wade Fletcher was sentenced to twenty-five years in prison, rather than being hanged. But over the years I learned that the vagaries of frontier justice could not be predicted on any sort of consistent basis.

Of course, neither can the actions of the female of the species, yet I wasn't surprised when I heard that Dinah Macauley refused to have anything to do with Tanner Moody from that day forward. True, Fletcher had been the villain of the piece, and Miss Macauley would have found herself married to a killer and a thief if not for what Tanner Moody had done. But in her mind, he would always be associated with that awful moment in front of the altar when something that should have been solemn and joyful had turned into something bloody and terrible instead. And so she turned away from him in order to put that behind her.

It was several years later when he stopped carrying a badge, but I think the events of that day had something to do with his decision.

As for me, I never saw him again after I left Flat Rock and returned to Washington, but I never forgot him, either. Tanner Moody had saved my life up there in the Prophet Mountains, and in those endless seconds of thunder and flame, a bond was forged between us that could never be broken. After that, Tanner Moody would always be my friend . . .

And the best man with a gun I ever saw.

Five

The New York Morning Telegraph, Feb. 8, 1903
The Legend of Tanner Moody
Fifth in a series by Bat Masterson
Exclusive

Pete Conway paid his respects to Tanner Moody, whom he hadn't seen since that time in the Prophet Mountains. After that he collected William Pinkerton from the bar and they left. Conway tossed me an eyebrow, but Pinkerton left without giving me a second look.

I took a few minutes to jot down another note or two concerning Conway's story and then put my notebook away. At this point in my life all I'd written for the Denver newspaper was some sports stories—mostly boxing, a little horse racing. I had a pocketful of notes, enough for four columns, but I wasn't even sure I'd even know how to write it down later. Alfred Lewis and his brother, William, thought I had writing talent. I hoped not to disappoint them.

I spotted Jack Allison in the lobby of my hotel the next morning. He was an unsmiling man in his mid-forties, a shock of dark hair falling forward almost into his eyes every time I saw him. Allison and I had crossed paths many times over the years. When you moved around as much as we did, you either never crossed paths or did so over and over. In our case it was the latter, and neither of us could ever explain it.

He saw me immediately and came walking over. I knew he was glad to see me, though he was a man who rarely—if ever—smiled, and he did not grace me with one now.

"Bat."

"Jack."

As I said, we had run into each other many times over the years, so it was hardly ever a surprise—and I'd already seen so many people whose attendance had surprised me that we simply shook hands and accepted each other's presence.

"What brings you here, Jack?"

"Same as you, I imagine," he said. "The Tanner Moody wake."

"I didn't know you knew Moody," I said.

He looked at me. "It was a long time ago, but it made me who I am today."

"Then you don't talk about it much," I said. We'd been drunk together enough times that I might have heard it, otherwise.

"No," he said, looking down at his boots, "like I said, it was a long time ago, when I was on my way to becoming somebody . . . else. He saved me from that."

"You want to talk about it now that he's gone?"

He eyed his boots a little longer, then looked at me and said, "Maybe it's time."

"Before you do . . ." I went on to tell him what I was doing there, and what I was planning. "Maybe you can tell me about it over breakfast?"

He thought it over for a while, then said, "Sure, why not. I haven't actually been hiding it all these years, the time was just never right . . ."

Tanner Moody
And the Bad Hombres

by L. J. Washburn

Oh, we were bad hombres, all right. No doubt about that. The judge told us we were. An old gent with a face like a prune, he was, and he sat up there so big and high above us behind that bench and whacked on it with a wooden mallet and said we were all hooligans. Incorrigible, he called us, and I didn't know what the word meant. But I do now, and he was on the mark. We were downright incorrigible.

There were eight of us in the gang. The Gambrell brothers, Stan and Wilmer, were the biggest but also the dumbest. We had two Freds, last names of Milton and Cheever. Fred Cheever was a little fella, so naturally we called him Little Fred and the other one was Big Fred, although he wasn't anywhere near as big as the Gambrell brothers. George Newman had the biggest ears I ever saw, and he hardly ever stopped grinning, even while the judge ranted and raved at us and told us how bad we were. Bill Stone never said much, so he hung around with Teddy Jessup, who never shut up. Bill was the smartest of the bunch and more than likely could've made something of himself if he'd wanted to. That left me, Jack Allison, and I didn't say much, either. People said I never smiled much, that I always glared out at the world from under that black hair that kept falling in my eyes. The way I saw it, the world hadn't given any of us much to smile about, although you'd never know it from the silly grin pasted on George's face. We were all around fifteen years old, the children of drunks and pimps and whores and gamblers, and our school was the St. Louis riverfront.

A rough school it was, too, so it's no surprise we were rough boys. I won't deny it. We bullied those younger and smaller than us. We rolled drunks. We broke into stores to steal and sometimes we snuck aboard the riverboats tied up at the docks and robbed what we could from the passengers' cabins. The Gambrell brothers were bigger than some grown men, so Bill and I, who sort of ran things between the two of us, hired them out when somebody wanted a beating handed to a business rival or something like that. The St. Louis police got to know us pretty well, and finally we got hauled into court to face charges of burning down a warehouse for money.

The funny thing is, we didn't do it. We did plenty of other things, some of them just as bad or worse than arson, but we were innocent of that one. Still, it didn't matter. The judge said we were guilty and wanted to send us to prison, only he couldn't on account of we weren't old enough. But when he got through fussing at us he said he was going to send us to the reformatory until we were twenty-one, and he was about to bang that wooden mallet on the bench to make it official when somebody behind us in the courtroom stood up and asked if he could say a word.

That was how we met Mr. Roland Sweeney.

I looked over my shoulder at him. He was a short, heavyset man about forty years old. He was balding and had a thick brown mustache. He carried a broad-brimmed brown hat in his hand and wore a brown suit. I could tell from the cut of the suit that he was from out west somewhere. He looked like a cattleman, the sort who would come to the big city once a year or so.

The judge was testy because Mr. Sweeney had kept him from smacking that mallet down, but he said to go ahead. Mr. Sweeney introduced himself and said, "Your Honor, I have a small ranch near Abilene, Kansas, and I'm in need of hands to work that ranch. It occurred to me that I might be able to help both myself and this court."

"Don't be long-winded about it, Mr. Sweeney," the judge advised him. "What are you suggesting?"

Mr. Sweeney waved a hand at the eight of us. "That I take these boys off your hands. I've heard what crowded, squalid conditions exist in that reformatory you were about to send them to. Why not let me take them to my ranch and make something of them?"

I could see right off that the idea appealed to the judge. But he hemmed and hawed and said, "What you propose smacks of indentured servitude, sir. We no longer have such things in this country."

"Not at all, Your Honor," Mr. Sweeney said, just as slick as you please. "I've heard that it's actually a common arrangement in other jurisdictions. The state pays me a small fee, a reasonable amount to cover the cost of transporting the lads to my ranch and caring for them while they're there, and—"

The judge held up his mallet. "Let me get this straight. *We* pay *you* to take them?"

"Yes, Your Honor. A reasonable amount."

"So you get 'em as ranch hands and get paid, to boot."

Mr. Sweeney said, "Your Honor, you'll find that the sum I'd require is far less than the cost of feeding and housing them in the reformatory until they turn twenty-one. Far less, Your Honor. What I really want, though, is to expose these poor boys to some fresh air and hard work. That'll make all the difference in the world for them, Your Honor. They'll leave my ranch honest, productive citizens, instead of coming out of the reformatory with all the criminal knowledge they would glean there."

The judge played with his pointy chin for a minute, and then he said, "I'm going to call a recess before I determine the final outcome of this case. Mr. Sweeney, if we could discuss the matter further in my chambers . . ."

"Of course, Your Honor," Mr. Sweeney said, and he was grinning as big as George Newman.

So that's how we came to head for Kansas with Mr. Roland Sweeney. I've always been convinced that the judge found some way to get his hands on some money out of the deal, but I don't know about that for sure. All I know is that we were what they call remanded to the custody of Mr. Sweeney, loaded onto a wagon, and sent to Kansas with him. Hardened criminals that we were, we had to wear handcuffs and leg irons until we got out of Missouri.

Not that we would have tried anything funny if we hadn't been wearing them, because not far out of St. Louis, Mr. Sweeney stopped the wagon, turned around on the seat, and pulled out the biggest gun any of us had ever seen. The barrel was so long and big around it looked like a cannon. He pointed it at us and said, "Just in case any of you little bastards feels like runnin' off, I want you to know I'll blow your ass to kingdom come if you try it."

That was when we started to get the idea that no matter what he had said in court, Mr. Roland Sweeney did not have our best interests at heart.

Still and all, the trip wasn't so bad at first. Hot as blazes, because that wagon didn't have any cover over the back of it, but we were used to being uncomfortable. And the air out on the prairie smelled better than it did along the riverfront, too. I got to thinking that maybe there was something to the way people talked about fresh air be-

169

ing good for you. Mr. Sweeney didn't feed us much, but we were used to going to sleep with empty bellies, too.

A couple of weeks went by, and we rolled through Missouri, past the town of Independence, and on across the Missouri River into Kansas. We followed the railroad tracks most of the time, and I spent a lot of hours staring at that pair of shiny rails disappearing into the distance to the west. Back in St. Louis, I'd never thought about much beyond the few square blocks where we ran wild. Now I found myself wondering what was out there past where I could see, over the horizon where those railroad tracks led. Every time a train rumbled past, belching smoke from its stack, I wished I could get on it somehow, so that it could carry me to places I'd never been.

But that wasn't going to happen, of course. I was going to spend the next few years stuck on Mr. Sweeney's ranch with the rest of the gang, probably working like dogs from dawn to dusk for nothing more than our keep.

We swung southwest from Abilene. The country was mostly flat, with a few rolling hills. It had been a dry summer. Many of the creeks were nothing but narrow trickles. The grass was brown and waved gently back and forth in a hot breeze. A couple of days went past in which we saw nothing and nobody. We were well and truly in the middle of nowhere.

It was hard for us to keep our spirits up. At first the whole thing had seemed like an adventure, but we were tired of it now. Teddy tried to keep us cheered up by telling jokes, and Big Fred and Little Fred sang some songs. Both of them had good voices. But mainly we just sat in the back of the wagon, rocking along with our heads down, wondering when we were going to get to Mr. Sweeney's ranch. Obviously, it wasn't as near to Abilene as he had made it sound.

Finally one day he pulled the team to a stop and said, "I reckon this'll do."

I looked around and didn't see a ranch or anything else. Nothing except that damned old empty prairie. It occurred to me then that maybe Mr. Sweeney intended for us to *build* his ranch for him, but I sure didn't know what we'd build it out of. There wasn't a tree to be seen.

He stepped down from the wagon and pulled that big revolver of his from its holster. "Get out of there," he snapped at us.

The eight of us climbed out. We were stiff from riding for so long. Little Fred said, "Where are we, Mr. Sweeney? Where's your ranch?"

"I bet we're nearly there," Teddy said. "Ain't we nearly there, Mr. Sweeney? Will we be there later today, or maybe tomorrow?"

"You've gone as far as you're goin'." Mr. Sweeney waved the gun at us. "Back off from the wagon. Go on."

We were all mighty puzzled, but we did what he told us. When he started to get back up on the seat, Teddy said, "Where you goin', Mr. Sweeney? You goin' to get somethin', and then you'll come back for us? Is that it?"

Bill and I figured it out about the same time, but Bill

spoke up first. "He's not coming back. He's leaving us here."

The others looked at him, surprised and scared. "Leavin' us here?" Stan said. "But . . . he can't do that!"

"We're supposed to work on his ranch!" Big Fred said.

Even George had stopped grinning.

"There's not a ranch," Bill said bitterly. "Or if there is, he doesn't need us to work it. All he needed us for was the money he chiseled out of that old judge."

"That's right, sonny boy," Mr. Sweeney said with a big smile. He looked like he was mighty satisfied with himself. "And there'll be another bank draft next year, and the year after that and the year after that, to pay for your keep. Only there won't be no keep."

"You're nothing but a crook," Bill accused him. "You're just like us."

"The hell I am. I'm a lot smarter than you whelps." Mr. Sweeney picked up the reins with one hand while he kept that big pistol trained on us with the other. "So long, boys."

"But where'll we go?" Teddy asked. "There's nothin' out here!"

"That's your problem, son, not mine."

With that, Mr. Sweeney got his team moving, and the wagon rolled off, turning in a big circle back toward the north. We watched him go, knowing there was nothing we could do to stop him. I looked at the other boys. We were a tough mob, but there were some trembling lips among us, and eyes that shined a little more than normal from tears. We were a long way from civilization, and chances were we would starve to death or die of thirst before we could walk that far.

"What are we gonna *do?*" Teddy wailed.

"Follow that son of a bitch," Bill said, "and kill him."

He meant it, too. Right then, he would have put a bullet through Mr. Sweeney or cut his throat without blinking. Most of us would have. But it seemed to me that there was a mighty slim chance of ever catching up to the man.

"Let's go," Bill said. He took off walking, heading in the same direction where the wagon had disappeared. The rest of us hesitated, but then we went after him.

There was nothing else we could do.

We couldn't keep up with a team of big strong horses, of course. I knew that Mr. Sweeney was getting farther and farther away with each minute that passed. Bill's dream of taking vengeance on him was just that, a dream. But maybe if we kept walking, we'd come across somebody who could help us. That was my hope, anyway.

By nightfall, though, I wasn't sure we were even going in the right direction anymore. We were headed north, I could tell that by where the sun set, but we had lost the trail left by the wheels of Mr. Sweeney's wagon. The ground was hard, the grass was sparse, and we weren't frontiersmen or anything close to it.

We were a bunch of scared little boys a long way from home, that's what we were.

None of us wanted to show that, though, so we kept on walking even after it got dark. Looking back on it now, that was a mighty stupid thing to do. Without the sun to steer by, we got lost good and proper. None of us knew how to find a direction by the stars. We should have stopped and waited for the sun to come up again. If we could have kept walking north, we would have struck the railroad sooner or later. Then we could have waited for a train to come along and flagged it down. But I was convinced that we were walking in circles in the dark.

We hadn't had anything to eat since the morning before, and not much then. We had no water. We'd been able to suck up a little from some brackish puddles in a mostly dried-up creek bed, but that was all we'd had in hours. On top of that, our feet were sore. Our cheap shoes were rubbing blisters. We were in piss-poor shape.

When I said as much, Bill got mad. "If you're so damned smart, why don't you figure out what to do?" he yelled at me.

"Sit down right here and wait until morning," I said.

"Then we'll never catch that bastard Sweeney."

"We're never going to catch him anyway. He's long gone, Bill."

"The hell he is! Nobody pulls a trick like that and gets away with it."

I didn't tell him that people pull tricks worse than that all day, every day, and get away with it. The world even seems to reward some of them for being so tricky and downright mean. Some folks say that people like that get their comeuppance in the next world, but I don't know about that. I have enough trouble figuring out this world.

Before I could argue any more with Bill, big ol' Wilmer Gambrell pointed and said, "What's that?"

We all looked and saw an orange glow in the sky, low down on the horizon. It made a sort of half-circle of light. "Looks like a fire," Big Fred said after a minute.

"If something's on fire, there's got to be people there, don't there?" Teddy asked hopefully.

"Maybe, maybe not," Bill said. "Maybe lightning set the grass on fire."

I hadn't seen any lightning, but sure enough, as soon as Bill said that, it flickered in the sky, bright silver fingers leaving trails in the darkness. The wind picked up, and a few minutes later, big fat drops of rain began to fall, pattering down around us and smacking us in the face.

The sky opened up after that, and nobody wanted to walk in such a downpour. We all sat down close together so we wouldn't get separated in the darkness. One good thing about the rain, it washed away the tears on our faces as soon as they welled from our eyes, and the racket of the storm was enough so that we couldn't hear each other sobbing.

But we heard the hoofbeats that came pounding toward us out of the night, and we heard the gunfire that was louder than the thunder, and we saw the muzzle flashes that were brighter than the lightning.

"Everybody get down!" Bill said as all hell broke loose around us.

I threw myself on the ground and felt it shake as horses swept by. I couldn't see anything, didn't know if the rest of the boys were all right or if some of them had been trampled by the wild riders rushing past us. When I glanced up, bright flashes blinded me. I didn't know if what I saw was lightning or more muzzle flashes. The roaring sound was constant now.

Even with all that racket going on, I heard somebody yell. Something crashed to the ground close beside me. I hollered in fear and jerked away. Another flash showed me a man lying on the ground, either senseless or dead. His bearded face was turned toward me.

I saw something else in that split second: the man wore handcuffs. He was a prisoner, just like we had been until Mr. Sweeney abandoned us.

A man's voice shouted, "Fletcher! Damn it, Fletcher, where are—"

I scrambled to my feet as a horse's hooves thudded against the ground right beside my head. Panicky, I tried to lunge away, but a hand grabbed my collar. Suddenly, as if I didn't weigh much at all, I was jerked off my feet. I sailed through the air and slammed down on my back. A knee drove into my belly and forced all the air out of my lungs. As I gasped, a hand closed around my throat and made sure I couldn't breathe. I thrashed around some, but the man who had hold of me was so strong I was just wasting my time. Lightning flashed again and showed me his face. It was hard and blunt and had several days worth of beard stubble on it. Rain dripped from the broad-brimmed hat he wore. He jammed the long barrel of a gun into my jaw under my left ear and said, "Who the hell are you?"

That was how I met Mr. Tanner Moody, though I didn't know his name until later.

I couldn't answer his question, of course, not with his hand around my throat. In fact, I was about to pass out from lack of air. He must have figured that out, because he let go of me. He kept the gun barrel pressed against my head, though.

He had already put aside the question he'd asked me. He had something more important on his mind.

"Have you seen a man wearing handcuffs?"

I pointed. My arm and hand shook pretty bad. But Mr. Moody looked around and saw the man on the ground as more lightning lit up the night.

About that time I heard more horses and some whooping. Mr. Moody's horse spooked. It reared up, whirled around, and ran off into the darkness. Mr. Moody made a grab for the reins before the horse took off, but he was too late. Once the horse was gone, Mr. Moody stretched out on the ground beside me and that unconscious—or dead—man.

"Keep quiet," he hissed in my ear.

I intended to. I didn't have any idea what was going on, but I knew without thinking about it that we were in danger.

As I lay there, I gradually figured out that there were Indians racing around on the prairie nearby. I had heard about wild Indians, of course. Everybody had. The cavalry was fighting them down in the Texas Panhandle and up north in Dakota Territory. Being in St. Louis, I never figured to run into any of them.

But as I was rapidly learning, things were a whole lot different out here on the Kansas plains.

I don't know how long we stayed there, flat on the ground. I lay in a little hollow, and the rain started to collect in it. I was soaked to the skin and shivering, and I had to lift my head to keep it out of the muddy water. The rain finally stopped and the thunder and lightning tapered off, though there was still quite a show going on in the heavens as the storm moved on to the south. After a while, Mr. Moody pushed himself to his feet and looked around. The clouds had begun to break up overhead, and that let some starlight through. Mr. Moody said, "I reckon they're gone. Get up, boy."

I stood up, still shivering, and watched as Mr. Moody reached down and hauled the other man to his feet. The man was groggy and only half-awake, still stunned from the bad spill he had taken, but he managed to stay upright. Mr. Moody said, "What the hell happened to your horse?" but I didn't think he sounded like he expected an answer.

He didn't get one. The handcuffed man was still too much out of his head. Mr. Moody kicked his feet out from under him. The man fell and lay there breathing heavily.

Mr. Moody turned to me. "You know how to use a gun?"

I didn't know what to say. I had shot a pistol a few times in my life, but most of the hell-raising the boys and I got up to involved clubs or knives. Finally I nodded and said, "Y-yeah. I reckon."

Mr. Moody took something from his belt and pressed it into my hand. It was a short-barreled revolver. The grips were hard and cold and slick.

"I'll find the horses. If he tries to get up, shoot him in the leg."

The authority in Mr. Moody's voice made me think he was a lawman of some kind. Now, I didn't like the law. Growing up as I had, I distrusted and hated anybody who packed a star. But I was alone on the prairie, on a dark night, with wild Indians around, and Mr. Moody was not only a grown-up but a grown-up who seemed strong enough and smart enough to take care not only of himself but of me and the rest of the gang as well. So I nodded and said, "All right."

Mr. Moody started to stomp off. He had gone only a couple of feet when a dark shape rose from the ground and leaped on his back. Mr. Moody stumbled a little from the impact but caught himself quickly. He reached up, grabbed whoever had jumped on him, and flung him through the air.

179

I heard Bill shout, "Get him!" More shapes bounded up from the grass and leaped at Mr. Moody. I yelled for them to stop it, but nobody paid any attention to me.

I didn't have to worry about Mr. Moody. Like a bear being attacked by a bunch of yapping dogs, he grabbed some of those boys and threw them every which way. The others he batted back to the ground. After he'd shaken himself free of them, he said, "Hold it!"

They listened and stayed where they were, sprawled around him. The moon peeked out through a rip in the clouds and cast even more light over the prairie. I counted the boys—one, two, three, four, five, six. Somebody was missing.

Before I could think too much about that, somebody grabbed me. Hands caught hold of my ankles and jerked my feet out from under me. With a yell, I went over backward. But I managed to hang on to the gun Mr. Moody had given me, and as the handcuffed man tried to swarm over me, I lashed out with it and smacked it hard across the side of his head. He fell to the ground with a groan.

Mr. Moody loomed over us. He said, "Didn't I tell you to shoot him if he tried to get up?" He sounded mad.

I don't know what made me bark back at him, but I did. I'm not sure how I knew what to say, either. The words came out anyway. "A shot'll draw those Indians right back down on us mighty quick!"

For a second Mr. Moody didn't say anything. Then he chuckled and said, "You're sure right about that, son. I reckon you're thinkin' straighter than I am right now." He leaned over, took hold of my arm, and helped me to my feet. "The way you walloped him, Fletcher won't give any trouble for a while." He took a key from his pocket, unlocked the handcuffs, jerked the man's arms behind his back, and cuffed his wrists together again. "Now he can't get up to as much mischief," Mr. Moody said as he straightened.

Bill and the rest of the boys had gotten to their feet by now, but they stayed back warily. "Who are you, mister?" Bill asked.

"Tanner Moody." That was the first time I ever heard the name.

"Why'd you try to ride us down?"

"Didn't. Just tryin' to get away from that bunch of Pawnee."

That was what I had figured out, too. Mr. Moody and the other man had been running away from the Indians when they nearly trampled us. The other man—Fletcher, Mr. Moody had called him—had fallen off his horse. And then Mr. Moody's horse had run away. But the Indians had gone on chasing Mr. Moody's horse, maybe thinking that he was still on it. That made sense to me, anyway.

I had a feeling we were still in danger. The Indians had left, but they could come back any time. We couldn't just stand around.

But there was something else that had to be checked on. "Bill," I said, "somebody's missing."

He looked around, saw that there were only seven of us, and said, "Who's not here?"

They sounded off, Stan and Wilmer, George, Teddy, Big Fred. I waited for Little Fred to say something, but he didn't. He was the one who was missing.

"Spread out," Bill said, his voice shaking a little. "Look for him."

While they did that, Mr. Moody said to me, "Keep an eye on Fletcher for me, and do a better job of it this time. We're in trouble if I don't find those horses."

It seemed to me like we were in trouble anyway. Two horses couldn't carry nine or ten people. If Mr. Moody found the animals, he and Fletcher could ride off and leave us boys in the same pickle we'd been in when they found us accidentally. But Mr. Moody might not do that, I thought. Somehow, he didn't seem to be the sort of fellow who'd abandon a gaggle of youngsters in the middle of nowhere.

Teddy found Little Fred lying on the ground with his head stove in. That was enough to shut Teddy up and take the grin off George's face. Big Fred sniffled some when he found out that Little Fred was dead. They had been pretty good friends.

"Horse must have stepped on him," Bill said as he got up from where he had knelt to examine the body. Bill looked toward Mr. Moody, who was a dark figure moving around about a hundred yards away. I saw Mr. Moody come up to a dark, bulky shape that lay huddled on the ground. A moment later there was a shrill scream cut short after only a second. I wasn't sure what had happened. Mr. Moody got up and walked back toward us while we used our hands to scoop out a shallow hole in the ground. We put Little Fred in it as gentle as we could and then pushed the dirt back over him. It was all we could do for him.

Mr. Moody had taken off his hat as he stood there watching us. When we were done, we stood up and wiped away tears, leaving dark smudges of dirt from our fingers on our faces. Bill turned toward Mr. Moody and said, "It could have been your horse that stepped on him and busted his head open."

"Could've been," Mr. Moody agreed. "Might've been any one of a dozen other horses, too. We'll never know. He was your friend?"

"He was one of us," I said.

Mr. Moody nodded like he understood. "Then I'm sorry for your loss. That don't change our situation none."

"Did you find what you were looking for?"

"Fletcher's horse must have fallen," he said. "Leg was broke. The brute managed to get up and go a little farther, but then it fell again. Had to cut its throat to put it out of its suffering." He looked at me. "Since I didn't want to draw those Indians' attention with a shot."

That made me feel a little better. But only a little, because I knew that it meant we were in an even deeper hole now.

"No tellin' where that horse of mine's got to," Mr. Moody went on. "He took off for the tall and uncut, and he was so spooked he's probably still runnin'."

"Mister, who *are* you?" Bill said.

"Told you. Tanner Moody."

"Are you a lawman?" I asked.

He looked at me. "Bounty hunter," he said curtly. "Used to pack a badge. Not any more."

I pointed at the prisoner. "What about him?"

"He's an escaped convict named Wade Fletcher." Mr. Moody's voice had been flinty to start with, but it had an extra edge to it now. "He wound up in prison a while back because of me, so when he broke out, I figured it was up to me to bring him back. Besides, there's a five thousand dollar reward on his head. He killed a couple of guards when he broke loose."

So the man was a murderer. Somehow, I wasn't surprised. Mainly, though, I was thinking about that reward Mr. Moody had mentioned. Five thousand dollars! Lord, I had a hard time believing there was that much money in the whole world. It was more than I had ever seen or even hoped to see, that was for sure.

"Now, answer a question for me," Mr. Moody went on. "What are you boys doin' out here? And have you got any horses?"

"That's two questions," Teddy said.

"Shut up," Bill said to him. He looked back at Mr. Moody. "No, we don't have any horses. We're after the man who left us out here."

"Huh," Mr. Moody said. "Sounds like an interestin' story. Tell me about it while we're walkin'." For the second time tonight, he reached down and pulled Fletcher to his feet. With a shove, he started Fletcher walking. Mr. Moody's hand on his arm kept him from falling and kept pushing him along. The rest of us trailed along because there was nothing else we could do. I hoped Mr. Moody knew where he was going, because none of us had any idea.

I glanced back over my shoulder at the place we had buried Little Fred. I wished we'd been able to do a better job of it. Sometimes you just can't do what you want, though.

As we walked, Bill told Mr. Moody about what had happened to us. The only thing Mr. Moody said in response was, "You say this fella Sweeney headed north after he left you?"

"That's right."

I didn't know why that was important, but it seemed to be. We kept walking. Mr. Moody looked up at the sky from time to time, and I knew he was steering us by the stars.

The prisoner, Fletcher, had regained his senses now. I saw him looking around, shifty-like, from time to time. But he didn't say anything, just stumbled along with the rest of us.

The hard-baked ground had turned to gumbo from the rain, and it sucked at our feet with each step we took. That got mighty tiring mighty fast, and we'd been worn out to start with. But Mr. Moody kept going and so did we, because we didn't want him to leave us behind. At least I didn't. The sun finally came up, and when it did, we saw something black ahead of us.

It was a wagon, I realized, or what was left of one after it had been burned, anyway. Mr. Moody stopped and looked at the wreckage for a long time, and the look on his face was darker and colder than any expression I had ever seen on the face of a human being. It just got worse when Fletcher started to laugh.

Mr. Moody turned and swung his left arm in a backhand that knocked Fletcher sprawling. Fletcher cursed and spat blood and then went back to laughing. "Remind you of something, Tanner?" he asked, just like he and Mr. Moody were old friends.

Mr. Moody drew his gun and pointed it at Fletcher, and for a second I was convinced he was going to shoot him. We hadn't seen hide nor hair of those wild Indians, so maybe Mr. Moody figured it would be all right to risk a shot. But then he lowered the long-barreled revolver and slid it back into its holster.

"Reward dodgers say dead or alive," he told Fletcher. "You'd best remember that."

He picked up the prisoner and shoved him toward the burned-out wagon. We stumbled on and finally got there a while later. It was Mr. Roland Sweeney's wagon, just as I had thought it might be, and I knew the light we had seen in the sky before the storm hit the night before had come from the flames that had consumed it.

Mr. Sweeney hadn't burned up with the wagon, but he might have wished that he had before he died. He lay on the ground with his naked skull glistening in the morning sun where the scalp had been cut off. The rain must have washed away all the blood. Other things had been cut off of him, too, and he was torn up pretty bad. I figured it had taken him a while to die, and that must have been a mighty bad time for him.

The horses were dead, too. Mr. Moody shook his head in disappointment. "Saw the fire last night and figured the Pawnee had jumped somebody else before they came after us. I was hopin' they'd left some horses alive. They didn't have any interest in those big draft animals, though. But they could've left 'em for us to ride, those inconsiderate red bastards."

We poked through the ruins of the wagon, hoping to find something useful. But the Indians had taken Mr. Sweeney's gun and all the food he carried.

Mr. Moody peered off toward the north. "It's about twenty miles to the railroad," he muttered, as much to himself as to any of us. "We can walk it. Got no choice." He turned around and looked at us, waved a hand at what was left of Mr. Sweeney. "You want to bury him, too?"

Bill spat, and it came close to landing on Mr. Sweeney's body. "Leave him where he is," he said.

Mr. Moody nodded. "Your decision. Don't reckon it matters one way or another to him."

We trudged on. I saw that Mr. Moody and Fletcher were wearing riding boots, which were even less suited to walking than our shoes. Their feet had to really hurt. After a while Fletcher started to complain about that very thing, but Mr. Moody looked at him and he shut up.

The sun climbed higher and sucked up the moisture that the storm had dropped the night before. That made walking easier, but the heat sucked the moisture out of us, too. We lapped the muddy water out of some little puddles before they dried up completely. Around the middle of the day Mr. Moody stopped to let us all rest.

"Come maybe five miles," he muttered. "Push on all day, make the railroad sometime tonight."

By then our feet would be bloody stumps and we'd have holes in our middles from our empty bellies eating themselves. But what else could we do?

Moving awkwardly because his hands were cuffed behind his back, Fletcher sat down cross-legged on the ground. He was so tired his head drooped forward on his chest. He didn't look up until Teddy came over to him and said, "Hey. Hey, mister."

"What do you want, kid?"

"What'd you do, mister? You're an outlaw, right? You wouldn't have been in prison unless you were an outlaw. I guess you could say we're outlaws. This ol' judge was gonna put us in a reformatory. That's like a prison for kids, ain't it? So we're outlaws, too, sure enough. But why were you in prison? Did you rob a bank or something like that?"

I was about to tell him to take a breath, for God's sake, when he stopped long enough for Fletcher to get a word in. Fletcher grinned and said, "You want to know the real reason I was in prison, kid? I'll tell you. It was because I stole the sheriff's girl. And you know who that sheriff was? His name was Tanner Moody."

And with that, he threw his head back and laughed, just like earlier.

Mr. Moody didn't wallop him this time or pull a gun on him. He just ignored Fletcher and stood there with his thumbs hooked in his gunbelt, staring off to the north.

Right from the first, I had gotten the feeling that there was something between Mr. Moody and Fletcher, some special hate that went beyond Mr. Moody being a bounty hunter and Fletcher being a fugitive. I was sure of it now. But it was none of my business. I was more worried about whether we were going to live to make it to the railroad.

That worry got even stronger a moment later when Stan pointed off to the south and said, "Somebody's comin'."

Mr. Moody turned around fast and peered in that direction, and after a few seconds he said, "Some of those Pawnee doubled back."

I got cold all over despite the heat of the sun overhead. I remembered what the Indians had done to Mr. Sweeney. We had two guns, the one Mr. Moody carried and the short-barreled one he had given to me. It was tucked behind my belt. I figured it had been Fletcher's, and that Mr. Moody had taken it away from him when he captured him. I didn't know how many bullets Mr. Moody had, but I was willing to bet not enough to fight off a war party of wild Indians.

"There's only a few of them," Mr. Moody said as he yanked Fletcher to his feet. "Come on."

"Get these cuffs off me, Moody," Fletcher said in a ragged voice. "Give me my gun back and let me die fightin'."

"Nobody else is gonna die." Mr. Moody shoved Fletcher into a run and then glanced at me. "You want to give somebody else that gun?"

I swallowed, knowing that he was asking if he could depend on me. "I can handle it," I said.

He jerked his head in a nod. "I think I spotted a buffalo wallow about a quarter of a mile up ahead. We'll try for it."

I wasn't quite sure what a buffalo wallow was, but Mr. Moody sounded like it would be a good thing if we got there before the Indians caught up to us. So we all forgot about how bad our feet hurt and started running. We stumbled and staggered some, but we kept running. Fletcher was unsteady on his feet, so Bill moved up beside him and grabbed his arm to keep him from falling.

I wanted to look back, but I was afraid to. I didn't want to see how much the Pawnee had gained on us. But finally I had to see how many of them there were. They were close enough I could make a rough count. I thought there were six of them, or maybe just five. That was about half the size of the band that had chased Mr. Moody and Fletcher the night before.

I didn't see the buffalo wallow until we were right on top of it. It was a shallow, circular depression in the earth, no more than three or four feet deep at the deepest spot, and maybe fifty yards across. I learned later that it was just what it sounded like, a spot where thousands, maybe millions, of buffalo had wallowed over the years. We half-fell into it and rolled down the gentle slope.

Mr. Moody caught himself and scrambled back up to the lip of the depression, gun in hand. I went with him and dropped onto my belly beside him. I saw the Pawnee warriors maybe a hundred yards away, galloping toward us on their wiry little ponies. Mr. Moody looked over at me and said, "Make your shots count. I got a box of shells in my pocket, but we don't want to waste 'em."

I nodded. My lips were dry and my heart was pounding so hard in my chest I thought it was about to bust out. I'd never been more scared in my life.

"I never fired that gun you got," Mr. Moody said, "but Fletcher took a couple of potshots at me with it when I caught up to him. My best guess is that it shoots a mite high and to the right. Better allow for that."

I nodded. I wanted to lick my lips, but my tongue wouldn't work. It was just a dried-out husk of meat right then.

Mr. Moody lifted his gun, drew a bead, and started shooting.

His shots were spaced out, not too slow, not too fast. I tried to make mine the same. I aimed at the Indian on the right end of the line. I squeezed off a shot and felt the gun jump in my hand. I used both hands on it then as I cocked the hammer and fired again.

The Indian jerked and started to fall off his horse. He grabbed the pony's mane and hung on, but he was hurt.

I wanted to yell in excitement at scoring a hit, but there were still more Pawnee attacking us. I changed my aim and fired again. Mr. Moody had gotten off five rounds by now, and he had knocked one of the Indians off his horse. The other four Pawnee stopped, turned around, and rode off in the other direction.

"My God," I said, my voice shaking. "We beat 'em!"

"The hell we did," Mr. Moody said as he opened the cylinder of his revolver and started replacing the spent shells with fresh ones from a box he took from his pocket. He handed some of the cartridges to me, and I knew the two guns were the same caliber even though Mr. Moody's had a longer barrel. "We wounded one and maybe killed another. They'll be back."

I looked at the Indians. They had ridden off some three hundred yards and stopped. I saw them milling around on their ponies and knew Mr. Moody was right.

"I didn't know there were still any wild Indians out here in Kansas," I said, maybe just to hear myself talk.

"There's not near as many as there used to be. A lot of them were put on reservations down in Indian Territory, south of here. But some of the bands jump the reservation sometimes and go out raidin'." Mr. Moody nodded toward the Indians in the distance. "Like this bunch."

I looked over my shoulder at the others. They were all

watching Mr. Moody and me with wide, staring eyes, knowing that the two of us were all that stood between them and the Pawnee. Except for Bill. He lay next to Fletcher, and he was listening as the outlaw talked to him in a low voice. Every now and then Bill said something, but I couldn't understand either of them.

I didn't like it, though. I didn't figure Bill ought to be listening to anything a man like Fletcher had to say. We'd done some bad things in our short lives, but Fletcher was a killer and God knows what else. Every time I looked at him for too long, I got the same squirmy feeling inside I got whenever I saw a water moccasin gliding through the river back home.

I heard whooping and looked at the Indians. Here they came again.

I dragged in a deep, shaky breath and held it. Mr. Moody didn't start shooting, so I didn't, either. I waited until the gun in his hand roared, and then I drew a bead—allowing for the fact that the gun shot high and to the right—and pulled the trigger.

I could tell there were four of the Indians left. One of them toppled off his horse. I never knew if I hit him or if Mr. Moody did. But losing a man didn't make them stop this time. They just kept coming, guiding those ponies with their knees while they fired at us with repeating rifles. Bullets hit around us, kicking up dust so that I couldn't see as well. Once or twice I heard a loud humming sound right beside my ear and knew I'd come that close to being hit.

I didn't know I was out of bullets until the hammer

clicked on an empty chamber, and by that time the Indians were right on top of us.

Mr. Moody came to his feet and shot one of the Pawnee at a distance of no more than five feet. I saw blood fly as the Indian went backward off his horse. Another Pawnee let out a whoop and swung his rifle at Mr. Moody like a war club. Mr. Moody ducked under it and reached up to grab the Indian's arm. He hauled that Pawnee down and started to wrestle with him.

That left one more Indian, and he was right there in the buffalo wallow among us, his pony circling wildly. He fired right at me, and to this day I don't know how he missed. But I jumped up and grabbed the barrel of his rifle and hauled down on it as hard as I could. The Pawnee let go of it before I could jerk him off his horse. He snatched a big knife from a sheath at his waist.

He might have gotten me with the knife if Stan and Wilmer hadn't jumped him right then. Like I've said before, those Gambrell brothers were uncommonly big boys. They knocked that Indian down, horse and all. One of them let out a howl as the Pawnee writhed around and cut him.

The other boys swarmed over him, grabbing his arms and holding him down. I had dropped my pistol, but I still had the rifle in my hands. I stepped forward, waited a second, and then leaned over to smash the butt of the rifle against the Indian's head as hard as I could. I didn't care right then if I killed him or not; I just wanted to make him stop fighting.

194

I killed him, all right. His skull caved in and blood came out of his mouth and nose as he jerked around for a second. Then he fell back on the ground, limp.

A yell that I instinctively knew was a war cry came from the last Indian. I whirled around and saw him jerk some sort of short-handled ax out of Mr. Moody's shoulder where he had just sunk it. Mr. Moody stumbled back, and the Pawnee raised the ax to hit him in the head.

I shot him in the back with that repeater before the blow could fall. It was a good thing there was a bullet already in the chamber, because I didn't have time to work the lever under the breech. The slug smashed into him and knocked him against Mr. Moody. Both of them fell. I ran over and pulled the Indian off Mr. Moody. He looked up at me and seemed a little surprised. I don't know if he was surprised to still be alive or surprised that I was the one who had saved him.

Then his eyes rolled up and he was out cold.

Times come along in a fellow's life when he has to do some things, and he doesn't have the luxury of wondering whether or not he *can*. He just does them. It was like that for me, the day we fought the Pawnee in the buffalo wallow.

The first thing was to make sure all the Indians were dead. They were. After that we got busy patching up Mr. Moody and Stan, who was the one who'd been cut by the Pawnee during the fight. Stan's arm had bled a lot, but once we wiped off the blood, it didn't look too bad. We tore strips off our shirt tails and used them for bandages.

We did the same thing with Mr. Moody's shoulder. He was hurt worse than Stan and had lost more blood. But I thought he might be all right if we could get some help for him.

The closest help was at the railroad. Our destination hadn't changed. And we still had to walk it, because after about half an hour of chasing those wild Indian ponies, we admitted that we couldn't catch them and gave up trying.

During all of this, Bill hadn't been much help at all. He just sort of sat to the side, watching the rest of us work and talking to Fletcher. I didn't like that. Bill and I had always run the gang, sort of splitting up between us the things that needed to be done. Now he was leaving it all on my shoulders. But I didn't want to waste any time or energy arguing with him, so I just ignored him and got on with it.

Stan and Wilmer got Mr. Moody on his feet. He was so big they were the only ones who could lift him, and it took both of them. But when he was up he sort of came back to his senses. He was able to walk with their help.

One thing we'd done was to gather up all the rifles and ammunition we could find that had belonged to those dead Pawnee. So we were a lot better armed as we started toward the railroad. If we ran into more trouble, I was hoping we could shoot our way out of it.

Bill had taken one of the repeaters for himself, and I wished he wouldn't walk so close to Fletcher. I hadn't forgotten how the outlaw had jumped me earlier. If he got his hands on Bill's rifle, he might kill us all.

Fletcher didn't try anything, though. He just trudged along like the rest of us.

After a while I started to wonder what it would be like to sleep, or eat, or drink some clear, cool water. It had been so long since I'd done any of those things I had just about forgotten how, I thought. The sun slid down the sky and our exhaustion and misery grew. It must have been worse for Mr. Moody, since he was hurt, but he never said a word about it. He just kept walking like the rest of us.

The sun went away, and I barely noticed at first. But then I looked up and saw the stars beginning to show against the sky as it shaded from deep blue to black. I was walking beside Mr. Moody, and he pointed and said in a tired, raspy voice, "You see that star up yonder?"

There were a lot of stars, but I thought I could pick out the one he meant. "I see it," I told him.

"Keep walkin' toward it . . . and you'll hit the railroad tracks . . . sooner or later."

"You'll keep us going in the right direction," I said.

"But if I can't . . . you know which way to go."

"Sure," I said, because I thought he wanted to hear it. "I know which way to go. I'll get us there."

"Figured you would, Jack," he said.

I had told him my name earlier in the day, but I

didn't know until then whether or not he remembered it. I was glad that he did.

We walked on. Some of the boys had to help each other keep going. We sort of straggled out. I forged ahead, not really meaning to, but I kept my eye on the star Mr. Moody had pointed out. I was sure we were going the right way.

And after a while, after hours of stumbling along that seemed like years, I tripped on something and fell and cried out when the sharp rocks of the roadbed cut one of my hands. The smooth, hard rail barked my shins. It hurt like blazes, but at the same time it felt wonderful.

"The railroad!" I croaked. "It's the railroad!"

So it was. The rails shone in the moonlight. Everybody sat down beside them to rest.

Mr. Moody was out of his head again. I asked him if he knew when the next train would be along. I had to ask several times before he came around enough to give me an answer. He had me take a big silver turnip watch out of his pocket and open it to check the time. It was a little after two o'clock in the morning.

"Be an eastbound . . . a little before three," he said. "Better get some brush . . . pile it up beside the tracks. Got lucifers . . . in my pocket. When you hear the train comin' . . . set the brush on fire. Engineer'll see it . . . stop the train . . ."

That sounded like a good idea to me. The boys and I got to work on it as soon as we'd caught our breath. Again, Bill didn't help. I told myself he was just keeping an eye on Fletcher, and that that was an important job, too.

Mr. Moody lay down on his good side to rest. I got the matches out of his pocket and got ready to light the brush we piled up beside the tracks. I thought it would make a pretty good blaze, plenty big enough to get the attention of the engineer and show us waving for him to stop the train. I just hoped he wouldn't think we were wild Indians.

I was sitting on one of the rails, so I felt the train coming before I heard it. I jumped up when the steel started vibrating. A minute later I heard the faint rumble of the engine. I hurried over and knelt at the brush pile.

I was so nervous it took me a couple of tries to get one of Mr. Moody's matches lit. Then the brush didn't want to catch at first. The boys started yelling at me to light the fire as the train's headlight appeared to the west. I fumbled with it some more, and then the flames started to lick at the brush. I stood up and backed off as the fire grew.

Just like I had hoped, it made a big blaze. And just like Mr. Moody had predicted, the train came to a stop with a squeal of brakes and a hiss of steam as we jumped up and down beside the tracks and waved our arms over our heads. As the conductor hurried forward from the caboose, the engineer called down from the cab, "What in the name o' the bonny blue flag are you boys doin' out here?"

"We've got a man hurt, mister," I shouted back at him. "We need help!"

"Hang on, hang on," the engineer yelled over the steam that was still escaping through the relief valve. He and the fireman climbed down from the cab as the conductor came trotting up.

I wanted to sit down and cry in relief. Somebody else could take care of things now. But I had to stay on my feet for a few minutes longer, so that I could tell the train men what had happened and get them to help Mr. Moody. I turned toward Mr. Moody, intending to take the conductor to him. He was still lying there motionless on the ground, and the horrible thought went through me that maybe he had died.

Things got even more horrible a second later as Bill stepped in between me and Mr. Moody and said, "Stand still, Jack, or I'll shoot you." He pointed the rifle in his hands at me.

Fletcher moved up beside Bill, and he had a gun, too, the short-barreled pistol I had dropped back in the buffalo wallow. I had clean forgotten about it. Bill must have picked it up back there without me ever noticing.

I was almost too shocked to speak. Finally I managed to say, "Bill, what are you doing?"

Fletcher pointed his gun at the conductor, the engineer, and the fireman and answered the question I had asked Bill. "We're takin' over this train, that's what we're doin'. My and my new partner. Ain't that right, Bill?"

"Damn right," Bill said. "I'm not going back to any reformatory."

I hadn't even thought about that. If we went back to St. Louis and told what had happened to Mr. Sweeney, more than likely the judge would send us to the reformatory. I didn't want that, either. But we didn't have any choice. We had to have help for Mr. Moody.

Fletcher laughed that ugly laugh of his. "The rest of you kids can come with us if you want."

"No, sir," I said. "Those days are behind us." I didn't know how I knew that, but I was sure of it.

"Don't be a fool, Jack," Bill said. "This is our chance to get away and start over."

"Start over as bigger criminals than before," I said.

The conductor spoke up. "You can't do this, son," he said to Bill. "The railroad will hire detectives to hunt you down."

"Shut up, old man!" Bill said, and he sounded so mad I thought he was going to shoot. "You're going to uncouple the locomotive and the tender so we can leave the rest of the train here."

"That's a good idea," Fletcher said. "We'll have 'em run it a few more miles down the line, until we get someplace we can steal some horses. You ready, kid?"

The barrel of the rifle in Bill's hands came up a little. "Yeah. I'm ready."

"Then if that conductor don't do as you say, shoot him. I'll bet the fireman would be glad to do the un- couplin' for us then."

As I looked at Bill's face in the light from the burn- ing brush, I knew he would do it. He would gun down the conductor in cold blood if he had to. He had been around Fletcher for only a day, but that day had been enough to change him forever. He wasn't my friend anymore, wasn't the boy I had grown up with and trusted with my life. I knew he would kill me, too, if I got in his way.

But I had to do it anyway.

"I won't let you do it," I said.

"You can't stop me," Bill said. "You left your rifle on the ground. All of you did."

It was true. Bill and Fletcher were the only ones with guns in their hands.

The repeater was at my feet. I put out my hand. "Forget it, Bill," I said. "I'm going to pick up my rifle, and you're going to put yours down."

The barrel swung toward me. His voice shook a little as he said, "Are you crazy? I'll kill you, Jack!"

"Then you'll have to kill me, too," Stan said.

"And me," his brother Wilmer said.

"And me," George said, and there was no smile on his face now.

Big Fred and Teddy chimed in, too. Teddy said, "You can't kill all of us, Bill. You can't shoot that fast. Nobody can shoot that fast."

Fletcher said, "I can." He started to turn toward us, and I knew he was about to pull the trigger. If he and Bill both started shooting, there was a good chance they *could* kill us all.

But that was when Mr. Tanner Moody got up off the ground and said, "Fletcher."

The outlaw turned and Mr. Moody's hand came up and both of them fired at the same time, flame licking from the muzzles of their guns. Mr. Moody staggered, but Fletcher doubled over and blasted another shot into the ground as he collapsed.

By that time I had lunged forward and grabbed the barrel of Bill's rifle and twisted it aside. I swung a punch and landed it clean on his jaw. He went back and down to the ground, and when I flexed my hand pain stabbed through it. I knew I had busted a knuckle.

It was worth it.

Mr. Moody walked over to Fletcher and would have turned him over, but the conductor beat him to it. "Dead," the conductor announced. He looked up at Mr. Moody. "Who are you, mister?"

"Tanner Moody." The gun went back in the holster.

"Heard of you. Let's get you back to the caboose. Looked like this fella hit you with his first shot."

Mr. Moody leaned on the conductor and the fireman. Before they took him back to the caboose, though, he looked over his shoulder at me. "You did fine, Jack," he said. "Figured you would."

I had only known Tanner Moody for a day, but just like with Bill and Fletcher, that day had changed me, too.

We didn't go to the reformatory, not even Bill. I don't know for sure, but I believe Mr. Moody had something to do with that. But we weren't a gang anymore. Stan and Wilmer Gambrell rode in the cab of that locomotive, found that they liked it, and went to work for the railroad and did fine for themselves. Big Fred took to singing in saloons and wound up in opera houses; he always did have a fine singing voice. Teddy talked himself into a job with a company that sold barbed wire and traveled all over the West doing it. George sold newspapers, started writing for one later on, and by the time he was through he was the editor and publisher. I ran into all of them from time to time, seeing as I traveled quite a bit in my job, too. I was a deputy United States marshal.

As for Bill, I don't really know. The last anybody saw of him, he held up a train in New Mexico back in '92 and took off into the Sangre de Cristos with the loot. Maybe he got killed, maybe he's still alive somewhere, leading a law-abiding life. I'd like to think so. Yeah, he went bad, but I remember a time when we were closer than brothers. He just followed the wrong star.

It's damned easy to do unless you're lucky like I was, lucky enough to meet a man like Tanner Moody.

Six

The New York Morning Telegraph, Feb. 9, 1903
The Legend of Tanner Moody
Sixth in a series by Bat Masterson
Exclusive

We had breakfast in the White Elephant's restaurant and then Jack—Marshal Jack Allison, still—went to pay his final respects to Tanner Moody. I had another cup of coffee and waited until he'd gone before going back in myself. Telling me his tale seemed to embarrass him, so I resolved not to let him see me again . . .

I was going to save this story for last, but as I have been writing these columns and telling these tales in order, I shall persist in this manner.

As I entered the White Elephant saloon I could see that the third day of the wake had brought no fewer people in. There were more coffee cups than beer mugs and shot glasses due to the hour, but people were still milling about, trading stories if they had them, listening to stories if they had none of their own. I went to the bar and collected still another cup of coffee from a bartender who was new to me. Perhaps the other had decided to get some rest and come in later, or he might even have taken the day off.

I took my usual spot at the bar, where I could see people as they entered and they could see me. A case in point was one particular young man who entered the room and paused in the doorway, as many had done before him. It was a sight to behold, the number of people who had turned out for Tanner Moody's wake. This young man, however, stood out for me, for what reason I did not know then. He seemed barely in his twenties. He was not a large man, but was strikingly handsome and attracted the eye of many of the women in the room.

I was standing at the bar, holding a partially filled cup when the young man suddenly seemed to look directly at me. I wasn't actually sure, however, until he walked right over to me and presented his hand.

"Bat Masterson, I presume?"

"You've got me at a disadvantage, young fella," I said, accepting his hand nonetheless.

"I'm sorry," he said. "My name is Jack London. I'm a writer. I was told you were in attendance here."

"Is the word getting around?" I asked.

"Apparently so."

"What can I do for you, then?' I asked. "Did you know Tanner Moody?"

"Actually," London said, "I only met him at the beginning of this year. I've just recently returned from England and heard of his passing. I rushed here from New York."

"I'm impressed," I said. "In fact, I'm leaving for New York after the funeral." I explained briefly to young Mr. London what I was doing there, and what I was planning to do with these articles.

"I'd actually heard you were doing that. I've heard of Alfred Henry Lewis," London said. "I'm a novelist myself."

"Are you?"

"My first three novels came out this year," he said, with no hint of ego.

"Three? You're very prolific."

"I keep to a strict regimen of one thousand words every morning," London said.

"What are the titles?" I asked out of politeness. I don't think I was quite aware at the time of what a monumental output of words that was.

"My first was called *Daughters of the Snows*. That was followed by *Cruise of the Dazzler* and *Children of the Frost*."

"I'm sorry," I said honestly, "I haven't read any of them." Or heard of them, for that matter.

"That doesn't matter," London said. "The book I've just finished is the reason I'm here. You see, I was working on it when I met Mr. Moody. I had heard of him, of course, but I had no idea of the type of man he was until he was kind enough to dine with me one night."

"And where was this?"

"In New York. I was there to see my publisher and he was there to see Colonel Cody."

"Buffalo Bill Cody?"

"Yes," London said, "I believe the colonel wanted him to join his show."

Tanner in Cody's show? That would have been a sight.

"I'm sure Tanner refused."

"He did, but that night we met in the Yale Club—a gentlemen's club. Mr. Moody was with the colonel and I was with my publisher. They were both members, and both had to leave before dinner, but they took care of the check and Mr. Moody and I dined together."

"How old are you, Mr. London?"

"Twenty-six, sir," he answered. "Why?"

"I'm just wondering what you and an old reprobate like Tanner Moody had to talk about."

"Actually," London said, "we talked quite a bit about him, and about my book. You see, I titled it *The Call of the Wild*, and when I told Mr. Moody what it was about—the theme was—he seemed to identify with it."

"What is the theme?"

"Basically, the struggle to survive with dignity and integrity. You see, I believe the proper function of man—or any living creature—is to live, not just exist."

"And Tanner identified with that?"

"Yes, he did."

"He would."

"You see, I was at an impasse in my book. I didn't know what Buck—that's my main character, a wolf named Buck—should do next. But listening to Mr. Moody talk about his childhood, and his own battle to survive all his life . . . well, it was inspirational."

Having just recently heard the story of Tanner's childhood, and of some of the other travails of his life, I could understand why the young man would have been impressed.

As if reading my mind, London said, "I was more than impressed, I was inspired." There was a fire in the young man's eye at this time, one he would become quite well known for.

"That was why I had to come here today to pay my respects, and why when I heard that you were here— and what you were doing—I wanted to tell you my story."

"Well, I appreciate it, Mr. London," I said sincerely. "I've been listening to people's stories about Tanner Moody and how he affected their lives. Yours is . . . unusual."

"In what way?"

"Well, a literary figure such as yourself," I said, "and a man like Tanner, who lived most of his life by the gun. I may just be an old lawman myself, but I appreciate the irony of the sword inspiring the pen."

"Yes," London said, "yes, that's exactly it. You do understand!"

"I do, indeed."

What I couldn't know then, as young Mr. London shook my hand and went to pay his respects, was what a talented writer Jack London truly was. As I write this, dear reader, I hold in my hand an advance copy of Jack London's *The Call of the Wild*, and while I am by no means a literary critic, I believe it is a brilliant piece of work. I cannot recommend it to you more highly. And as an old westerner myself I'm proud to think that one of us had even a small part in inspiring it, if you read this, Jack London, I say thank you and good work.

When Alice Bickerdyke walked into the White Elephant Saloon she was a complete stranger to me, and yet I knew who she was instantly. Perhaps, of all the mourners who had come and gone, she was the one I had been expecting.

I knew the story of her and Tanner Moody. He had told me about it once in Arkansas, not long after he and Alice had met, spent time together and gone their own ways for the second and final time in their lives . . .

Liars Three

by John Jakes

Of all the vicious, mean-spirited sons of bitches who disturbed the West as the frontier was closing, one of the worst was William Molesworth. Everybody took it for granted that Bill Molesworth, a Georgian, was secesh, but in truth he never espoused any cause or belief except as it suited him, to distract some hapless victim he intended to rob or murder. Tanner re-encountered Bill on a night of hard rain and thunder, in the main street of the slippery spot on the side of the Montana mountain named Two Mile—or so it was told afterward.

Before his death, Tanner often said to close friends, "Bill Molesworth was vermin and I did the world a service that night."

The lady involved repeatedly said at the funeral, "I can testify that I saw Tanner Moody shoot and kill William Molesworth."

Frankie Fat said to anyone who asked, "I don't

know any Bill Mozeworth, I live here in Sacramento since a little boy."

When Bill Molesworth drifted into Two Mile in the autumn of '87, the gold vein was already played out. Half the claims were abandoned. The editor-publisher of the Two Mile Trumpet, popularly known as the Two-bit Trumpet, had taken down his sign and freighted his press to what were, presumably, greener journalistic pastures. The only lawman within thirty miles, down at the county seat, had died the previous July of a social disease acquired at a Two Mile crib. A third of the town's dilapidated shops and stores were shut up: higher education was not needed to see that the rats were running down the lines to a safer, brighter shore before the boat sank altogether.

Tanner Moody was already in town, having stopped when his weary paint could not go farther on the long journey back to Texas, where Tanner hoped to transfer from the life of a bounty hunter to the no less rigorous but somewhat less nerve-wracking calling of rancher. It was as necessary for him to stop as it was for the worn-out paint: influenza was battering his bones and burning his forehead.

Dripping muddy water from his soaked duster and big sombrero, he staggered into the empty lobby of the Golconda House dragging his saddle bags. He signed the book, asked the clerk, George, for a quiet room where he could recover, and thereupon slid down in a faint in the center of a big self-made puddle.

Bill Molesworth was just at this hour riding into the godforsaken little town, and Alice Bickerdyke was putting wet cloths on bruises on her arms up in room twelve, next door to the room given to Tanner. As yet she didn't know Tanner was there, though to have known would have pleasured her: she and the legendary gun artist had shared twelve blissful nights in Santa Fe when they were younger and the torch in her bosom had never quite burned out, although Alice had plunged into matrimony four times since the New Mexico idyll. Most recently, she had fled from spouse number four, S. S. Haddfield, a gambler, whose fits of depression when he lost were worked out in giving weaker mortals a brisk tattoo with his fists.

He tried this on Alice but twice; the second time, she seized a large flower pot in which bamboo was struggling to survive and broke it, dirt and all, over his luxuriant wig. Though eminently respectable, not to say wholesome and trustworthy, in her appearance—this was why she never lacked for employment—Alice was no hothouse lily. She'd spent most of her adult life dealing cards in better-class sporting houses, and was at least marginally proficient with stilettos, hideout pistols and, on occasion, flower pots. In her room in Two Mile she was using the damp cloths to soothe the most recent and, she vowed, the last purple and yellow stigmata left by Haddfield, whom she hoped was still lying on the floor.

Tanner and Molesworth had likewise met previously, in Kansas. In fate's peculiar style of weaving, these three people were suddenly bound together that rainy night in a played-out mining town in Montana.

Bill Molesworth tied his stolen horse at Frankie Fat's Canton Café and stumped inside, leaving the inevitable water trail. Frankie's mild-tempered hound dog followed, dancing around Bill's boots in an attempt to be friendly. Scowling, Molesworth shooed him away. A couple of idlers took one look at Molesworth's baleful eyes and stubbled jaw and promptly lit out, never mind that they didn't have rain gear to protect them from the downpour.

Molesworth ordered his supper from the slender Asian proprietor. The mutt continued to caper around Bill's feet good-naturedly. Frankie said, "He won't hurt anybody, he just likes people."

"What's his name?"

"Rex, old Rex."

"Well, Rex," Molesworth said, patting the dog's head, "my boots is surely dirty enough without you mucking them up some more." He reached under his duster, drew a revolver, jabbed the barrel into the mouth of the hapless pet, and fired.

"Oh, my Lord," Frankie moaned, wiping his face of gore from the dog's head. "Why you do that, mister?"

Molesworth gave him a grin—the full shot of his handsome store-bought porcelain teeth. "I never liked

214

dogs, they always turn on you. Now if you don't want to go out the same way, clean up the mess and bring my fucking food."

Alice partially disrobed in her room and, overcome by weariness, put her head down on the hard bolster. She slept about an hour, wakened not by the lulling rain but by persistent moans reaching her through the thin wall. With some annoyance, she concluded that the clerk had given her a room next to a couple indulging their carnal appetites.

She heard but one voice, however, and that rather deep and sonorous. It struck her that perhaps she was hearing the plaint of a man in pain, not the amorous bellowing of a Romeo. She lit a candle, drew her wrapper from her valise, and trudged downstairs.

George the clerk stumbled from the back room in answer to the bell on the counter. "I'm afraid your guest in the room next to mine is making a lot of noise," Alice said. "I would appreciate a different room."

"Oh, sure," George said, half awake and fumbling for another key on the board behind him.

"And you might look in on him, he sounds like he's in pain."

"Sick," was George's quick, indifferent reply. "When he walked in here he fainted right in front of me." He indicated the slow-drying puddle.

"The poor man," Alice said, ashamed of her preoccupation with her own sleep.

"Yeah, took me ten minutes to wake him up enough to boot him upstairs. Some saddle bum," he concluded, handing over the new key. "Just move your things and give me both keys in the morn—lady? What's the matter?"

The matter was that Alice's eyes were big and round and black with astonishment; her gaze had fallen on the guest register. The last, wobbly signature was *T. Moody*.

"Moody?" she said.

"You know him?"

"I am not sure. Did he give his first name?"

"Tucker, Trapper, something like that."

"Is it possibly Tanner?"

"Possibly," George returned, sublimely uninterested.

Why, she wondered, would he sign his real name? Then she asked herself, *Why would he not?* Men feared Tanner Moody, not the other way around.

She was gone up the stairs before George could blink more than once. She was in such a transport of confusion and excitement, she left both keys on the blotter.

Alice reached the threshold of the room adjoining hers. Sure enough, although the rain again pelted the shingles loudly as peas bounced on a drumhead, she heard him moan. She patted her gleaming if disarrayed hair; tapped gently on the door and whispered his first name.

In response to a grunt she whispered it again, louder, and he responded with a distinct *"Gnnngh,"* which she took to be permission to enter.

Her inamorata lay half covered by a blanket in the midst of a disorderly bed. She had no doubt of the sick man's identity, for his room had two windows, not a single tiny one like hers, and the blinds had not been drawn; feeble lamps of the main street cast just enough secondhand light for recognition.

"Oh, Tanner, Tanner, it's you." She flung herself on her knees beside the bed, an unlikely, almost prayerful position for a lady of her temperament and history.

"I know you?" he said, rolling his head side to side as he tried to sit up and failed.

"It's Alice, Alice from Santa Fe."

"Here? Montana? How—?"

"Circumstance. Sheer chance. Oh, my dear, how grand to see you again, even when you're ill."

Her hand unconsciously flew to his brow. He was boiling with fever. She interpreted his next grunt as the start of a question. "I saw the register," she said. "I must put cold cloths on you." The room had nothing but an empty ewer; Alice ran next door, fetched hers, and sped back to Tanner, who lay tossing and muttering about the vagaries of fate.

While this transpired, Bill Molesworth strode into the lobby of the Golconda House, leaving an even larger puddle than the one drying near the desk. He banged the bell so hard that it flew behind the counter and plonged on the floor. George came stumbling from his cubicle. "Now who in the goddamned—?" His eyes focused on the baleful face of the stranger gripping the register with two hands. Molesworth's dirty thumb squished down on the crooked signature.

"Moody—you got a Moody staying here?"

"Yeh, a mighty sick one, too. Passed out cold when he walked in. Who is he? Sure does get a lot of notice."

Molesworth helped himself to a handful of George's flannel nightshirt. "What's his first name? What's the *T* stand for?"

"I think it's Topper or Tanner or something like that. You're the second one who—"

But Molesworth was already halfway out of the lobby, nearly insensible with fear and wrath. He staggered into the rain and turned right two blocks to the livery where he'd put up his nag after killing the pooch and finishing his meal at the Canton Café. He lurched into an empty stall and squatted in the dark, sniffling and cursing under his breath as he prepared himself for killing the man he hated while at the same time guaranteeing his own survival.

About an hour later, as he tirelessly scraped grease from his stove top, Frankie Fat mourned his murdered dog and wondered why he had left the Pearl River in exchange for punctured dreams in America. A single lamp burned in the café kitchen, but it was enough for Frankie's work. The alley door opened suddenly, admitting a gust of rain and Molesworth, visibly armed.

"Hello, Mr. Chink," Molesworth said with a smile as heartwarming as a prairie blizzard. "Step away from the stove, put up your hands, and do like I tell you and maybe you'll still be slinging hash in the morning."

Fear abridged Frankie's churning emotions to three words. "What you want?"

"Just a little errand, won't take you long." Molesworth's gun hand, his right, was in the open, full of deadly blue metal. Frankie Fat gasped when Molesworth's left hand appeared suddenly through a slit in his rain-spattered duster; ambidexterity was one of Molesworth's few non-lethal talents. Frankie Fat stared at the sheet of paper, folded once, with a name written on the outside.

"Had to wake up the livery boy for this," Molesworth said, shaking the paper in his left hand. "You take it down to the hotel and deliver it personally to the gentleman whose name is written here. See? *Moody*. You wake up the clerk, find Moody's room and hand him the paper. If you so much as peek at what's inside, I'll know. I'll find you tomorrow morning and blow your fucking head to Saskatoon." How exactly the cadaverous man with rain still dripping off his sugar-loaf hat would effect his promised act of telepathy eluded Frankie; he was too scared, as any normal person would be, to think about it much.

"I find him. I give it to him. I no look," Frankie assured the visitor.

"Make sure," Molesworth warned, and slipped

away into the night, leaving only an echo of the closing door, and spots of water on Frankie's none too sanitary floor.

In the meantime, Alice had been zealously applying damp clothes to Tanner Moody's naked chest and extremities. He lay with half-lidded eyes, mumbling questions too feverish for her to understand. Her every reply was, "Plenty of time for that later."

In the course of her vigorous bathing, she discovered that the dear, sick man was not as lethally ill as she'd imagined. Or maybe it was just that certain parts of a man responded no matter what. In any event, as she would characterize it to herself many times in the years that followed, his manly prowess revived. He spoke with unexpected clarity.

"It really is you, isn't it, honey lamb?"

He bore her backward. The cloth dropped from her hand. Despite the rain and damp, it was Santa Fe all over again.

Much later, in a thrilled haze of satisfaction and satiation—sick or not, he was the same old Tanner—she heard someone knock at the door. She yanked the coverlet over her exposed bosoms while Tanner, equally bare, tottered around the footboard to answer the peculiar, almost tentative hiss of inquiry from the corridor.

Tanner Moody closed the door and, near the window, squinted at the paper. "I'll be a red-eyed albino son of a bitch," he said with a good deal of husky catarrh in the sentence. "I thought I killed that no-good."

Alice cried, "Who? Where? When?"

"Bill Molesworth. Bison Wallow, Kansas. Must be, oh, fourteen years ago." He slapped the paper. "I can't believe this. He expects to meet me in the main street in one hour." He sank down on the bed beside Alice. "How did he get here? Sometimes I wonder if there's a God ordering the universe, damn if I don't."

"Tanner, you can't possibly accept a challenge like that."

"He suggests as much," Tanner replied with an empty jerk of his lips passing as a smile. "He says he recognizes that I may yellow out and if I do, he'll come after me here in the hotel." He gave her the paper. "Read for yourself."

"You're too sick to face him," Alice insisted, stroking his brow with fingers that were quickly damp and heated by his fever. She noticed, not incidentally, that his manly prowess had all but disappeared into his loins.

"Nevertheless," he began, resuming a minute later after a fit of coughing, "nevertheless, I must go." And somewhat like a dying swan she'd seen in a ballet performance in Denver, he fell back on the bolster in a swoon.

Alice contemplated the unconscious man. In one night of chance circumstance, all of his exploits, real and fabricated, would be rendered as nothing if William Molesworth got away with whatever he was planning. Which certainly wouldn't be a fair fight; she didn't know the challenger but she knew the type. She hit her knees with her fists.

"This won't do. This won't do at all."

At a few minutes before one A.M., a person walked out of the Golconda Hotel with face shaded by a big sombrero. A stained duster dragged in the mud puddles. A block up, the only other visible inhabitant of the sleeping street was Bill Molesworth, likewise attired in duster and sugar-loaf hat. The rain fell, not hard, but it created a ghostly murk.

"Hallo," Molesworth called, unbuttoning his duster with his right hand, throwing it open, and dropping his hand suggestively toward his holstered revolver. His opponent from the hotel raised a left hand to signal reception of the message.

"We each take six paces forward and draw," Molesworth called out above the hiss of the rain. "Six paces, understand?" Again the left hand signaled that the message was heard.

"All right, then, you crawling, lizard-bellied hot air bag," Molesworth cried, and began to pace and count at the same time. "One. Two. Three. Four—"

On the four count, Molesworth's other hand and accompanying hideout pistol popped from the slit on the left side of his duster. His opponent was way ahead of him. A hand flew up to the brim of the sombrero; the hat sailed away in the rain. One shake of the head, and shimmering dark hair flowed to the shoulders of the duster. Dumbstruck, Molesworth let his right hand fall while the left drooped in the slit.

"Godamighty. He's yellower than I thought. He sent a *woman?*"

"The man is sick. His reflexes are slow. His eyesight is blurry."

"I don't give a fuck if he's the emperor of China with the dropsy. I may be a skunk but I won't stand for this. Go back and tell him to get out here, crawl out if he has to, in the next ten minutes, or I'll burn down that fucking hotel."

Stomping mud to dramatize his ire, Molesworth spun about. "I'll wait yonder on the porch, where it's dry." A shot rang out.

Bill Molesworth turned around slowly, mouth open, eyes big as coffee cups. The pistol in his right hand misfired and he was forced to resort to the other gun half in, half out of the slitted duster. His bullet buzzed away harmlessly. She shot him again. He fell face forward into a puddle and made a big splash.

Frankie Fat ran off a porch where he had been hiding and clapped his hands, exclaiming, "Hooray, hooray." By next morning, he would rethink the desirability of appearing as a witness to the slaying.

The shrouded figure of Alice Bickerdyke, got up in Tanner Moody's boots, jeans, coat, and hat—people always commented on the resemblance—slowly retraced a path to the Golconda Hotel.

Which didn't explain why Bill Molesworth died with one bullet hole in his back and one more in his chest. Certain residents of Two Mile remarked on this curiosity, but it was never reported or noted in an official way, there being a temporary absence of law in the vicinity.

Alice Bickerdyke and the slayer of Bill Molesworth left Two Mile late that day. She handled the buckboard's reins while he held on, swaying and coughing. They didn't stop running until Little Rock, Arkansas, by which time it was blowing across the landscape like a blue norther that Tanner Moody had shot and killed the notorious William Molesworth in Two Mile, Montana.

"Shouldn't of done it," Tanner Moody complained through chattering teeth. "Weren't you scared?"

"To death. But it wasn't as if I'd never had reason to plug a man before. If you'd stepped into that street, you'd have stayed there for good. You were a sick puppy."

"Don't let that get around."

"I don't intend to. Don't you either."

Alice and her lover parted after two months of carnal bliss in Arkansas; he was always too fiddle-footed to be tied down. He went on to Texas, she to whatever lay over the next hill.

But she had good memories.

The late Tanner Moody often said to close friends, in rather a hushed tone, "Bill Molesworth was vermin and I did the whole world a service when I shot him down that night."

Alice Bickerdyke, his inamorata whom he never saw after they parted in Fort Smith, declared at the funeral, "I saw Tanner Moody shoot Bill Molesworth in the street of Two Mile. He was so brave. I will stand by the story forever."

Asian restauranteur Frankie Fat said, "I don't know any Bill Mozeworth, I live here in Sacramento since a little boy. You order, please, I need the table."

Seven

The New York Morning Telegraph, Feb. 10, 1903
The Legend of Tanner Moody
Seventh in a series by Bat Masterson
Exclusive

It was the resemblance to Tanner Moody that identified Alice Bickerdyke to me. That and the way he had described her to me. Odd that I'd remember that fifteen years later. Moody and I had never been close friends, but that day he'd been in the mood to talk.

I decided not to ask her name, or even speak to her. I'm telling you all here in this article that she was Alice Bickerdyke, the only woman who had ever saved Tanner Moody's life. I'm telling you that I *know* that—and even if I'm wrong . . . it's still the stuff of legend.

* * *

Late in the afternoon I had still not found another story when I became aware of some commotion outside the main door. There were raised voices, but it did not sound like an argument or a fight, it just sounded like . . . excitement.

Other folks in the saloon noticed and we were all watching the door when a man I recognized entered, and suddenly I knew what all the excitement was about.

The man who entered was named William Brady, and trailing behind him was a photographer with a huge camera up on his shoulder.

"Where's the casket?" Brady asked loudly, speaking around his ever present stogie, and then he spotted it. "Over there, set up over there. Hey, excuse us, please? We got some business here."

William Brady had only one business and that was boxing. At that time he was managing just one fighter—the heavyweight champion of the world, Jim Jeffries. Jeffries had just KO'd Bob Fitzsimmons a few months earlier to claim the title. I knew that Jeffries and Fitzsimmons were now touring the West together. Jeffries was taking on all comers, and in the absence of any, he and Fitzsimmons were fighting exhibitions.

Brady was a good fight manager, but what made him good at his job made him a rude human being, and he was exhibiting all of that at the moment, pushing people out of the way so his photographer could get set up. It was clear now what the excitement outside was about. Where Brady went, the champ was not far behind and, sure enough, Jim Jeffries entered the saloon next, followed by his little trainer, Billy Delaney.

Jeffries was already one of the most popular champions in history, and there was a crowd of people following him, trying to talk to him, to just touch him. Since there had already been a crowd of people in the saloon for Tanner Moody, the place was now bursting at the seams—and I was sure that many of the folks following Jeffries had no idea what was going on in the White Elephant.

"Champ, champ!" Brady called. "Come on, in front of the casket."

"I don't know about this, Brady," Jeffries said. "This just doesn't seem—"

"Trust me, champ," Brady said, cutting the big man off. At six foot two and a half, the champ towered over both his trainer and manager.

I knew all three men, because I had been at the fight where Jeffries knocked out Fitzsimmons. I knew that Jeffries had gone into that fight at a fit two ten, but he seemed to have ballooned up to about two hundred and fifty pounds or so.

"Tanner Moody was one of the most famous gunmen of all time," Brady said to his fighter, "and you're the most famous fighter of all time. This is a natural!"

Mourners were being shunted to the side by the champ's fans, and Brady was busy pushing people out of way, and I finally had seen enough of it.

"Jim," I said, stepping forward.

Jeffries turned and looked at me, and recognized me immediately. So did Brady.

"Mr. Masterson?"

"Bat!" Brady said. "By God, this is great! We can get you in the picture, too."

"There's not going to be any picture, Brady," I said, then turned my attention to Jeffries. I had learned a long time ago that it did little good to talk to Brady. Jeffries was the one who had concern for others. Brady had none. That's probably what made him a good manager but, as I alluded to before, not much of a human being.

"Jim, this isn't a good idea."

"That's what I thought, too, Mr. Masterson," Jeffries said, "but Brady said—"

"Brady's not always right," I said. "Maybe he is most of the time, because he's thinking of what's good for you and your career, but this time, Jim, he's way off."

"Hey, wait—" Brady started to say, but I ignored him. Jeffries was the one to reason with.

"Get him out of here, Jim," I said. "Now."

"Yes, sir," Jeffries said. "I'm real sorry about this."

"Now look—"

I turned away from Brady and looked at the photographer.

"You know who I am?" I asked.

Looking confused, the man said, "Not really."

"My name is Bat Masterson. Now do you know?"

The man swallowed and said, "Yes, sir."

"Get out of here," I said. "Take your equipment and get out."

"But sir, Mr. Brady is paying me—"

"Nobody is taking any pictures in here today, son," I said. "Get out before I put a bullet in your lens."

That seemed to do it. He started collecting his apparatus. I turned and ignored him, looked at the hangers-on who had entered the saloon with Jeffries and his people.

"I want you all to get out," I said. "This is a man's wake, goddamn it, not a circus. Git!"

I heard my name muttered by someone, and Jeffries was talking to Brady, guiding him toward the door. It was probably that more than my actions that made those folks move. If the champ was going to leave, they were, too.

As they went out the door the trainer, Billy Delaney, turned and tossed me a grateful smile, then followed them out, as did the rest of the entourage.

When I turned to face the people who were there for the right reasons they suddenly put their hands together and applauded. I tipped my hat, waved at them to quiet down, and went back to my place at the bar.

I wondered what the newspapers would say about all of that the next morning.

Bob O'Dell, the reporter from the local paper, was still making the rounds of the room. He wasn't looking at me, though. Either he didn't take me seriously as a journalistic threat, or he was simply afraid to look my way for some other reason. Perhaps he was a firm believer in reputations and legends.

In any case, I hadn't found myself a likely candidate for an article for some time, but O'Dell had cornered a young man who seemed to have a lot to say. They were standing at the end of the bar and I decided to sidle up as close as I could and give a listen. O'Dell's back was to me, and the young man was too engrossed in what he was saying to notice.

Maybe I was about to become a real journalist by stealing a story . . .

Tanner's Diamond

By Jory Sherman

A few minutes after I walked into the White Elephant
Saloon, it struck me that I had landed in the middle of
Tanner Moody's life after he was plumb dead.

It was an odd feeling, seeing all those people there,
people he had spoken of, had told me about during his
last days in Vickery. I didn't know their names and I
had never seen their faces before, but Tanner had told
me about them and as I stood there staring at that
long, long bar, it seemed that pieces of his life were
walking around, talking, whispering, nudging, belly-
ing up to the bar, drinking, swearing, maybe even
praying.

Yes, praying—for a scoundrel and a killer, for a
man who had lived by the gun but had not died by the
gun. I could almost hear Tanner laughing, the way he
laughed on the porch of my father's house where he

had rented a room to pass his final days. That laugh, it seemed it was there in that room, like an undercurrent, or like some vagrant sound snatched away by the wind that blows into a man's ear when least expected, when all about him is utter silence.

The smell of cigar, cigarette, and pipe smoke was thick in my nostrils. The people in the room were shadowed by a blanket of blue haze that hung in the air over their heads like a pall of cannon smoke over a battlefield.

The casket stood on a pair of draped sawhorses in one corner of the saloon. A few curious ladies peered into it, then after hankying their eyes to dab away tears or smoke, walked on past, and one or two old galoots went up to it and took their hats off, sniffed the corpse, then ambled over to the bar as if they had gotten their six bits' worth of viewing for the day. The casket was placed as far away from the bar as it could be and, even from where I stood, just inside the saloon, it seemed like a magnet that turned both ways, both to attract and repel.

I was going to walk over and take a look inside that homely casket, just to see how much the man I had known only for a little time had been changed by death, a death that he had known was coming even back there in Vickery at my mother's modest boarding house.

But, as I took a step toward that part of the room, a man approached me. He was wearing a rumpled seersucker suit that seemed almost glaring in its whiteness against the predominance of black suits milling around in the room. He had a sheaf of papers or a notebook sticking out of the side pocket of his jacket. He wore a Panama hat that had greasy finger smudges on it, and was starting to tatter at the edges as if it had been chewed by straw-eating moths. His face was ruddy from drink and his slightly bulbous nose underlined his Irishness with spidery crimson scrawls that were a roadmap of all the saloons in Dallas and Ft. Worth. The little bow tie attached to his collar lay askew and drooped with much the same sag as his jowls.

"A moment of your time, sir," the man said. "That is, if you were acquainted with the deceased."

"What?"

"Mr. Moody. Tanner Moody. Was he a friend of yours?"

"I don't know."

"Well, did you know him? Ever have a run-in with him?"

"No, I never had no run-in with Tanner."

"Come to pay your respects, eh? I just need a few moments of your time, sir. I'm Bob O' Dell from the *Fort Worth Telegraph*."

I started to feel at home, or at least not so much the stranger.

"My pa worked for the *Dallas Sentinel*," I told him. "He was a reporter and typesetter."

"Oh, yeah. What's his name?"

He started guiding us to a table in the corner next to the front window, well away from the long bar.

"Raleigh. Raleigh St. John."

"Rolly?" O'Dell slipped his notebook out of his pocket and laid it on the table, flipped the pages to a blank one.

"As in Sir Walter," I told him.

"Most of the folks I've talked to here didn't actually know Moody. They heard about him or know someone who supposedly knew him. And those I've met who did know him don't want to talk about him. Curious. My editor thinks there's a story here."

"But you don't."

"I didn't say that, son. I'm looking for the truth. There seems to be very little of it in evidence at this gathering. If you believe all the stories about Tanner Moody, he was as legendary as Daniel Boone, or Davy Crockett, maybe even more notorious than Jesse James."

I didn't say anything. O'Dell lifted a hand to a waiter and held up two fingers in a beckoning gesture that showed O'Dell had some familiarity with ordering beers in saloons. The waiter nodded and a drop of sweat beaded up on the tip of his nose. His white shirt was soaked through with perspiration and his apron was stained with spilt beer.

Tanner came to our place when he was seventy, or he said he was that old. He didn't look it, then, but as I got to know him, I could believe it. His memory was good for some things, but he had trouble remembering names. He said he couldn't see as well as he once did and his hearing wasn't what it was.

"I don't need no ear trumpet, yet," Tanner told me, "but sometimes I can't hear the middles of words."

"The middles?" I asked him.

"Or maybe it's the tones. I have trouble understanding what women say in their squeaky voices. Sometimes it all sounds like gibberish. You got a good even voice, Toby, and I don't have no trouble hearin' you."

Tanner had a manly voice. It was kind of deep, and had a throaty rasp to it as if it had to fight its way through the phlegm in his throat, or maybe the tissue inside from a scar he had just above his Adam's apple.

"Well," I said, "it's probably going to be hard to find someone who knew Tanner real well."

"Why's that, son?"

"I don't think he let anyone get that close to him."

O'Dell scribbled something in his notebook. I couldn't make out what it was. Whatever he wrote didn't look like a real word, just a scrawl, like maybe he was just doodling.

"But you lived in the same house with him, right?"

I nodded.

"So, did you get close to him? Did you talk to him?"

"Mostly I just listened. He paid me to read books to him. Four bits a book."

"Books, what books?"

O'Dell scribbled. He didn't look down at the paper. He just looked at me.

"Schoolbooks I had at home. Readin' books. Parts of books. Parts of the Bible and such."

"You read to Moody from the Bible?"

"Some parts. He didn't like the parts that had all the begats and he liked the Old Testament mostly."

"Well, what parts of the Old Testament did he like you to read to him. What's your name, anyways?"

"Toby. He liked Ecclesiastes. And Job."

"What other books did you read to him, Toby?"

"Plato. *Ivanhoe. The Count of Monte Cristo.* Other stuff."

There was a light in the reporter's eyes that was fading with his interest. He had stopped writing on his notepad and I knew Mr. O'Dell didn't want to hear any more about the books I read to Tanner. It was just as well, for I didn't feel like talking about the books anymore. Tanner, despite his advanced age, had a mind that roamed far and wide.

"What about the gunfights, Toby? Did he ever talk to you about them?"

"No."

"What about his crimes? Did he ever talk about those with you?"

"No."

My father had told me once that there was nothing worse than a reporter who came to an interview with all the questions asked and answered in his mind. He said that the best skill a reporter had was the ability to listen. O'Dell, I realized, wasn't really interested in who Tanner Moody was, or why he had become so notorious. He was just interested in the sensational aspects of Tanner's life, of which I knew nothing first-hand. I knew some of the stories. Everybody did. But I doubt if anyone else knew what I did about Tanner Moody. And, now that he was dead, probably nobody cared much.

The waiter brought two big glasses of beer and O'Dell paid him in coin. The beers had heads on them that were at least two inches deep. O'Dell lifted his glass and swallowed. When he set his glass down, he had a mustache of foam just above his upper lip.

I looked at my beer and saw the light shine through the light amber liquid. The depths sparkled with tiny motes that danced like dust in a beam of sunlight.

"Drink your beer, Toby," O'Dell said.

"Why?" I asked. "Do you think it will loosen my tongue so you can ask me more questions about Tanner?"

An odd look came over O'Dell's face and he cackled a small nervous laugh. He squinched up his face so that his eyes nearly disappeared from their sockets and I could see that I had struck bone.

"Naw, naw, not at all, son. The beer's good and it's cooler than anything in this room."

I took a sip of the beer, let it ooze through the foam. It tasted of hops and malt and musty fields of alfalfa and lespedeza that had been shorn so that the smell of hay lingered in the air like the dust in an old barn. And maybe its warmth in my stomach did serve to loosen my tongue a little.

"He mostly talked about souls," I said.

"Huh?" The light of interest came back into O'Dell's eyes, but the expression on his face told me that this was not what he wanted to hear. It certainly was not what he *expected* to hear.

"Did you say 'souls,' Toby?"

Right sudden, then, I wished I hadn't said what I said. I nodded and picked up the glass of beer again, sipped from it so that I didn't have to speak.

"Can you explain that?" O'Dell asked.

I shook my head and kept drinking. If the tongue could be loosened by drink, it could also be stilled by drinking, by swallowing, by keeping the mouth filled with liquid so that the tongue lay silent like some basking lizard on a mud bank.

Tanner took me into his confidence after I had read a couple of books to him. He began wanting to discuss some of the stories, the characters, and his mind would drift back in time as if he was trying to piece together people he had known with those in the books. Some of the ancient Greek writers, like Socrates, had mentioned souls and this seemed to fascinate Tanner.

"Toby," he said one day, "do you believe people have souls?"

"I don't know, Mr. Moody. I don't rightly know."

"Well, I believe they do. The injuns believe that everything has a soul, birds, animals, people, rocks, trees. They don't call it a soul, like them Greeks did, but spirit."

"The Greeks thought it was in the breath, Mr. Moody."

"Yeah, I know. And what is breath, anyways? You

can't see it 'cept on frosty mornin's or when you put smoke to it. Point is, a soul is somethin' you can't see, but it's in every damned thing, and maybe it stays around after a body's dead and rotted, eaten up by varmints or worms."

"Could be, Mr. Moody. I just don't know."

When he talked like that, of souls and spirit, Tanner got a faraway look in his eyes and there was a vein under his temple that ridged up and looked blue under his skin and the muscle in his face made the vein throb like a worm trying to get out from under the skin.

"Tanner never sat in the rocking chair," I said.

"What?"

"On our front porch. Tanner never sat in the rocking chair nor in the swing. He sat in a hard straight chair."

"Son, you makin' a point?"

"He said the noise would keep him from hearing what he had to hear."

O'Dell leaned across the table, hanging on my every word. That gave me a feeling of power. Just a little bit. His questions were making me remember little things about Tanner Moody, little things that later added up.

"You mean Tanner was listening for something when he sat on your porch, or do you mean he couldn't hear you when you read to him if he was rockin' or swingin'?"

I think I smiled.

"I read to him in a real low voice, Mr. O'Dell. That way he could hear if anyone was coming down the street. And when he talked, he talked soft, you know. Not whispering, but his voice low and I'd have to lean real close to him so I could hear. His voice was like purring, sort of, it rippled like water over smooth stones in a creek, or like a slight breeze rustling the leaves in a steady rhythm. He could make me sleepy with his talk if he'd kept it up long enough."

"Well, now," O'Dell said, "what would Tanner talk about that made you so sleepy? The gunfights? The men he'd killed?"

I sighed and downed another swallow of that beer, which was getting warm in that big room. The talk around us was an unsteady drone, and it rose and fell from softness to loudness like the sound of beating wings when the geese were wheeling over a cornfield in late summer.

"No, he talked mostly about Plato. He wanted to talk about what Plato wrote at the end of *The Republic,* when he writes about the myth of Ur."

"You're way over my head, son," O'Dell said.

"Did you not read Plato in school?" I asked.

"I heard about him. Why in hell would a man like Tanner want to hear what some old Greek wrote thousands of years ago?"

"I never asked Tanner about that. But, gradually, when I'd read to him and we'd talk when I came home after my classes, I began to understand why Plato's myth of Ur was so fascinating to him."

"Where did you go to school?" O'Dell asked.

"I studied at Teacher Training Institute."

"Was that the place that used to be called Texas Normal College?"

"Yes, and after I left it was called North Texas Normal, and now they're going to call it North Texas State Normal College. They keep changing its name."

"I know about it," O'Dell said. "So what was it about this Plato that Tanner was so interested in? Can you tell me?"

I laughed, remembering.

"Plato speaks about the daemon," I said. "At first Tanner called it *the diamond* until I showed him the word and then he called it *the demon*."

"The demon? What in hell is that?"

I laughed again. I wasn't used to drinking beer and evidently it loosened more than my tongue. I didn't expect Mr. O'Dell to understand these things about Plato and Tanner, but I was born to be a teacher and if I could teach Tanner, I could certainly enlighten Mr. O'Dell a little.

"Plato said that each of us has a soul and that each soul is given a unique daemon. That daemon shapes us, shapes our lives. We live according to that daemon in our souls."

"Toby, son, you're beginning to sound like a crackpot philosopher."

I laughed once more.

"Well, you wanted to know what Tanner talked about. That's what he talked about. A lot."

"I don't get it, son."

"I think Tanner was looking back at his life and trying to find reasons for what he did, how he lived. Plato said we must live this myth so that we could work out our destinies."

"Destinies?"

"Tanner thought that he had lived according to a plan that was given him before he was born and that he was just following the, ah, instructions, if you will, of his own personal daemon."

"Or demon," O'Dell said.

"That's what Tanner called it. But then he started calling it his *diamond* again. He said he would follow his diamond."

"So, you're saying he didn't feel responsible for any of the things he did in life."

"I'm not saying that at all, Mr. O'Dell. He just believed he was supposed to do all the things he did in life."

"Destiny, you mean."

"I think Tanner believed in destiny, yes. And, he was pretty sure how his destiny was going to wind up."

"How?"

"He never spelled it out, nor spoke of it in so many words. But all the time he stayed with us, he was waiting for something. For someone."

"Who?"

I took in a deep breath as if to clear my mind, to try and bring back into focus those last days when he stayed at our boarding house. Tanner became more restless. He listened to the street noises when he sat on our porch. He watched the kids shooting marbles in the dirt of the lot across the street. He watched the girls playing jacks on their porches and he looked far down both ends of the street, as if he was waiting for someone. Someone who would surely come one day.

"We all got souls," he said to me one day. "I know I got one."

I didn't say anything. This was one of those times when Tanner was going to talk in that low-pitched hypnotic voice of his, that rhythmic rumble that came from his chest like the distant drum of a prairie chicken, or the murmur of thunder so far away you could barely hear it.

"Old Plato knew it, too," Tanner said. "He knew that it was in your breath and that diamond lay sparklin' in the center of it, catchin' the sunlight and then sparkin' it back out when you look real deep into it, like lookin' down into a well and seein' your face way down there in the black water, shinin' back up at you, like your twin brother, or another part of you that was a-lookin' on at what you done or was a-doin' and never sayin' nothin', but lookin' on, ever lookin' on."

I just nodded, wondering what Tanner was trying to say, wondering if he could find the words to explain something that could not be explained.

"I took a man's woman," Tanner said. "Took her from him, 'cause she used to be mine. He's an old man, like me, and I know he's got his own diamond and he's comin' after me one of these days. Him and his whelp."

"What will you do?" I asked.

"I will do what my diamond done give me to do, Toby, boy. And, he'll do what his diamond tells him to do."

244

"Toby," O'Dell said, "you trying to think of something more to tell me about Tanner and his diamond?"

"No, Mr. O'Dell. I was just thinking of something Tanner said on the last day he stayed with us. I knew he was going to leave and he knew he was going to leave. But I didn't know how he knew. And I still don't."

"What did he say, son?"

O'Dell's voice was very soft and it seemed the whole room quieted down while waiting for my answer. It was just a feeling, but there seemed to be a hush in the saloon, like the hush that comes when you're about to blurt out a secret and don't want anyone besides the person you're talking to, to hear it.

"There was a man coming to kill Tanner," I said. "Tanner said his name was Fred Benson. 'I took his woman from him,' Tanner told me. 'And she died. She was an old woman by then, and she had a nearly growed son named Billy Joe. And, he's a-comin' too, 'cause he don't know no better.' "

"And did this Fred Benson come, and his boy?"

"I was sitting in the swing, reading my schoolbooks. I wasn't swinging though. I knew Tanner didn't like the noise of it."

"And what happened?" O'Dell asked.

"An old man and a young boy rode up the street, headed straight for our house. Tanner didn't say anything, but he loosened the pistol in his holster and he watched them coming."

"Go on."

245

I went on, seeing it in my mind as clear as if it was yesterday. The two riders stopped in front of the house. They were both wearing pistols, the old man and the boy, and they walked up close to the porch.

"Tanner, you sonofabtich," Benson said. "I'm going to kill you. For takin' Lurlene from me."

"I didn't take nothin' from you, Fred. Lurlene wasn't yours to take in the first place."

"By God, she was my woman, Tanner. My wife."

"You was married to her, but she was my woman. Always was. I was just takin' her back in, takin' her back to home."

"And you killed her," the boy said.

"No, I didn't kill your ma, son. She died of a heartbreak 'cause you didn't come with her."

The images flashed in my mind, like the faces and numbers on a deck of cards when you flip through them. Benson and the boy went for their pistols. Tanner hardly even moved, but his hand flew to the butt of his pistol like a hawk diving to its prey and his pistol jumped into his hand. He fired twice, so fast, it seemed almost like a single gunshot, and then Benson's pistol went off and his bullet went through a window, missing both me and Tanner. Then Benson and the boy both crumpled, their chests spouting blood for just a minute or two. I dropped my book and stared at the two people Tanner had shot and killed. I knew they were dead.

"That was like seein' myself," Tanner said softly.

"Both of my selves. Me, as a young man, and me as the old man I am now. I reckon our souls knowed each other a long time."

"What did Tanner do after that?" O'Dell asked.

"He walked down the steps and took something from Benson's hand. He reloaded his pistol and shoved it back in its holster. Then he walked over and stood by the young man and he took his hat off. I could see his lips moving, but couldn't hear what he was saying."

O'Dell licked his dry lips and breathed deeply. I heard the clink of glasses and the piano start up again. Chairs scraped on the floor. Someone coughed. A woman at the casket fainted and someone called out for water.

"Tanner walked over and picked up his carpetbag, which sat on the porch, already packed, and said good-bye to me."

"Is that all?" O'Dell asked.

"I saw what it was he took off of Benson's hand. It was a diamond ring. A big diamond."

"He stole Benson's diamond ring?"

"He took it. Then he said to me something that sent shivers up and down my spine. He said it just as he was walking down the steps to go out back and get his horse out of the stable."

"What did he say, Toby? Exactly."

"He said, 'The boy's name is Billy Joe Moody. He was my son. Mine and Lurlene's. That ring I took from Fred was the one I gave Billy Joe when he turned sixteen. That was his diamond and now it's mine."

"And he left?" O'Dell said.

"He looked at the diamond for a long time and held it up close to his face and it sparkled in the sun. And then he left. I never saw him again. I told the constables what happened and I don't know if they went after Tanner or not."

"They did," O'Dell said.

I got up from the table.

"Where you going, Toby."

"I'm going to say good-bye to Tanner. I know he's over there in that casket."

"You mean his corpse."

"Yes, his corpse. But, he's there, too. His soul is."

O'Dell followed me over to the casket.

I looked down at Tanner's corpse, the skin darker than I had known it to be, his face drawn and haggard, a celluloid collar jutting up out of the black frock coat the undertaker had put on him. His hands were folded across his chest.

"There it is," I said to O'Dell. "Tanner's diamond."

"Sure enough," O'Dell said, staring down at the ring on Tanner's shriveled brown finger. The diamond seemed to sparkle even more as I stared at it and it seemed there was a slight smile on Tanner's lips. A trick of the light, perhaps, but I looked up at the ceiling and I thought I could feel Tanner's old soul peering down at me.

"I've got to go," I said to O'Dell.

"Back home? Back to your folks?"

"My ma died last week," I said. "And my pa, he died the day Tanner left our house."

"What?"

"That shot that Benson got off went through the front window. My pa was standing there, staring outside. Benson's bullet hit him in the heart. I didn't know it until after Tanner had left."

"So, Benson killed your pa?"

"His bullet did. Tanner didn't know it. Neither did I, as I said. But Tanner had said something to me a few days before and I just remembered it."

"What's that, Toby?"

"Tanner said I should take good care of my ma and pa, that there would come a day when their souls would go back home. He said they'd be waiting for him."

"Waiting for him?" O'Dell's face was drained of blood as if he had seen a ghost.

"Yes. I think Tanner knew they would both die before he did."

O'Dell swore and I left him there to think about those things I had told him. I don't know if he would ever learn the truth about Tanner Moody, or even enough to write about him. None of us ever would.

But Tanner knew who he was and why he did all the things he had done.

It was all written out a long time ago, before he was even born, and set deep into that diamond of his like a map for his soul to follow in this life and perhaps the next.

Eight

The New York Morning Telegraph, Feb. 11, 1903
The Legend of Tanner Moody
Eighth in a series by Bat Masterson
Exclusive

I have to admit the boy's story shocked me. It isn't often you hear a story about a man killing his own son. I couldn't imagine Moody carrying that around with him those last few years. I wondered if that was the reason for the decline in his health.

O'Dell and the boy separated, went their own ways. O'Dell didn't look too happy with the story he'd gotten. Maybe he didn't understand it. Maybe he wanted to interpret it and couldn't. All I've done here is put it down the way the young man told it. Maybe I'm not doing the right thing journalistically, but you, the reader, can interpret it yourself.

* * *

The next story is an odd one. I warn you, there are inconsistencies with the rest of the stories, but this is a tale we all heard. The story of the piano player ran through us like a chilled breeze, and nobody knew what to believe and what not to believe.

But perhaps you should decide that for yourselves . . .

The Man Who Let the Devil Out

by Kerry Newcomb

On the last day of his death, Jesse Banks roused himself from sleep, images of blood and fire and struggle still clinging to the edge of his mind. *Lie still a moment. Allow the last of the dream to fade into impotence, to a place where, for a little while, it can't hurt you.* He climbed out of bed and stumbled across the room and lit a lamp, then added a scoop of coal to the small iron stove in the corner. He poured water over his head, gasped as the cold droplets found his spine, dripped from his sallow features into the washbasin. He ran a brush through his close-cropped brown hair.

He studied the man framed in the small mirror over the washstand. The face that peered back at him was craggy, older than his age, etched by a past that included any number of failed ventures, a past like a maze: down this corridor the hardscrabble ranch where the water fouled and cattle died; follow that corridor and find the time he wore a badge and backed Tanner Moody and carried justice into places where the seeds of law and order had yet to take root; follow this turn and see a sweet, gentle lass who deserved better than her rough and tumble lover; here now, another turn, another path, find the final grand adventure that cost Jesse Banks his pride and the life of his beloved. Oh God . . . Oh God . . .

Come back. Find your way back. It's only a mirror. And the man, only a shadow of a life once held and lost.

In the bed he had left, Crescensia Bazan stirred, yawned, opened her eyes, stretched like a cat then lay back on the brocaded pillow while she studied the man by the mirror. She patted the warm space where he had slept, nestled against her. She scratched her hip and sighed as she studied the older man. Crescensia considered the piano player handsome, but in a broken sort of way. Beneath his lean and craggy frame, she sensed his damaged soul. But what attracted her to him was his kindness, toward her and those like her. He asked for nothing, expected nothing, and yet, she was certain Jesse cared for her, as much anyone could care for another in Hell's Half Acre. And he was gentle, a rare quality these days.

Jesse gasped as a rivulet of water snaked down his bony torso, tickled his spine and bled into the waistband of his flannel long johns. He closed his eyes, waited, opened them again. No change. Everything was the same as it had been the day before and the day before that. A mind-numbing progression broken by momentary lust, release, remorse.

The faded damask curtains that framed the one window overlooking Calhoun Street had been drawn against the setting sun. No matter. The sight of billowing storm clouds crowding the bitter hues of a February sunset were lost on him. His hours were a preordained ritual, a structured half-life fueled by a destructive mixture of troubled dreams and cork barrel whiskey, bitter as rattlesnake poison and damn near as lethal.

Crescensia Bazan rolled onto her side, her coppery colored hide, all dusky and warm from sleep, the soft and willing flesh of her comforting bosom, concealed by a fold of patchwork quilt and the faded embroidery of her cotton gown. "Did I hear thunder?"

"Looks like rain," Jesse said. Thunder in February was an unusual event. Then again, this was Texas.

She yawned and sighed, glanced at Banks's gold pocket watch, the one with the inscription, hoping to discover its intricate puzzle of springs and tiny wheels in motion at last, but of course, the timepiece had long since frozen, the shorter hand edging past eleven and the longer caught between the three and the four. Time had stopped at eleven seventeen, to be precise, when a 7mm bullet from a Spanish Mauser struck the timepiece dead center, then glanced off, imbedding itself in Jesse Bank's side, fracturing a rib.

Crescensia squinted and peering at the inscription, proudly read it aloud. "To Captain Jesse Banks, Fort Worth Volunteers . . . with gratitude, Colonel Tanner Moody."

Jesse Banks pulled on his worn woolen trousers and a faded shirt that Crescensia had mended, then a black vest, and donned his one and only frock coat, which was threadbare but serviceable. He returned to the bedside and distracted Crescensia with one hand while with the other he collected the watch and tucked it away in his vest pocket. His fingers were still nimble, could pluck an unsuspecting tinhorn clean as a whistle, take wallet or money pouch or jewelry and never ruffle a coat flap.

"I know what it says." Banks did not bother to explain how the timepiece had saved his life one hot, murderous, pandemonium-filled morning in Cuba, on the slopes of Kettle Hill.

The forty-three-year-old piano player had just revisited that murderous incline in his tortured sleep, glimpsed the indistinguishable brown features of the Spanish regulars on that first of July morning back in '98, heard the wild hurrahs of his comrades at arms, heard himself exhort the company of Volunteers to hurl themselves forward onto the battlements of the Spanish defenders.

His dreams had replayed the carnage. One moment he had been as full of piss and vinegar as any of his *compadres*, and then, staring through the heat and haze at the hilltop lined with guns, the clouds of powdersmoke and dust parted, permitting him a glimpse of what waited for him at the top of Kettle Hill.

Death.

An end of him.

The noise was terrible. Explosions. Rattle of weapon fire, like the crack of splintered bones. Then a thunderous roar. And there above him on the ridge, the Reaper awaited, clothed in the dust-caked tunic of a Spanish marksman.

Bullets whined about him; one of the volunteers fell, choking blood. Jesse could not move. His legs had taken root. His gut went hollow, mouth dry, breath shallow in his throat. His courage failed. Blind, muscle-numbing fear engulfed him. No power on earth was going to propel him up into those guns.

He was no coward. My God, think of all the times he had backed Tanner Moody, faced down countless miscreants and highbinders. But this was different. This promised to be a wholesale slaughter on the slopes. And he had a wife waiting for him, a future. And suddenly "high adventure" seemed far less important.

Crescensia Bazan saw the man standing before her shudder as he relived the impact of a Spanish slug, and experienced anew the flash of white hot pain. He was watching himself spin, topple, lose his place in history as the others passed him by, charged into glory, to rise victorious and drive the Spaniards from the hilltop. Rough Riders, men like Tanner Moody and the Fort Worth Volunteers, had stormed that summit, survived the battle, and carried the day.

But Jesse Banks's legacy was a busted watch, a fractured rib, a near mortal wound, and a bout of malaria that further broke his health while he recuperated aboard a hospital ship. At war's end, Colonel Tanner Moody brought his company home to Texas, the living and the dead, and those men like Jesse Banks, ravaged by illness and beset by memories they would carry to their graves.

Home . . . Jesse could still see Tanner Moody—a towering, ashen-haired man in a long gray duster, whose stern features looked as if they'd been chipped from stone by an angry sculptor with a vendetta against marble, so seamed and weathered was that face. The two men were standing by a grave marker . . .

ELIZABETH MARIE BANKS
BORN? DIED—MAY 17, 1898
MAY SHE REST IN PEACE

"If you'd told me your wife was pregnant, I would have never accepted you into the Volunteers, Jesse."

"Lizzie didn't tell me. She knew what it meant for me to join the lads, to be part of the adventure of it, so she kept her condition to herself. But I knew something was on her mind. Maybe I even suspected, but I never came out and asked her. I don't think I wanted to know for sure. That's a hell of a thing for a man to do, leave his wife to die in childbirth. Leave her to be buried by strangers. Speaks well for me, eh, Colonel? Well doesn't it . . . ?"

"Senor Tanner is dead." Crescensia wasn't certain how much Jesse had been drinking or how well his memory served him. Moody's passing had left a mark on the city. Tales of his exploits filled the local papers. Word had spread across the state and folks had been drifting in to Fort Worth to pay their respects to a man and a legend.

"I know that too."

"He was your *companero*?"

"A lifetime ago. More like a teacher, I suppose, looking back on it. I was a headstrong young pup when our trails crossed. Didn't have a father I could call by name. So Tanner Moody fit the bill. For a while I thought the sun rose and set in him. But our trails parted. After . . . Cuba."

"But tonight you will go to the White Elephant, to honor him? And you will play the sad songs on the piano?"

"It's a wake," Jesse explained. "And yes, I will play. But not all my songs are sad. Just the Irish ones." Playing piano and picking pockets both required nimble fingers and were the two things Banks could still do tolerably well. Drink and dissolution had yet to rob him of these talents.

"I do not understand. Why did you not go to Senor Tanner when he was sick?"

"Friendships are like a field. Sometimes a drought hits, and everything sort of just dries up for a spell. But a man's dying has a way of patching over the cracks in the earth."

Crescensia shrugged.

She had always been fascinated by the watch with the shattered case, intrigued by things people treasured. Sometimes the men who paid for a poke at her, left the young woman a trinket with their crumpled bills. That made her feel special, that she meant more to them than the other whores. "One day you said you would tell me why you keep a watch that doesn't work," she reminded him.

Crescensia pretended to make a grab for the watch and snatch it from his vest pocket. With far more gallantry than a prostitute was ever accorded in Hell's Half Acre, Jesse Banks caught her hand and tenderly kissed her knuckles and nodded.

"What do you mean, it doesn't work? I'll have you know, this old bullet-riddled relic still can tell the correct time, twice a day." He grinned. "And so can I."

Crescensia Bazan playfully scowled—it took her a moment to catch the joke—and then she laughed softly, brushed her long black hair back from her youthful features and leaned forward, allowing the quilt to fall away from her ripe bosom. She was a quarter of a century younger than him. But that didn't matter. Her profession would age her soon enough. For now, her eyes still held the glow of youth. But every year the warmth dimmed. It would be gone in another couple of seasons on her back, that sweet gaze and fragrant flesh were destined to become cold and impenetrable. Jesse briefly considered marrying her. And then what? The two would make a life for themselves, the broken-down piano player and the prostitute? Anyway. He'd already been married. And yet she mattered to him. Being concerned for her, in a way, kept him sane and helped him make it through the night.

"Don't work tonight," he said. All sorts of miscreants would be prowling the streets tonight, they had been drifting into town, drawn to North Texas by the death of a legend. "I'll tell the Irishman you are not well. I won't be gone long. And then we can be together."

"Senor Jesse, we have *been* together."

"I mean . . . well . . . in another way. Just together."

She swung her legs over the side of the bed, straightened the cotton gown she wore for him—simple, unprovocative, not like what her customers demanded of her when they climbed the stairs to her room, hungry for her body, eager to have her, to claw at her in the dim light, to demand she moan endearments while they spent themselves in sweaty excess beneath the sad watchful face of Our Lady of Guadalupe on the dresser.

"I like you Senor Jesse. Because you see . . . more than who . . . or what I am. Because when you look at me, I feel like it was before I knew of men. But I also know what I must do to survive."

She picked up a bottle of tequila from the floor and lifted it to the lamplight, sighed with disappointment to find it empty. Crescensia had a powerful thirst gnawing at the pit of her belly. It would have to be appeased.

"Go now. Play for your friend, Mister Tanner Moody." She blessed herself, making the sign of the cross. "And may he hear you in heaven."

Jesse nodded. People like Crescensia had no illusions and somehow had learned to handle it. That was

Hell's Half Acre, a place of carnal fantasies and dreams, but a place without hope.

Banks took care to conceal his few possessions in a battered carpetbag, then slid it beneath her bed. The last of his things, a letter from his wife, fell from a leather packet that had come untied. Jesse hesitated, teased himself, pretended maybe he was going to open it and read the sentiments for the first time. But in truth, he had already memorized the words.

My Dearest Jesse—There is no easy way to tell you this, and not have some small part of you resent me for not telling you before you left. But you so wanted to go to your splendid little war, to have your adventure, that I could not hold you back. Not even for our son—yes, I am certain it will be a son. Don't ask me how. A woman sometimes knows these things. Yes, my dearest, you will be a father before the year is out. So you see, now you must come back safe and whole, I will not have it otherwise. And never fear. I am well. Rosarita comes over from Mister Moody's house to check in on me everyday. So you see, I am having my own adventure as well as you. God bring us together soon. And forgive me for not telling you sooner. Have your adventure, Jesse Banks. Because I will never let you go again.

"My splendid little war," Jesse muttered to himself. He glanced up as if expecting to find Tanner Moody seated across from him, admonishing him to stiffen his backbone. He knew what Tanner would say: *If a man is broken, it's because he's brittle. Ride it out, Jesse. Ride it out and let it go.*

Banks shivered, felt a chill pass through him. "You didn't love her like I did, Moody. You didn't need her . . ." Then he straightened and wiped a forearm across his face, embarrassed that he had spoken aloud.

Crescensia heard him, but pretended not to notice. The woman watched Banks tenderly fold the letter and tuck it inside his frock coat. If her heart had not already been broken long ago, perhaps that simple gesture on his part would have finished the job.

"I'll leave, then," Jesse said to her. "But do this for me, stay away from the likes of the Tolan brothers. Hec and Orville are on a losing streak and looking for trouble. And keep clear of El Muerte. The madness is on him again. I heard he knifed a man, left him dying down by the bend of the Trinity, right there below the courthouse, split belly to throat."

"And you did nothing?"

"None of my business, not any more. Hell, not even the law will touch him, as long as he stays in the Half Acre. Proper folks figure we get what we deserve."

"Perhaps we do," the prostitute added, with a shrug.

"Mind my word, senorita. You have no business with that peyote eater. To hell with what Iron Mike says."

"I am not afraid of El Muerte. Beneath the sheets all men are the same."

"Don't be a fool."

"Fool?" Crescensia glanced about the room as if berating an imaginary audience. "Listen to him talk.

262

Enough. Now go before I regret that I like you, Jesse Banks."

A man who is lost has to want to be found. It is the same with a woman. There was nothing more to be said. And Crescensia was right. Who was Jesse Banks to spout platitudes and warnings? He shrugged, opened the door and stepped into the hall, leaving the woman to her satins and bows and lace, the trappings of her "work" clothes.

As rain mixed with pea-sized hail began to patter on the rooftop, Banks made his way down the gas-lit corridor, the air thick with the smell of cheap perfumes, of whiskey and opium, sweat stink and spilled drink. A door opened at the far end of the hall and another of the "soiled doves" stepped out of a room that overlooked the alley out back. Frenchie was a buxom, brassy woman with a ready smile and a coarse laugh who had seen it all and done it all and approached every night's work with forced enthusiasm. Her cheeks were heavily rouged, her features powdered, a black beauty mark applied to her cheek. Her blond hair was pinned up in layered curls. She wore a slim long-waisted dress of pale green satin with a layer of sea green taffeta ruffles from her knees to the floor.

"*Bonsoir,* Mister Banks." A wave of heavy perfume carried to him as she approached and slipped her arm through his. She leaned into Jesse and kissed him on the lips. "What does your child whore do that I cannot do better?" She tasted of sherry, which masked the

263

bitterness of the laudanum she was known to consume. Banks extricated himself from her grasp. He was in no mood to be taunted, especially by an addict.

"After you, Frenchie," he said with a gesture to the stairway. The whore studied him with her hard eyes. She smiled, gave him a wink, glanced over his shoulder at the door to Crescensia's room.

"Tell your little tart to mind her manners tonight." She wagged a finger in his face. "She is no better than the rest of us. The sooner she learns that, the better for us all." The woman almost lost her balance, gripped the rail, and then, laughing, made her way downstairs.

The narrow steps were always a daunting prospect, especially when the world was already slightly skewed. But with a hand firmly clasping the rail, Jesse left the L-shaped hallway and managed to follow Frenchie, descending like some two-bit Orpheus into the smoke and the clamor of the bawdy house below.

Banks was greeted by a chorus of drunken, albeit good-natured patrons, ranch hands and feedlot workers, down-on-their-luck drovers with a few spare coins to lose, lonely men eager for a few moments of lust, an escape from a hard day's work. They came to Hell's Half Acre to squander the contents of their meager purses on gambling and quarreling, on cheap drink and willing flesh.

Come one come all. Hell, yes! Banks licked his lips and decided to play them at least one tune while he had his usual breakfast. Break a couple of eggs into a shot glass, fill it with a measure of rye whisky, slug it down, and hang on to the piano bench.

He waved to a few of the more familiar revelers, his mind a blank for names. Business was good despite the wintry wind and the unusual storm scouring the streets of the city. El Matadero was a sanctuary for the nameless. Downstairs, the cantina was no more than a broad, open room with heavy velvet curtains drawn across the windows, a room where painted women sashayed about in revealing attire, paraded their "wares" past a long wide bar, entertained, cajoled the patrons, carried on as if every night were a party. An irregular selection of round and rectangular tables and ill-matched chairs littered the room, left for the gamblers and highbinders to gather around. El Matadero was a temple of vices, with lurid lithographs adorning the walls above a pair of curiously worn high-backed couches. The bawdy house was open to one and all. No denizen of the street was ever turned away as long as there was folding money in his pockets.

Two wood-burning stoves at either end of the room tempered the north wind that moaned through the alleys and streets and sent its wintry tendrils exploding into the room every time the front door swung ajar. A chorus of curses erupted whenever someone entered the room from Calhoun Street.

Thankfully, the piano was located near the stove at the rear of the cantina, across from the unadorned bar behind which El Matadero's glum-looking proprietor, Iron Mike Kilkenny, glared at Banks disapprovingly and took out his pocket watch from beneath his apron to make a show of "just how tardy" the musician was.

Still scowling, Iron Mike brought over Banks's

breakfast in a double shot glass, left it on the piano, near the yellowed ivory keys. It was obvious the Irishman resented the fact that his piano player intended to spend part of the evening at the White Elephant Saloon just south of the vice district. But tonight Kilkenny didn't have the stomach to make too much of a fuss. The Irishman was obviously nervous, and with good reason.

"Well then, have your drink, Banks. But mark this paddy's words, you might want to tarry here a while longer. We've a most unwanted guest, tonight. I hope you've told your whore to be on her best behavior." Kilkenny straightened. He wiped a stained cloth across his hairless skull. "We've trouble about." He nodded toward the rear of the saloon.

A chill crept the length of Banks's spine as the back door that led off to the privy in the alley creaked open and an all too familiar figure lurched out of the blackness into the amber glare of the cantina. No one knew him by any other name except El Muerte. He was a mix breed, part Mexican, maybe some black Irish and Apache thrown into the bloodline; that morbid name, *the Death,* had been hung on him more as a warning to the wise then some misguided tribute.

El Muerte hesitated, wavering, unsteady on his feet. Then he found his balance and swaggered across the room to snap an order in Kilkenny's direction. He stood with his back to the bar as if surveying his domain while Iron Mike set down an unopened bottle of tequila and gave the breed a warm and generous welcome.

El Muerte fished a crumpled bill out of his pocket

and tossed it back toward the proprietor without bothering to glance around at the man. One of the prostitutes, a horse-faced old girl on the downside of her best years, hurried to his side, struck a match and lit the cigarillo that dangled from the corner of his mouth. Smoke trailed from the glowing tip like the ghost of a rattlesnake uncoiling toward the soot-stained ceiling overhead. El Muerte muttered an aside that sent the harlot in retreat. He grinned at Frenchie who waited for an invite but did not wave her over to him.

The breed surveyed the interior of the bawdy house as a lion examines his domain. El Muerte was average in height, barrel-chested, thick-necked, with a long powerful reach. His glossy black hair, partly concealed by a bowler hat, spilled to his shoulders. His eyes were like pools of black oil floating on the surface of some stagnant pool. The thick mustache that scrawled across his upper lip trailed down to his jawbone. He was dressed in a faded blue woolen shirt, his brown canvas Levi's were tucked into mud-spattered boar hide boots. Moisture dripped from the hem of his full-length canvas duster and puddled on the wood floor underfoot.

The breed had been handsome once, but years ago, down in Old San Antone, a crib girl, protesting his rough advances, had raked his right cheek with her long fingernails and left three puckered rows of scar tissue across his cheek, below his left eye. It was said that afterward, the unfortunate prostitute had come to a bad end.

The revelers might jostle one another, but they gave

El Muerte a wide berth, fearing to crowd a man of volatile character. From his position, the breed's presence dominated the room. He liked the effect he was having, a benign if somewhat contemptuous smile lit his face, contrasting with the bleak promise of his eyes.

Suddenly his gaze settled upon Jesse Banks. El Muerte tucked a thumb in the wide leather belt circling his waist, then turned and muttered a few words to one of the men standing alongside him—words to the effect that his bottle of tequila was not to be touched—then shoved clear of the bar. He shambled across the room toward the piano player.

Banks suddenly felt nauseated. Men like El Muerte, who were dangerous and unpredictable as nitro, made his ass knit barbed wire. Jesse wished he had forgone "breakfast," continued straight out the front door and made his way across Hell's Half Acre to the wake at the White Elephant Saloon. El Muerte was feeling his oats now, with the likes of Tanner Moody gone under. Bullies grow bold when brave men die.

Banks gulped his breakfast; the whiskey burned a path to his belly. He hunched over the keys for a moment, then proceeded to play a lively reel. His fingers nimbly coaxed a merry tune from the sounding board despite the fact that the instrument, like the player, was "out of tune." The melody carried to the street, through the closed doors and shuttered windows. It merged with the lonely keening wind and rain that scoured the gambling dens, saloons, crib houses and bordellos from Ninth to Front Street and from Jones to Throckmorton. The nether world of Hell's Half Acre was a no man's land crisscrossed by sinister looking alleys where life was cheap, vice was easy and the night belonged to the quick and the dead.

"Play a *tarantos, amigo,*" said El Muerte, his lips pulled back in a feral grin as he batted Jesse's hands away from the keyboard, interrupting the reel. He glared around at the painted women who were already beginning to work the room for Iron Mike. The half-breed spied Crescensia on the stairway, dressed in crinoline and lace bustier and button shoes. He gestured toward the young woman as she descended into the cantina like a carnal gift from pagan gods.

El Muerte leaned in toward the piano player, so as to keep his voice menacingly soft. "No. Play a *villancico*. And I will dance with your *puta,* eh?"

Jesse could smell the liquor on the man's breath. When the breed leaned forward, the folds of his duster parted to reveal the grip of the double action Colt jutting from a worn leather holster worn high on his waist. "Then I take her upstairs. What do you say to that?"

"I say you will do as you please," Jesse replied. "And that you have mistaken me for one who gives a damn."

"As I please!" El Muerte grinned, oblivious to Banks's aside. The breed raised his voice so that it topped the rest of the noise in the room. "As . . . I . . . please . . . !"

Glancing past El Muerte, Jesse noticed Crescensia

269

approach the unopened bottle of tequila El Muerte had left on the bar. Ignoring Iron Mike's protest, she uncorked the bottle and tilted it to her lips and gulped twice, then set the bottle down, halfheartedly replacing the cork. She met Jesse's stare as the piano player shook his head "no" in an effort to warn her away.

Instead, she laughed and began to cajole the other men at the bar, her gaze full of invitation, her lithe frame and generous bosom fueling their fantasies. She was a flirt, a coquette, enticing and yet somehow innocent, convinced her youth and beauty would protect her. Crescensia stroked her luxuriant hair that she had gathered back from her features and tied with a chartreuse ribbon in a style that only accentuated her high cheekbones and prominent nose. Her eyes twinkled in the gaslight. Her Yaqui heritage, the flared nostrils and coppery cast of her features, could not be disguised by her rouge and perfume and ribbons.

El Muerte sauntered back toward the prostitute, who pretended to ignore him as he approached. She kept her back turned toward him. He grabbed her by the arm and spun her around and whispered in her ear. Crescensia laughed in his face and told him he was too ugly for her. However, if she could see the color of his gold . . . maybe . . .

The breed noticed the slanted position of the cork capping his tequila. He flicked it off with a snap of his finger. "What is this? Who has let the devil out?" El Muerte glared at Iron Mike who paled, retreated. He stared malevolently at the men who stood bellied up to the mahogany bar.

Crescensia picked up the cork and ran her pink tongue along the smaller end. "*Aqui ella está.* Here she is. I am the one who let the devil out. What do you say to that?"

El Muerte laughed.

She laughed.

Then he shot her.

The explosion startled everyone in the room. A whore's muffled scream . . . men frozen in place, Jesse Banks staring in disbelief, everyone startled by the breed's sudden savage response. One moment Crescensia had been standing with the cork in her slender hand, playful, taunting. Then El Muerte had reached inside his coat and his hand reappeared with the double action Colt. The woman collapsed like a marionette whose strings had been cut, she slumped against the bar, blood spurting from her throat. She clutched at the wound, eyes wide with disbelief as she slid to a sitting position, the weight of her head tilted to the side, dragging her torso over until her forehead rapped the hard floor.

"Someone take the garbage to the alley," El Muerte growled.

He glanced around at the faces, the stillness hanging heavy, overpowering. He sensed their fear. No one in the cantina was gonna do a damn thing. He turned and glared at Jesse Banks. The piano player knew if he made the wrong move, the breed might shoot him down like a dog. Jesse focused on the keyboard. His fingers found the appropriate notes, the sharps and flats responded to his touch. Somehow he coaxed a melody from the sounding board. But his hands felt numb and he could not hear the tune, no matter how hard he played. Only the sound of the gunshot roaring in his ears and the thud of her head striking the floor.

El Muerte took his time. He ambled across the room, stood staring for a moment at a couple of stove-up drovers who had been in the process of courting the amply endowed Miss Frenchie. The harlot started to shrink back from the breed, then took a second glance at the body on the floor and reconsidered. The drovers retreated out of harm's way as El Muerte brushed them aside and reached for the woman who hurried into his arms, laughing, muttering coarse asides in his ear. He grabbed another bottle, slapped Frenchie's ample derriere, and followed her up the stairway. The killer vanished from sight like a bad dream, leaving in his wake a chill to rival the silver rain, the rumbling night sky.

One by one the patrons began to gather around the fallen woman. Jesse rose from the piano, hands trembling, expressionless. He walked across the room, stood over Crescensia's body as Iron Mike knelt by the woman and touched her wrist, feeling for a pulse.

"She's dead." Iron Mike stood and nodded to a couple of the men standing nearby. "What's done is done. It was her own doing. I don't want any trouble. Help me take her out to the lot across the alley. There's a bottle of 'Who hit John' for any man who helps."

He looked at Banks. It seemed they were all looking

at Jesse, who had to steady himself against the edge of the bar. *She looks so small, so childlike. So broken. . . . What do they want of me? She was not my woman. Damn them all.* Banks turned, and digging his hands into his coat pockets, preceded Iron Mike and his cronies through the back door. Once in the alley, and momentarily safe from prying eyes, he doubled over and retched against a weathered wood fence.

The downpour had eased to an icy drizzle, moisture worked its way down his collar. He shivered. He stood there listening to the keening wind. It sounded like a lost soul, like a poor fool's soul. *Oh God, oh God. For nothing.* He squeezed the bridge of his nose, rubbed his eyes as if to erase the imprint her death had left there.

The foolish girl. What had she been thinking? Why, he asked himself. Why? She had died for nothing. And that's exactly what he had done for her. Nothing.

The back door opened and he watched as the drovers, bathed in the yellow glare from within, carried their lifeless burden out into the alley, crawled through a break in the fence and hauled her out into a lot overgrown with weeds. Iron Mike appeared in the doorway and waved the two men back. They lost no time in scurrying back through the fence. One paused to look in Jesse's direction then hurried inside, returning with his friend to claim his whiskey.

Well, what the hell. She was just a whore.

"Son of a bitch!" Jesse muttered aloud, his voice hoarse, tortured. A stray mongrel began to bark for-

273

lornly. Above him, a window opened. El Muerte's voice carried from the darkened interior of Frenchie's bedroom. The breed cursed whoever was making all the noise. Within the room, Frenchie could be heard entreating the brute to return to her bed and finish what he had started. El Muerte, unable to identify the figure below, brayed "Go to Hell" and slammed the window shut.

Thunder rumbled across lowering black sky. A board creaked, something scurried out of the shadows and as quickly vanished. A sudden shriek, then something died.

"I'm already there," Banks grimly muttered.

He didn't know how long he walked. But she haunted him all the way, past shuttered windows, lamplight filtering into the street, he heard her laugh, glanced up in alarm as a carriage hurried past. Not her, of course—the horse and rider sped on, heads lowered against the elements. He walked as one benumbed by grief, the same pace that had carried him from his wife's grave, out of the living world, out of daylight and into Hell's Half Acre. The foolish girl, the poor foolish girl.

What was that? He turned, peered along the boardwalk, uncertain of his direction, head low to the wind, shoulders hunched. He was standing at the corner of Eleventh Street. Or was this Tenth? And was this the Waco Tap or the King's Ransom, both brothels and as indistinguishable from each other as El Matadero. He paused at the corner, underneath a street lamp that cast a feeble pool of light and turned the vaporous mist into a golden tinted shroud. He could not bear the light and took off for the alley, seeking the embrace of the darkness, hoping to conceal his shame. A cat raced across his path. He thought he heard the crunch of boot heels behind him and turned back the way he had come. And for a fleeting second he thought he saw a tall, imposing silhouette of a man watching him from the street.

Jesse gasped with recognition and wiped the moisture from his eyes to clear his vision. "Tanner?" No it couldn't be. He shrank back and tripped over a pair of outstretched legs. A drunken old timer, nestled against a rain barrel to block the wind's bite, howled, startled awake.

"Don't hurt me, lads, Old Cutter ain't got nothing but the clothes on his back and I'm sharing them with the crawlin' critters." A face like wrinkled parchment eased out of the shadows. Jesse hurried off without bothering the old one. But when he looked over his shoulder, the face had changed, became *his* face.

"No!" Jesse charged back toward the man by the rain barrel who held up his reed-thin limbs to ward off a blow. Jesse halted in his tracks and stared at the poor soul, who was Old Cutter and no one else.

Jesse waved for him to be quiet. "Do you hear that?"

The old man listened. "What?"

Tick . . . tick . . . tick . . .

"The clock, the watch."

"Son, if'n I had a watch I'd have traded it for a room out of this goddamn rain."

Jesse grabbed the watch from his pocket. No, it couldn't be. He couldn't see in the dark. Got to find the light. Find the light. He stumbled off toward the center of town.

"Sonny, you're as crazy as me, maybe crazier, cause I got sense to hole up," the old man called out.

An icy gust sprang up, clattering a pair of loose shutters.

Jesse . . .

Banks whirled about, breath labored now. It was her voice, calling him.

Jesse . . .

He told himself it was only the storm playing tricks on him, calling in her voice. He glanced over his shoulder and spied movement. The alley lengthened, became a long black tunnel, yawning wide. He turned and ran full out. Slipping, sliding, he rounded another corner and darted across the street. A carriage carrying its driver home for the evening almost ran him down. The driver cursed him, the horse pawed the air and came within inches of trampling him under its iron-shod hooves. Jesse careened past and darted off through the coming storm, hounded by voices and the ghosts of his guilt.

Then he was standing in front of the White Elephant Saloon, a big, bold, brassy-looking place, crowded with the friends and associates of Tanner Moody. There was a rather stiff photograph of the man himself, propped on an easel under the roof of the porch. Tanner Moody was standing against a painted backdrop that featured a pastoral scene of prairie and wildflowers and sagebrush. The scenery was fabricated. But the man in the image was real, was in the twilight of his years, still tall and straight, with an intensity of purpose and dignity of bearing. His silver hair was long and leonine in appearance. He wore the long frock coat he always favored, brocaded vest and stiff collar shirt. The thumb of his right hand was hooked in the gun belt circling his waist. His revolver, a Smith and Wesson .44 was holstered over his left side, the gun butt forward in the cross draw Moody always favored. He was no quick-draw artist but whatever he aimed at, he hit.

Jesse stood there in the street in front of the saloon, summoning the courage to enter the wake. He glanced back the way he had come. No one was chasing him now. It was all illusion, a momentary madness, none of it was real, he told himself. He closed his eyes and saw Crescensia collapse to the floor and slide over on her side, heard her skull slap the wood. Jesse stared down at his hands held palm upward. No more. He was tired of running, of losing, tired of the endless night.

A raucous chorus of cheers and jeers sounded from within. The sound of life drew him. The piano player gingerly climbed the steps, stared at the billboard someone had placed on a makeshift easel alongside the photograph of Moody.

The Galveston Gravedigger will take on all
comers.
Special Prize to the Cowtown son who can
emerge victorious:
A Smith and Wesson single action .44 pocket
pistol,
One of a Kind, like the man who owned it.
Offered from the estate of Tanner Moody
In whose honor and memory we conduct these
festivities.
Pay your money, take your chances.
Proceeds go to Sisters of Charity Orphanage.

No one could ever say the friends of Tanner Moody
didn't know how to give the local icon and legendary
figure a proper send-off. The wake had started at sunset and promised to carry through to morning with
plenty of spirits, music, dancing, laughter and tall
tales. And a proper display of fisticuffs. Tanner would
have approved.

Banks continued into the room. The sounds washed
over him, the volume nearly lifted him off his feet and
sent him staggering out toward the street. The White
Elephant was twice the size of Iron Mike's cantina
and the people within were an eclectic mix of Fort
Worth's finest families, vaqueros, shopkeepers, gamblers, lawmen, even a scattering of military officers.
Some of the faces Jesse instantly recognized, remembering them from the expedition to Cuba. Thankfully,
no one seemed to notice him standing near the front
door. Attention was centered on the makeshift arena

that had been constructed in the center of saloon.

Two men battled one another within the ropes. One of the combatants Banks recognized as Emil Sharene, the best blacksmith in the city and the owner of a stable and a feed lot. Emil, a heavyset, bear of a man, was standing toe to toe, exchanging blows with a slender, hammer-handed foe who could only be the Galveston Gravedigger, a man of seemingly boundless energy whose fists were methodically battering Emil into submission, much to the chagrin of the revelers. Sooner or later one of them would probably land a lucky punch and the Galveston Gravedigger would topple like a felled oak. A man could only take so much punishment.

"Jesse Banks, *Madre de Dios,* you are a sight. You look like a ghost," someone remarked at Jesse's elbow. "One that doesn't have sense to come in out of the rain to do his haunting."

Jesse turned to find a rakishly handsome figure from his past, standing at his side. The years had been good to Sixto Heredia. Once Moody's *segundo* and ranch foreman, Heredia had married a widow from Coahuila and invested his wife's dowry in real estate. He now owned a couple of city blocks in the prosperous business district on the south side of town as well as a horse ranch south of the border.

Heredia removed his Stetson and brushed a hand through his black hair that was thinning on top, silver at the temples. His clothes were carefully tailored, he smelled of lilac water and talc, his cheeks were smooth shaven from a recent visit to the barber. Sixto Heredia had sailed to Cuba with the Fort Worth Company of Volunteers, he had followed Moody to the top of Kettle Hill, charged straight into a hail of lead and emerged unscathed.

"I wondered if you'd come. Permit me to buy you a drink, amigo?"

He gestured toward the elaborate walnut bar, a polished wall of beauty, stained the color of black cherry and sporting a shiny brass boot rail along the base. The White Elephant had traded in its notoriety and become the kind of place where respectable men gambled and enjoyed the company of elegant ladies, where fine cigars were smoked and sporting events might be held within the great room or out back during the spring and summer months.

"Where is he?"

Heredia had taken a half step toward the bar, assuming Jesse would accept his offer. He did not look the sort of man to refuse a free drink. It took him a few moments to realize what Banks had asked. "Come see the lads. Several of the Volunteer Company are here; Rafe Garner, Digger Marlow, and you remember old Stack Stubblefield. He's come all the way from Denver." He raised his coat flap and patted the watch chain that was similar to Jesse's. "We were all *companeros* once."

"Where is *he*?"

Heredia frowned, thought a moment, then nodded, understanding. He gestured to a side room. "Tanner never missed a fiesta. We are here to celebrate life and to honor his passing." He gestured toward a side room that was reserved for high stakes gamblers who preferred a private game amongst their peers. "We will visit him together, *si*?"

"Alone," Banks said, catching Heredia by the sleeve of his expensive coat. He was staring at the open doorway. "Please. I'd like to see Tanner, alone."

Heredia shrugged. "As you wish, amigo. But afterward, it is time you joined your friends among the living." He clapped Banks on the shoulder, inspected Banks's appearance for a moment, smiled reassuringly, sadly, and repeated. "It is time."

Jesse Banks entered the room. It was dimly lit, a pair of gaslights flickered from the walls. Shadows danced upon the chromolithographs, played upon images of buxom maidens tending their gardens, flowers rampant. The room smelled of aged leather and finely polished wood—and sipping whiskey, smooth as mother's milk. Jesse's hand began to tremble as an old thirst started gnawing at his vitals. He tried to will it away, licked his lips, continued across the room. The thirst might have overwhelmed him had he not heard the ticking of the clock. He glanced around the room. It was devoid of furnishings save for an ornately carved mahogany table on which the coffin had been placed.

Tick . . . tick . . . tick . . .

The night wind moaned and rattled the window. Thunder rumbled. Another downpour was at hand. The blood in his veins turned cold. Banks gingerly approached the coffin. The ticking sound increased in volume. Slowly, he reached out, placed his trembling hand upon the wooden lid. Then drew back as if burned. He decided to ignore the sound. He lifted his gaze to the display that had been set up against the outside wall, below the window that overlooked the alley. Banks heard the rumble of far-off thunder, low and ominous as a growl. He shivered and crossed the room and quickly took stock of the memorabilia, the mementos of a man's life. Favorite rifles arranged in a rack, a framed certificate of appreciation signed by none other than Theodore Roosevelt. He recognized the military uniform, a favorite pair of spurs, a worn leather gun belt with Moody's revolver, a Smith and Wesson .44, looking shiny and freshly oiled, snug in its holster.

Someone had built a framed display box that contained several badges from Tanner Moody's career as a lawman. There on the purple felt were remembrances from towns like El Paso and Fort Worth, the tin star issued by the Texas Rangers, and oddly enough, a city marshall's badge from Durango and another from as far north as Miles City, Montana.

A braided lariat was coiled about the silver pommel of a hand-tooled saddle that had been Moody's pride and joy. Next to the saddle were a pair of branding irons with the T-Cross brand. There was more, but Jesse's gaze returned to the Smith and Wesson .44. He checked the door, listened to the festivities, expecting someone to enter the room at any moment and intrude on his privacy.

Take it.

He jumped, startled. Lightning flashed, and for a moment, reflected in the window, he saw a figure standing behind him. It was Tanner Moody, not old, but as Jesse remembered him from the past: forceful, vigorous, undimmed by age, eyes like an old curly wolf. Jesse gasped and whirled about.

He was alone in the room, with the coffin, with his memories. He heard the ticking of a watch, louder now, almost deafening. His head felt as if it were about to split open. Banks covered his ears with his hands.

"Stop!" he managed.

You know what you have to do. It was Moody's voice, unmistakable, reverberating in his skull.

"You're dead," he groaned. The wind rattled a window. He glanced up, thought he saw a figure standing in the far corner of the room. A coat hanging from a rack? Then why did it seem to move? No power on earth would drag him closer to investigate.

Tick . . . tick . . . tick . . .

He rubbed his forehead, tried to command the sound to cease.

That's why you came. So take it.

Jesse ran to the coffin and slammed his fist against the lid. "Damn you, Tanner. Leave me alone. What do you want of me?"

What you want of yourself. To stand . . .

The ticking . . . Jesse grabbed the watch from his vest. His eyes widened, his blood went cold, it was as

283

if the night wind had found him, and sliced through his chest to clutch his heart. The hour and minute hands were in motion, despite the shattered case. It was impossible. And yet the proof was in his hand, advancing toward midnight.

Follow me up the hill, Jesse. Follow me.

Banks shook his head. His strength left him, he slumped into a nearby chair, buried his face in his hands and began to sob. He wept for his wife, long dead, for the child he would never hold, for the moment when courage failed him at Kettle Hill, for the inability to forgive himself. And he wept for a poor fallen child, lying alone in an empty lot. And then he knew what he had to do, no matter the price.

Jesse . . . it's time.

Sixto Heredia balanced two drinks in his hand and tried the doorknob to the gambling room. He called over his shoulder to the lads who had exhorted him to hound Jesse until he joined them at the bar.

"Enough of this, Captain Banks! See here, amigo, if you don't . . ." His voice trailed off. The room was empty save for the coffin. "Where the devil are you?" Heredia crossed to the center of the room, his boots tapping the wooden floor underfoot; he slowly turned on his heels, checked every corner of the room. "Well I'll be . . ." Heredia shrugged, turned, raised one of the glasses in salute to the man in the coffin. "Rest easy, Senor Tanner. You were *muy hombre*." He drained the contents of one glass, sighed with satisfaction as the aged bourbon whiskey spread its warmth to his belly and fueled his limbs. He placed the second glass next to the coffin and reverently left the room, taking no notice of the display with Tanner Moody's gunbelt and its empty holster.

The quiet woke him. The absence of noise drifting up through the floorboards of Frenchie's bedroom. El Muerte bolted upright and reached for the revolver he had placed under the pillow after he had ridden the prostitute until she had begged him to stop and he had worked her even harder, forcing her to earn every penny. The woman stirred, muttered in her sleep, slurred something, an entreaty, pleading with him to let her rest, to not be so rough this time. The breed ignored her and swung his legs over the side of the bed. He dressed quickly, thunder rumbled, a flash of sheet lightning illuminated the window, permitted a glimpse of the alley. And in the lurid light, he thought he saw someone standing in the rain, staring up at the room, a man all in gray, flowing silver-white hair revealed in the flash of fire.

"Moody!" El Muerte whispered.

He blinked and rubbed his eyes and looked again. The figure had vanished. El Muerte shook his head, splashed water in his face. He reached for a bottle of tequila. Empty. But there was more where that came from. He pulled on his boots, tucked the Colt in his waistband. He leaned over the prostitute, considered waking her, then remembered the laudanum she had consumed. Well, the hell with her.

He walked from the room into the darkened hall. Light ought to be flooding up the stairway. El Muerte reached the top step, peered down into the cantina. It was brighter below, but not by much. The cantina ought to be awash with light and noise.

"Kilkenny!" Nothing. "You Irish bastard, the alleys are full of crib houses. You'll find another whore. No reason to close up for the night." He cursed and started down the stairs, almost lost his footing, stumbled and caught himself then made his way to the cantina.

The curtains were drawn back from the windows, the back door swung open, rocked by the wind that moaned through the doorway. Rain drummed upon the roof, the alley, the wooden boxes and discarded barrels. It sounded like boiling water in the muddy furrows out back.

The gaslights had been lowered. Their dim glare gave the room an almost reverential air, made ominous every time the lightning shimmered and lent its lurid cast to the faces of the women and men clustered in the far corner of the room. El Muerte hesitated, allowed his vision to adjust, then looked puzzled at the group crowded in the corner as if retreating from harm's way. He spied Iron Mike among them.

El Muerte started to speak, then noticed that the tables had been cleared back, leaving only the largest off to his left, in front of the bar. A sodden corpse had been placed on the table. El Muerte cautiously approached the deceased, recognized the rain-soaked body of Crescensia Bazan. Although her garments were spattered with grime and blood, her features had been lovingly washed clean, and were it not for the terrible wound puckering her flesh and the purple pallor of her face, she might have been asleep in innocence. A gold pocket watch on a slender gold chain, its casing shattered by a rifle slug, rested in her right hand. And near her feet, someone had left a full bottle of tequila.

"What the hell is this?" El Muerte growled.

"We are paying our respects," said Jesse Banks from over near the piano. "Isn't that right, Iron Mike?"

The Irishman, standing among his patrons, dutifully nodded. They hadn't moved since Jesse Banks burst into the room carrying the corpse. He'd ordered them at gunpoint into the corner.

El Muerte turned and spied him in the shadows. Muddy footprints trailed from the back door to the table and then over to the piano. Banks's trousers were mud-spattered, his boots caked from slogging across the lot out behind the alley where he had retrieved the dead woman's body and carried it into the bawdy house. Jesse looked soaked to the skin but the shivers had subsided. His hands were at his sides. "Do you hear the watch?"

"I hear nothing but the rattle of your bones, piano player. You brought your whore back. Now I think maybe you will join her."

Tick . . . tick . . . tick . . .

Jesse experienced a sudden burst of panic. Christ Almighty what was he doing? He stepped clear of the piano, moved to his left, easing toward the door to the alley. El Muerte chuckled softly. The sound of the breed's contempt cut through the sound of the ticking watch he'd left with Crescensia, stopped Jesse in his tracks. He would rather die here than dart through to the alley.

Tick . . . tick . . . tick . . .

El Muerte placed a hand on the revolver tucked at his waist. The other hand picked up the bottle of tequila and as he raised it, the cork stopper fell loosely to the tabletop and bounced to the floor. The breed sighed, recognizing the challenge. He even welcomed it.

"*¿Quién lo ha hecho?* Who let the devil out?"

"I did," said Jesse.

The breed smiled broadly and reached for his gun. Jesse took a step back and started to bring the Smith and Wesson to bear as El Muerte dragged the Colt into play. Jesse slipped in a mud smear and went down, inadvertently blasting a hole in the ceiling. El Muerte roared in triumph and charged across the room to blast Jesse Banks where he lay on his back. The breed flung a chair aside and had Jesse in his gunsight, point blank, dead on, and then lightning shimmered, filled the back doorway, and El Muerte, for an instant, glanced aside, distracted, and glimpsed a figure looming in the doorway.

"No!"

Tanner Moody . . . tall, and straight, hair the color of ashes, streaming in the night wind, his chiseled features vengeful, bathed in an unearthly light. El Muerte shifted, fired through the doorway as the image suddenly vanished with a flash of lightning. A second flash revealed the empty doorway. He had fired at nothing. El Muerte cursed aloud and turned to bring his gun to bear.

Jesse rose up on one arm and shot him.

The .44 caliber slug spun El Muerte and sent him stumbling back toward the bar. Jesse leaped to his feet and shot him again. The breed groaned and hit the bar, chest first. His arms splayed before him, the Colt skittered across the scratched wooden surface, shattered a couple of shot glasses in the process. El Muerte turned and reached for the Colt. It was just beyond his grasp.

He saw the piano player advancing on him, gun leveled. El Muerte coughed blood. He waved toward Banks. "Wait," he gasped.

Jesse closed his eyes a moment. *Tick . . . tick . . .* Then silence. He glanced over at the pocket watch clasped in the palm of that slender girlish hand.

"Wait . . ." El Muerte entreated.

Jesse raised the gun in his hand and squeezed the trigger. "I don't have the time," he said.

The story of that night changed in the telling, and retelling. Folks fabricated their own reasons for what had happened. How a man found his courage, how El Muerte's body, pawed over by dogs, came to be found in the vacant lot behind El Matadero. But some facts never changed: how Jesse Banks arriving at the burial site of his friend Tanner Moody, how the crowd parted as he approached, and the looks that were exchanged as Jesse knelt and placed the Smith and Wesson revolver upon his friend's grave. It was also told how, later in the day, Jesse saw to another burial, this one attended only by himself and a padre to speak the last words.

The ending was always the same. On a clear cool morning with the promise of spring in the air, Jesse Banks rode off astride *Death*'s horse, in search of the rest of his life. He left Hell's Half Acre behind him. And never returned.

Nine

The New York Morning Telegraph, Feb. 12, 1903
The Legend of Tanner Moody
Ninth in a series by Bat Masterson
Exclusive

I had decided I needed one more story. The last one I told was odd, I know, and I feel a responsibility to leave you, the reader, with something more traditional in nature. I did not know what that would be until, late that third night of Tanner Moody's wake, when the attendance had finally dwindled and folks had gone home to sleep in anticipation of Moody's actual burial the next morning. A lone figure slunk into the saloon and approached Moody's casket. He was slightly disheveled, bearded, and kept to himself, but I recognized him nonetheless, and was quite shocked at his appearance there.

291

I approached the casket as he finished paying his respects and when he turned and saw me he reacted first with surprise, but then with pleasure. The smile that split his face also illuminated it, and I was dead sure of who he was.

"Hello, Bat."

"Harvey," I asked, "what the hell are you doing here?" I looked around to see if anyone was close enough to hear us.

"Had to pay my respects, Bat," Harvey Logan said. "You know what Moody meant to the Syndicate."

"Over the course of the last three days this place has been crawling with law, and ex-law."

"I figured," Logan said. "That's why I decided to come at the last minute."

"Harvey, did you even know Moody?"

"Never met him, myself, Bat," said Harvey Logan—also known as "Kid Curry." "But Butch did. And since he ain't around, I figured it falls to me to pay respects."

Harvey Logan had ridden with Butch Cassidy when Butch had taken members of the Wild Bunch and both the Powder Springs and Hole-in-the-Wall gangs and formed the Train Robbery Syndicate. That was when Butch Cassidy had met Harry Longbaugh, "the Sundance Kid." Butch and Sundance, hunted by Pinkertons and lawmen, had supposedly moved on to greener pastures.

"I heard Butch and Harry left the country," I said. "South America, maybe."

"Maybe," Logan said.

"I also heard you were in prison over in Columbus."

Logan smiled and spread his arms.

"I look like I'm in prison?"

"I can't say that you do, Harvey." I didn't know if he had been in and escaped, or if his being arrested had been a rumor.

I did know one thing about Harvey Logan, though. He had a reputation for recklessness. I thought he was present as much for the thrill he got out of it as to do Butch Cassidy a favor.

Logan turned and looked into the casket at Moody one more time, then looked around.

"So, no lawmen around now?"

"Apparently not."

He nodded. Maybe I'd just taken all the fun out of it for him, but if he really wanted to be reckless he could have come earlier.

"You knew them both, didn't you?" he asked me.

"Yes, I did."

"Friends?"

As I explained in an earlier column, I could only claim Tanner Moody as a contemporary, not as a friend or even a colleague. With Butch it was even less than that. I simply had a history with both men.

"No," I said, "not friends."

"So then what are you doin' here?"

I explained about walking in on the wake in total ignorance, and my decision to write about it.

"Turnin' in your gun for a pen?"

"The times are changing, Harvey," I said. "We've got to change with them. Butch and Sundance both knew that."

"I guess they did," Logan said, "or do. Well, Bat, good luck with your articles."

"Good luck with whatever you're going to do, Harvey."

"I'm just gonna keep doin' what I do, Bat, until they stop me."

"Well, be careful going out, then," I said. "Somebody else might recognize you the way I did."

Logan stared at me for a few seconds, then said, "You got a story to tell, don't ya? I wish I could stay around to hear it . . . but hey, maybe I'll read about it."

"Maybe you will."

He touched the brim of his hat and headed for the front door. I listened and waited a few minutes, and when I didn't hear shouting or gunshots, I figured he'd made it away safely.

I turned and stared down at Tanner Moody. It was the first time in three days I had done so. Suddenly, I knew I was finished collecting stories, it was time to pay my own respects to the deceased.

Harvey Logan had been right. I did know both Tanner Moody and Butch Cassidy. In fact, the three of us had a history together. I suppose I should finish up this series of articles with that story, not only for you, the reader, but maybe Harvey Logan will enjoy it some day—even if it's from a prison cell.

And so, the last tale is mine.

Here is my Tanner Moody story . . .

Three-Handed Winter

By Robert J. Randisi

I was marooned in Lander, Wyoming, the winter of 1889–1890 like everybody else when the early snows came and cut off all the passes out of town. This was after the McCarty gang had hit the Telluride Bank. I had heard that the gang—the McCartys and Butch Cassidy—were holed up in the Star Valley, which was partially in Wyoming and partly in Idaho. Others said that the McCartys were there, in the valley, but that Butch had gone his own way. I didn't much care either way. I wasn't packing a star then, and had come to Lander for a private poker game. I had arrived early, but it seemed many of the players had not had the same notion, and so when I was trapped in Lander, they were trapped outside of it. Only one other man had arrived early for the game, and his name was Tanner Moody.

I had not met Moody at this point in our lives, but I

knew of his reputation as he knew of mine. He had, at various times in his life, ridden on both sides of the badge, been a rancher and a bounty hunter. This was the first I had heard that he was a gambler, as well.

The game was to have been run by a man called Dave Cole. According to a telegram I'd received from Cole several weeks before, the game was going to be big, drawing the likes of Luke Short and Ben Thompson, among others. Luke was my friend and I looked forward to seeing him whenever I could. Ben was a longtime acquaintance and a good poker player, as well as the best hand with a gun I had ever seen. We were never friends, but I looked forward to sitting across the poker table from him.

Unfortunately, neither of them made it into Lander before the snow. So that's how I came to be sitting in Cole's saloon, playing solitaire, when I first set eyes on Tanner Moody . . .

Just before Moody's arrival, though, I had been sitting with Cole himself, who was wallowing in despair.

"I'm in trouble, Bat."

"What kind, Dave?"

"This place. I'm gonna lose it."

"Dave—"

"I needed this game to bring me back, you know?" Cole said. "Without it . . ." He shrugged.

"Why don't you see if you can find some other players?"

"Would you do that?" Cole asked. "Play with other players?"

"Sure," I said, "why not? Poker's poker."

Cole stood up, ready to go out and find players.

"It won't be the same stakes, you know," he said. "The game, I mean."

"Go and find your players, Dave," I said. "It'll give you something to do."

Of course, I didn't know it was Moody when he walked in. Despite the fact that he was in his early sixties, he still cut an impressive figure as he came through the batwing doors. He was tall and lean then, still with a full head of hair that he wore long. He stomped some snow from his boots, walked to the bar, ordered a beer and exchanged words with the bartender, who inclined his head toward me. Moody collected a second beer from the man and walked over to my table with it. It was early; only a few other tables had occupants. Bored men with nothing to do but drink and wait out the snow.

"Bat Masterson?" he asked.

"That's right."

"Tanner Moody," he said. "I understand we're in the same predicament."

"Which is?"

"We came here for a poker game that ain't gonna happen," he said. "I notice your mug is empty, and I've got an extra beer."

"What a coincidence."

"Care to take this one off my hands?"

I hesitated only a moment, then said, "Have a seat."

He set the beer down next to my empty mug, and

sat across from me. He turned his chair sideways so he could see the door, or so he could stretch his long legs out. My money was on seeing the door.

"Where's our host?"

"He's around," I said. "Trying to scrounge up some players. Say, how did you get here if everyone else is snowed in and out?"

"Guess I'm made of heartier stock."

"Or have a better horse."

"That, too."

"Or maybe you were here even before me."

Moody shrugged.

"Odd we haven't run into each other before this," I said.

"We both travel around quite a bit," Moody said. "Jus' haven't found ourselves in the same place, I guess."

"Until now."

Moody nodded and worked on his beer. I looked around at the other men in the bar. There were two sitting together, staring morosely into their beers, and a young fellow sitting by himself in the corner, seemingly without a care in the world.

I gathered up the cards and started to shuffle them.

"I don't recall ever hearing that you play poker," I said.

A smiled creased Moody's weathered face and he said, "One of my minor talents."

"Care for a game?" I asked.

"Head to head?"

"Why not?" I asked. "It'll help pass the time—maybe until Cole comes up with some warm bodies."

"Guess it would," he said. "Okay, deal 'em out."

Cole didn't come up with any takers. Maybe it was because of Moody and me, our reputations. Maybe they were afraid they'd stop a bullet during a tense hand.

It took three days for the young fellow in the corner to stand up and walk over to us. Each day found me and Moody playing poker, and this youngster watching us from the corner. Finally, I guess he couldn't take it anymore.

"Got room for a third?" he asked. "Feller could go crazy round here within nothin' to do."

"If the stakes suit you," I said.

"What are they?"

We'd started with nickels and had worked our way up to dollars. Problem with a head-to-head game is that for long periods of time all you do is pass the same money back and forth. Having a third player would change that a bit.

"Dollar bet, dollar raise, up to five dollars on the last card."

"I can handle that."

"Could get steep," Moody warned him.

The young man smiled and said again, "I can handle that."

"Have a seat, then," I said.

He sat down, called for the bartender to bring three

more beers on him, and then took out a sheaf of money. Of course, right there and then I had no idea he was Butch Cassidy and that this was part of the money stolen from the Telluride Bank.

"What's your name?" Moody asked.

"Leroy."

"Well, Leroy," I said, passing him the cards, "it's your deal."

What I also didn't know when we started playing three-handed poker, was that there were others in town who did know who he was, and did know he had money from the Telluride Bank. A man named Lou Mathis had recognized Butch, and started planning to take the money from him. It seems Mathis had wanted to ride with the McCarty gang, but they wouldn't have him. Once he spotted Butch in Lander he knew this was his chance to impress the McCartys and make some money at the same time. Word had gotten out that the McCartys and Butch had made $3,500 each from the Telluride job. That was a fortune to folks struggling in the Star Valley back then.

First, though, Mathis had to collect enough men who would be willing to work with him. This was early in Butch's outlaw career, and while the man had recognized Butch, he had not quite become "Butch Cassidy" yet.

The only men in the saloon with the reps were me and Moody, and once Butch started playing cards with us this fellow Mathis must have decided he needed more men for the job.

First he had to start with his own partner, a man named Tim Grimes.

"You want to what?"

"I'll say it again slower," Mathis had said to Grimes. "Cassidy was in on the Telluride job, so he has to still have most of the money with him."

"And he's here? In Lander?"

"Yeah."

"How do you know?"

Mathis explained how he recognized Butch.

"The McCartys?" Grimes said. "That was before we became partners?"

"Yeah."

"So all we have to do is corner Cassidy and take the money from him?"

"Well," Mathis said, "there's a little more to it than that . . ."

Butch played poker with us for two days and held his own nicely. Also, I noticed that Tanner Moody actually could play poker, and play well. Of course, this didn't keep me from winning money from them pretty steadily. Still, the game continued to be more about passing the time rather than for anyone to make serious money.

"Leroy, we haven't learned much about you since you started playin' with us," Moody said on the third day.

"Ain't much to tell," Butch said. "Got stranded here just like the two of you. Saw you fellas playin' poker and figured it was a good way to keep from goin' stir crazy."

"What brought you up this way?"

Butch shrugged and said, "Just passin' through." At this point I didn't know whether Moody knew who Butch was or not. At this point there was a lot I didn't know.

Of course, we did other things besides play poker. We ate, we walked, we slept, but we did all of those things alone. The only thing we did that brought the three of us together was play poker in the same small saloon every day.

And while we played on during that first week, Mathis made his pitch around town . . . or so I heard later on.

"You gotta be crazy," Ed Thorn told Mathis. He looked at Grimes, who gave him nothing in return. "He's playin' poker with Bat Masterson and Tanner Moody, and you wanna take him in the saloon? Yer crazy, Lou." He looked at Grimes again, but still got no support.

"Moody is old," Mathis said. "Think about it. We take them and not only do we make some money, but we make names for ourselves, as well. The men who killed Tanner Moody and Bat Masterson."

"Tell him about the money," Grimes said.

"How much money?" Ed Thorn asked.

"And Masterson's best days are behind him," Mathis told Rich Dolan. Behind him Grimes nodded. He decided to take more of an active part in trying to convince this one. "He's been playin' a lot of poker and hasn't packed a star in years. Jesus, he's gotta be forty!"

To the twenty-five-year-old Dolan this sounded ancient.

"Think of it," Mathis went on. "We'll be the men who killed Bat Masterson and Tanner Moody."

Dolan did think about it, then asked, "How much money?"

"It's a small saloon," Mathis said, "no place for them to go. We walk in, start shootin', it's all over."

Chet Walker stared across the table at Mathis. Grimes didn't know what to say or do at this point, so he remained silent.

"How much?" Walker asked.

Mathis heard the same question from everyone else he approached, as well. When it came right down to it, I guess we should have been insulted, Moody and me, when we heard later that all they cared about was how much money was involved. Moody was too old, I was better with cards than with guns those days, and Butch was just a kid.

Everybody makes mistakes . . .

"What do you do, Mr. Moody?" Butch asked on the morning of the eighth day.

Moody looked at him. Butch smiled.

"Of course I've heard of you," he said, "and of Mr.

Masterson, too. I think I know what he does. You've had more of a . . . checkered past. I was just wondering what you were doing these days?"

"This makes me sound boring," I said, "predictable."

"Not borin', Bat," Moody said.

"Never predictable," Butch said, "but you've pretty much stayed on one side of the fence. I was just wonderin' which side Mr. Moody was on these days."

I looked across the table at Moody. He sat the same way every day. Sideways, long legs straight out.

"I guess that's a fair question," I said, dealing out cards for draw poker.

"I suppose it is," Moody said. He looked at Butch. "Pinkerton."

I don't know which one of us was more surprised at that moment, me or Butch.

"Pinkerton?" Butch repeated.

"That's right," Moody said. "They've been after me for a long time. I finally decided to give it a try. This is actually my first assignment for them."

"Doin' what, exactly?" Butch asked.

"Right now?" Tanner Moody said. "I'm lookin' for some bank robbers."

"Is that right?"

"Yep," Moody said, looking at his cards.

"Any bank in particular?"

"The Telluride Bank was held up a couple of weeks ago," Moody said. "Three men. We heard it was the McCarty gang."

Butch didn't comment on that, just studied his cards.

"You know the McCartys, Leroy?" Moody asked.

"Now why would I know the McCartys?"

"Your play, Moody," I said.

I was talking about the cards, but I think they both thought I was referring to something else.

Neither of them was in position to easily get to their guns. If they drew down on each other I wasn't sure what my reaction would or should be. The batwing doors slamming open saved me from having to make that decision . . .

Lou Mathis had managed to collect seven men. That meant whatever was left of Butch's $3,500 got split eight ways. That didn't sound like a lot of money to me, certainly not enough to risk your life for. Apparently, they thought differently . . .

Tim Grimes, Ed Thorn, Rich Dolan, Chet Walker and three other men followed Lou Mathis into the saloon. As soon as they were inside they fanned out and drew their guns.

"Damn," I said, and overturned the table.

Moody reacted very quickly for a man his age. He launched himself out of his chair and hit the floor. By that time his gun was in his hand.

Butch pushed his chair over backwards. It was a move only a young man could make. Me, I ducked down behind the overturned table and drew my gun.

By this time lead was flying, smacking into the table and—in some instances—right through the table . . . and my jacket!

The eight men were obviously surprised by our reaction. They expected to catch us flatfooted—or seated—in a hail of bullets. Now they had to deal with three armed men who all knew how to shoot back coolly while under fire—something they did not know how to do.

I fired twice, quickly, and two men spun and hit the floor. Moody fired the same number of times. He had a bigger gun than I did—longer barrel, heavier loads. One of his victims went flying through a window, and another was driven right back through the batwing doors. He pulled the trigger a third time, but his gun jammed.

Butch came to a stop on his knees and fired two shots. I hadn't noticed that Moody's gun jammed, but Butch did. Both his shots struck a man who was drawing a bead on Moody. I fired again, killing a sixth man, which left two more.

One of them—Mathis, who had started this whole thing—turned to run, but we weren't having it. Moody's gun unjammed at this point and all three of us fired at Mathis at the same time. The force of the three bullets striking him in the back sent him out the doors after his partner, and he was dead before he hit the ground.

The last man—Mathis's original partner, Grimes—tossed his gun to the floor, raised his hands and started shouting something.

I pointed my gun at him and ordered, "Kick it away from you! Put your hands in the air!"

He did, and when I looked at Moody and Butch they were pointing their guns at each other.

"You took that bank in Telluride, Butch," Moody said. "You and Tom McCarty along with Matt Warner."

Before Butch could answer I said, "He also saved your life just now when your gun jammed, Moody."

The man with his hands in the air watched all three of us, wondering if he was going to survive.

"I got nothin' against you, Moody," Butch said, "unless you try to take me in."

Moody stared at Butch, then risked a glance over at me.

"What the hell, Moody," I said. "Make a decision before the law shows up."

"Besides," Butch said, "Bat's got most of the money I had left from the job."

There were footsteps on the boardwalk outside as folks came running to see what had happened. One of them had to be the local law, who we had all stayed away from until now.

"Ah, hell," Moody said, lowering his gun, "I never did like the Pinkertons, anyway."

"Guess your first assignment is your last, huh, Moody?' I asked.

Butch lowered his gun, as well. By the time the sheriff walked in they had both holstered their weapons.

We went back to our game, and when the snow finally melted enough for us to leave, the money had worked its way around the table and we were about even. We went our separate ways, each to enhance his own reputation—probably no one as much as George Leroy Parker, who went on to become "Butch Cassidy."

Oh, and Dave Cole did not lose his little saloon, because folks came from far and wide to see where Bat Masterson, Butch Cassidy and Tanner Moody had stood off eight men and then gone back to their three-handed winter.

Ten

The New York Morning Telegraph, Feb. 13, 1903
The Legend of Tanner Moody
Last in a series by Bat Masterson
Exclusive

Violence is a bonding experience. It happens with men in war; it happens with men who have faced death together.

Hell, even poker is a bonding experience.

Our paths crossed a few more times, but that was the first meeting. I don't know if Moody ran into Butch again. I know I didn't. It probably would have been nice to run into Butch at Moody's funeral—then again, it might have just been odd.

Here's the oddest thing about Tanner Moody's funeral, though . . .

* * *

I awoke the next morning, pretty sure I had all the stories I was going to get, unless I heard some more around the grave site. I ate breakfast alone in a dining room that was damn near empty. As I walked over to the White Elephant, the damned street looked deserted. Turns out that all of the folks who had come to pay their respects during the wake had left.

There was only me and three or four others to follow the hearse to the cemetery where Moody would be planted. I didn't know the others, hadn't spoke to any of them during the wake. Didn't speak to them during the funeral, either. We all just sort of stood there with our hands folded while they dropped dirt on Tanner Moody's coffin.

I was thinking of my own wake and funeral, sometime in the—hopefully—far future. Had I commanded in life the same respect Tanner Moody obviously had? Would my death attract as many mourners? And how many of them would actually stay around to see me planted in the ground? Is burial the final tribute, or the final indignity?

When it was over nobody looked at anyone and we all walked down the hill.

LANCASTER'S ORPHANS
Robert J. Randisi

It certainly isn't what Lancaster had expected. When he rode into Council Bluffs, he thought he would just stop at the bar for a beer. How could he know he'd ride right into the middle of a lynching? Lancaster can't let an innocent man be hanged, but when the smoke clears and the lynching stops, a bystander lies dying on the ground, caught in the crossfire. With his last breath he asks Lancaster to take care of the people who had been depending on him—a wagon train filled with women and children on their way to California!